THESE DEFIANT
SOULS

A DARLING HILL
STORY

THESE DEFIANT SOULS
SPECIAL EDITION

A DARLING HILL STORY

L A COTTON

Published by Delesty Books

THESE DEFIANT SOULS
Copyright © L. A. Cotton 2022
All rights reserved.

This book is a work of fiction. Names, characters, places, and events are the product of the author's imagination or used in a fictitious manner. Any resemblance to actual persons or events is purely coincidental.

No part of this book may be reproduced or used in any manner without the written permission of the publisher, except by a reviewer who may quote brief passages for review purposes only.

Edited by Andrea M. Long
Cover Designed by The Pretty Little Design Co.
Cover Image: Michelle Lancaster

DARLING HILL

These Dark Hearts
A Nix & Harleigh Prequel

These Dirty Lies
Nix & Harleigh Book One

These Dead Promises
Nix & Harleigh Book Two

These Defiant Souls
A Darling Hill Story

1

―――――

ZANE

"I'M SURPRISED YOU SHOWED," I SAID TO NIX.

"It's Halloween, where else would I be?" My best friend grinned, grabbing a beer from the cooler by my feet and uncapping it.

"Didn't think you'd be able to drag yourself away from Birdie."

"We're not that bad."

I shot him a droll look. They were that bad and then some.

But I got it.

Harleigh Wren was his person. The other half to his tainted soul.

I might have been a skeptical motherfucker who had no intentions of ever letting a girl hold that kind of power over me, but I wasn't a total asshole. I knew love when I saw it.

And Nix and Harleigh had it in spades.

Didn't mean I didn't miss my best friend though. We still hung out with Kye, our other best friend, but it wasn't the same.

Everything was changing, and part of me hated it. Because there was no getting out of The Row after graduation for me. My life was tethered here. I would never leave Grams and even when she was gone, it wasn't like I had a fairy godmother waiting in the wings to make all my wishes come true.

Dreaming was for pussies.

I preferred to keep my feet planted firmly on the ground. And the truth of it was, I was stuck here. Darling Row was the rot that festered inside me, the poison that ran through my veins. And one day, it would claim my dirty black soul.

Kicking my feet out, I inhaled deeply on the blunt, letting the acrid smoke roll through me as I stared out at the carnage before me. Halloween at Darling Hill reservoir was always a big deal. Every kid on our side of the border turned up dressed for the occasion, looking to get fucked and-or fucked up.

"Check out Cherri and Darius, she really got her claws into him, huh?" I murmured, and Nix snorted at the sight of the two of them.

"He's welcome to her."

"Yeah, you had a lucky escape there," I said.

Cherri Jardin was bad news. But ever since Harleigh had transferred back to Darling Hill High, she'd kept a low profile where Nix was concerned. Probably scared of what Harleigh's old man, Michael Rowe, might do if she ever looked twice at his daughter.

Part of me still couldn't believe Harleigh was one of *them*. The rich, elite families that lived across the other side of town in Old Darling Hill. The very people we'd spent our entire lives hating. But she'd grown up with us, so despite the blue blood running through her veins, she was the exception to the rule.

"How's Grams?" Nix asked, pulling me from my thoughts.

"The usual. She puts on a brave face for me, but I can see the cracks. She isn't getting any better and the medical bills keep rolling in."

"The insurance—"

"Only stretches so far. You know that."

"Yeah." He blew out a steady breath. "If there's anything I can do…"

"It's fine. I'll figure it out."

I'd find a way to make sure Grams kept getting her meds and the help she needed. It was the least I could do after all she'd done for me over the years.

Kye appeared, sauntering over to us with his usual cocky swagger. "Look what the cat dragged in." Nix flipped him off, and Kye chuckled. "Didn't think you'd make it."

"Seriously, you make it sound like I've moved across the state. We see each other at school every day."

"When you're not dry fucking B against the wall."

"You're just jealous that I'm getting regular pussy, Carter." Nix smirked at Kye.

"He has a point, man," I added.

"Says you, Z." Kye pinned me with a knowing look. "When was the last time you got your dick wet?"

"You know I don't kiss and tell," I grumbled, handing off the blunt to Nix and reaching for a beer.

"And why is that exactly?" Kye taunted. "Having a little trouble—"

"Cut it out," Nix warned.

Kye backed off because that's how our trio operated. He was the joker, always putting his foot in his mouth. Nix was our fearless leader. And me, I was the quiet observer. A silent tempest who hovered on the periphery. There were only a handful of people I trusted. Even less I cared about.

Some people called me cold, but I liked it that way. The less people you let in, the less people who could disappoint you.

"Is it me or does this not have the same appeal as previous years?" Kye scanned the party, his brows furrowed.

"Yeah, I know what you mean," I said, glancing at Nix.

He was busy texting on his phone. I didn't need to ask to know who it was. He and Harleigh couldn't stand to be apart from one another for more than a few hours. It was hardly a surprise given everything they'd been through, but damn, I missed my best friend. Missed the days when life was simpler, and girls didn't enter the equation.

But we weren't kids anymore. Nix was as good as living with Harleigh now and we hadn't even graduated high school yet. Kye hooked up with a different girl every weekend, sometimes more than one. It wouldn't take long before one of them tied him down and demanded something more. And then I'd be alone.

"What?" Nix said, shoving his cell back in his pocket.

"Let me guess, B?" Kye asked.

"Yeah. They're heading to Strike One. We could always—"

"No," I barked. "No fucking way."

"Jesus, keep your hair on, Z." Kye flashed me a shit-eating smirk. "What's wrong with bowling? We had fun last time. Well, I did when I wiped the alley with your sorry ass."

"I need another drink." I got up.

"There's a six-pack right there." He tipped his head to the cooler at my feet.

"Need something stronger."

"Don't do anything stupid," Nix called after me, but I was already gone, winding my way through the crowd.

A few people clapped me on the shoulder, congratulating me on a good game last night. The Darling Hill Hawks were on a winning streak and if we kept it up, the playoffs were right in our grasp. But unlike

Nix and a handful of other guys on the team, football wasn't my ticket out of here. I was good—I knew my way around a football field—but I wasn't great.

Besides, even if a scholarship did come calling—and I wasn't holding my breath—I could never leave Grams. Moving her out of The Row and into a care facility wasn't an option.

So this was my hand. Senior year. One final season of football with the Hawks, and making as many memories with my friends as possible before graduation rolled around, and we all went our separate ways.

Shit, I needed that drink.

I was almost at the makeshift bar—really, the tailgate of someone's busted up truck—when a cute blonde stepped into my path. "Hey, Zane." She smiled up at me through her thick lashes.

"What's up?" I said, letting my eyes drop down her body. She wasn't my usual type. Too petite and small. Fragile. My hands looked like they would span her waist with ease. I liked a little more to hold onto.

"You played a good game yesterday."

"Thanks."

"I'm Freya. We have biology and history together."

"Yeah, I've seen you around." But I didn't tend to put a name to a face unless I needed to.

I left that to Kye. He could name every girl in our class, and probably recall their bra size and deep throating skills.

The guy was a fucking dog.

I preferred to keep my hookups to myself. Because sex wasn't a sport for me, it was a transaction. A way to burn off some steam and keep the anger and resentment living inside me at bay.

I liked sex. Sure. But I had no interest in all the other stuff that came with it.

"So…" Freya bit down on her bottom lip in that way less than subtle way chicks did when they wanted something. "I've been plucking up the courage to talk to you since the semester started."

"I don't bite."

"Not what I heard." Her eyes sparkled with interest.

"You shouldn't believe everything you hear."

Even if, in this case, there was a smidge of truth in it.

"Do you want to find somewhere quiet to talk?"

"No can do, sorry." I ran a hand through my dark hair. "I'm here with the guys."

"Oh, okay." Dejection washed over her. "Maybe another time."

"Maybe."

Without another word, I moved around her and went in search of liquor. At least liquor wouldn't talk. It wouldn't bat its eyelashes and try and lure me into its trap. It wouldn't misread signals that weren't there to begin with.

And liquor definitely wouldn't abandon you in your hour of need.

"YOU TURNED HER DOWN? The fuck is wrong with you?" Kye gawked at me as I told him and Nix about Freya.

I was buzzed. All the vodka running hot through my veins.

"She's not my type," I grumbled.

"But she basically offered to fuck you."

"You don't have to stick it in anything wearing a skirt, you know, Carter," Nix chuckled at him.

"You're an asshole," I added.

"Didn't know you cared about the fairer species?"

"I don't." I shrugged, nursing my beer. I wanted to keep the buzz, but I didn't want to be so wasted I couldn't rush home if Grams needed me.

"Not even a certain blonde-haired, blue-eyed genius from across the res?" He taunted, his eyes dancing with amusement.

"Fuck off," I grumbled.

She was the last person I wanted to think about.

Celeste Rowe.

Harleigh Wren's half-sister and a perpetual thorn in my side.

I'd known her all of a few weeks, but I'd learned enough to know that she was trouble.

Trouble with a capital T.

"Kye, man, leave it," Nix said, casting a weary glance my way.

"I'm fine," I snapped.

"You're wound tighter than a spring. Maybe you should speak to Bryson about getting in the ring."

Fat chance of that. Fighting was Nix's thing, not mine. I didn't mind sparring and going a few rounds with some of the guys who worked out at Buster's Gym, but I didn't get the same rush Nix did.

"Shit." Nix stared at his cell phone, his lips thinning with annoyance.

"What is it?"

"I'm guessing that." Kye pointed his finger behind me, and I glanced over my shoulder. "Fuck's sake," he said. "I told her to stay away."

Harleigh, and Kye's sister Chloe, made a beeline for us.

"The fuck, Clo?" he ground out. "You were supposed to be at the bowling alley."

"We were, but Miles showed up and he and Celeste got into it, so we bailed."

"She okay?" Nix asked, dragging Harleigh onto his lap.

"Yeah, Celeste can handle Miles." She looped her arm around his shoulder, her gaze sliding to mine. But I glanced away.

I didn't give a shit about Celeste and her on-and-off ex Miles Mulligan.

Even if hearing her name made me bristle.

No one got under my skin.

No one except her.

But Celeste Rowe was everything I hated. Smart. Beautiful... *Rich*. With the whole world laid out at her feet, she would never want for anything thanks to her parents' obscene wealth.

She didn't know what it was like to go hungry or to worry about how the fuck you were going to pay your bills on time. She didn't know what it was like to drown in medical expenses, wondering how you were going to help your ailing grams.

She didn't know.

And she never would.

So Celeste Rowe might have gotten under my skin, sure. But she would never worm her way into my heart. Because it was a cold, dead thing in my chest.

And I'd be damned if a rich girl from across the res would ever be the one to thaw it out.

2

CELESTE

I should have gone with my sister Harleigh and her friend Chloe.

That's all I could think as I sat in awkward silence with Miles, my best friend turned boyfriend. *Ex*-boyfriend since I ended things a couple of weeks ago.

It wasn't him. He was kind and sweet and he made me laugh. But I didn't feel it. That sparks-flying, toe-curling, heart-racing rush you were supposed to feel around your boyfriend. And life was too short to spend the rest of my junior year trying to convince myself that there was something more between us when there wasn't.

At least, not for me.

"I know I got a bit overprotective, babe." Miles finally broke the silence. "But I only care about you. I'll do better, I swear. If you just give me another chance, I'll—"

"Miles, we've been over this. We don't work together." I took his hand in mine. "You're one of my best friends. We work better as friends."

"We can't go back to being just friends, not after everything we've shared." His eyes twinkled as if he thought it might convince me of all the good times we'd had.

There had been some too. Fun dates and some hot and heavy moments over at his house. But something was always missing. And when my entire life was mapped out for me, I didn't want to settle for a relationship that didn't set me on fire.

Miles was safe. A good guy. The kind of guy who would hold open the door and pay the check. He was sturdy and dependable, and that was great... if I was looking for my future husband.

I wasn't though.

I wanted excitement. Something wild and reckless. Something extraordinary. I wanted my first great love to leave its mark on me. To be able to look back on high school in twenty years and remember the intensity and passion. I wanted—

"Celeste?"

"Sorry, what?" I blinked up at Miles, and he frowned.

"You weren't listening to a word I said just now, were you?"

"Sorry, it's been a long week."

He stood up abruptly and ran a hand through his hair,

dejection rolling off him in waves. "Obviously this was a mistake. I should go."

"I… if that's what you want."

"What happened to you, Celeste?" His lips pursed. "I can make you happy, I know I can. Yet, you won't even give me a chance."

"I gave you a chance, Miles. More than one. But if it's not there, it's not there." I gave him a sad, apologetic smile. "I don't want to fight with you, but that's my decision. If you can't respect that—"

"Yeah, whatever. I guess I'll see you around." He stormed away, taking the air with him.

I let out a heavy sigh, watching him leave the bowling alley. The couple on the next lane over gave me a sympathetic smile, obviously having overheard some of our conversation. Part of me wanted to ask them how long they'd been dating and whether they were both happy. But that would lead to me asking them if they were aware that over half of all marriages in the country ended in divorce or separation. Fifty percent. That meant that they had a less than one in two chance of making it.

It hardly seemed worth it.

Unless you were my half-sister Harleigh Wren and her boyfriend Phoenix Wilder. They had that once-in-a-lifetime kind of love. It was hard not to look at them and be overcome with churning jealousy. The way Nix looked at her, his eyes brimming with pure adoration. No way in hell would they end up a statistic. They were the real deal. A modern-day Romeo and Juliet but without all the tragedy and death.

As Michael Rowe and Sabrina Delacorte's daughter, my future was mapped out before me. I would graduate high school top of my class, attend Columbia, start dating a like-minded guy who instantly gained my parents' approval, and live the life they had always dreamed for me.

I was lucky.

At least, that's what everyone around me thought. I wanted for nothing and had the world and everything that came with it at my fingertips.

But lately, I felt restless. Confined by the expectations placed on me. Caged even. I had spent my entire life coloring inside the lines, being the daughter they expected me to be. There was so much more to me than the girl who knew the square root of pi to eight decimal points though.

After another minute of watching the couple, I grabbed my purse and left. Digging my cell phone out of it, I opened up my chat with Harleigh and her friend Chloe.

Me: Are you still at the res?

Clo: Yeah, why?

Me: Talk with Miles didn't end well. I'm heading over to you now.

Harleigh: Maybe you should go home. It's getting late and your parents will worry.

I rolled my eyes at that. Harleigh had recently moved out of our house and in with Nix and his stepmom Jessa.

I didn't blame her. Her relationship with our father was strained, and her relationship with my mom almost non-existent. For as much as I hated not having her around anymore, I knew it was for the best.

Me: It's not that late. I'm coming. See you soon.

Clo: I'll save you a drink.

Now she was the kind of friend I wanted in my corner. Chloe Carter was bold and brash and one hundred percent unapologetic. We'd become fast friends over the last few weeks.

I didn't make friends easily, so it was nice to have another girl to talk boys, shopping, and books with. And Chloe didn't judge me, not the way the girls at Darling Academy did. You couldn't sneeze in the halls of DA without someone dissecting it.

Maybe Miles was right.

Maybe I had changed.

Or maybe I'd finally realized I wanted more from life.

I HEARD the party before I saw it. Rowdy laughter and music carrying on the gentle breeze. It only made the nervous energy dance faster in my stomach.

If my parents knew I was here… well, that didn't bear thinking about. Harleigh might have grown up on this side of Darling Hill reservoir, with these kids, but I didn't belong here.

At least, that's what they all thought.

The truth was though, I liked it here, away from the elite of Old Darling Hill. Here, I could breathe. I didn't have to worry about what I said or who I said it to. People weren't dissecting my every move, scrutinizing my behavior, and judging whether I deserved the title of Michael Rowe and Sabrina's Delacorte's golden child.

It was exhausting—living the life laid out for you before you were even in grade school.

I burst through the trees and came to a halt, taking in the scene before me. It was Halloween and the kids of Darling Row had turned up determined to celebrate. Ghostface killers danced with sexy devils, zombie werewolves drank with zombie football players, and girls in leather and lace danced for the masked guys lingering in the shadows who watched their every move.

Hands wrapped around my eyes and a scream caught in my throat. "Guess who?"

"Kye! You scared me half to death." I jabbed him in the stomach, ducking out of his hold. He grinned down at me as I turned to scold him. "Not funny."

"Seemed pretty funny from where I'm standing."

"Jackass," I mumbled.

"Saw you standing over here and figured you might need a guide."

"I am quite capable of finding my way, you know?"

"Oh, I don't doubt it. But B would kick my ass if I didn't make sure you got to her in one piece." He crooked his elbow, and I rolled my eyes, shoving my arm through his. "So, what do you think?"

"It's… wild."

"Nah, you haven't seen anything yet." He winked at me, and nervous laughter vibrated in my chest.

Kye Carter slung his arm around me and guided me through the sea of bodies. And I soaked up the attention. He, Nix, and their friend Zane were three of the most popular boys at their school, Darling Hill High. They played for the football team and had that untouchable, bad boy thing working for them. Except, they weren't bad boys, not really. They were just three boys trying to survive the hand life had dealt them.

Sure, they made some questionable, less than lawful decisions at times, but didn't all teenagers?

My mother despised them. My father—since Harleigh was dating Nix—barely tolerated them. And the residents of Old Darling Hill would cry bloody murder if they ever showed up on our side of town. But I only saw a family: three brothers bound not by blood but circumstance. By survival.

The division and hatred between Darling Row and Old Darling Hill ran deep though. And it was going to take a lot more than Nix and Harleigh's relationship to heal the wounds caused by years of prejudice and rivalry.

"Look who I found," Kye said as we approached his friends. Harleigh offered me a small wave, but Chloe leapt out of her chair and ambled over.

"I'm glad you came." She grabbed my hand, pulling me away from her brother. "Let's get you a drink."

"Oh, no alcohol. I'm driving."

"Soda it is."

"You didn't dress up?" I asked Nix and Kye, and they shrugged.

"Not this year," Nix replied, kissing Harleigh's cheek.

A familiar ache spread through my chest. "I was thinking I could stay over," I said to them.

"No," Harleigh rushed out, as Nix said, "Fine by me."

"Oh, okay."

Tension descended over us.

"It's not that I don't want you to sleepover," Harleigh's expression softened, but the disapproval was clear in her eyes. She wasn't happy I'd come. "I just don't want you to get into trouble."

"I can handle Dad, Harleigh." We'd had this argument many times already but apparently, she wasn't going to let it drop.

"I know you can. But things are complicated enough without…" She trailed off, the disapproval giving way to guilt.

"Without me making things worse."

"Celeste, I—"

"It's fine." I waved her off. "I'll go, don't worry."

"You know you can come and hang out whenever you want," Harleigh said, and I managed a weak smile. "I guess it won't hurt if you stay a little while," she added, but it felt like an afterthought.

In the space of a year, I'd gained a sister and lost her again. At least, that's what it felt like. But Harleigh didn't belong with me in Old Darling Hill, and I guess she thought I didn't belong here with her either.

My stomach churned. I shouldn't have come. I should have gone home like she'd told me to. But I was so tired of always doing what people expected of me.

"Here," Chloe offered me a can of soda and motioned to the bench. I sat down beside her, and she whispered, "You good?"

"I guess. I probably shouldn't have come."

"Fuck that. I'm glad you came." She smiled. "It gets real boring watching them make out all night while my brother tries to fuck anything in a skirt."

"Thanks." Strained laughter spilled from my lips. "No Zane tonight?" I asked, trying to keep my tone casual.

"He's around somewhere. Why?" Her brow arched.

"No reason." I shrugged, glancing at the ground.

"You, Celeste Rowe, are a terrible liar."

Just then, a trickle of awareness went through me. My gaze lifted just in time to see him step out from the crowd. His black hoodie and black jeans combo made him blend with the shadows, the piercing in his brow glinting in the moonlight as his icy gaze fixed on me across the bonfire.

He stalked toward us, his long, lean legs eating up the distance as he ran a hand through his dark hair. It was longer now, falling into his eyes a little. He didn't grin like Kye or offer me a small smile like Nix had.

No. Zane Washington glowered at me like I was nothing more than dirt on the bottom of his boot.

"Z, my man. Look who showed up," Kye said with a hint of amusement.

But Zane wasn't amused.

Not in the least as he spat, "What the fuck is she doing here?"

3

ZANE

"Zane, don't be an ass," Chloe glowered at me. "Celeste has as much right to be here as you do."

I snorted at that. Because that was utter bullshit if ever I'd heard it.

Little Miss Goody Two-shoes belonged on the other side of the res, cloistered away in her ivory castle, better known as the Rowe-Delacorte's huge, gated estate.

"It's okay, Clo," she said, glaring at me.

The air crackled between us as everyone waited to see what I'd do.

But fuck that.

I wasn't here to get into it with Harleigh's sister. I was here to forget the shitshow waiting for me when I got home.

Dropping into my chair, I grabbed another beer from

the cooler and uncapped it. So Celeste was here, I didn't have to acknowledge her presence.

Nix watched me out of the corner of his eye while Kye chatted to his sister and our unwelcome guest. Harleigh didn't seem too impressed with Celeste's presence either, watching her half-sister like a hawk. The feeling was mutual. She and Harleigh might have shared fifty percent of their DNA but that was where the similarities ended.

"You look like you want to murder her... or maybe fuck the life right out of her." Kye smirked, his eyes crinkling with silent laughter.

"She shouldn't be here."

"And yet, you haven't taken your eyes off her since you saw her."

"That's not..." I trapped the response behind gritted teeth.

He was right. But I wasn't glaring at her because I wanted her. I just didn't want her here. Pretending to be one of us. Pretending that she somehow fit in with the kids from The Row.

Because she didn't.

Little Miss Money Bags probably hadn't experienced a day of hardship in her life. And if she had, no doubt Mommy and Daddy had waved their magical wand and fixed it.

There were kids in The Row literally starving. Their families unable to put food on the table. Yet *they* went on with their lives across the res like we didn't exist.

They disgusted me, all of them.

"Mom wanted to know if you and Grams will be joining us for Thanksgiving this year?"

"It's still four weeks away."

"So, you know what she's like. She likes to plan."

"A lot can happen in four weeks," I murmured, feeling the weight of the words lying heavy on my chest.

"Did something happen?" Kye shot me a concerned look.

"Nothing more than usual."

"You need to ask for help, Z," he said quietly.

"I can handle it."

"You keep saying that. And it's admirable, it is. But what happens when you break?"

"I won't." Because it wasn't an option.

Grams needed me.

I was all she had left in this world. And after everything she'd done for me, I wasn't about to force her into some mediocre care facility who cared more about their next paycheck than the people they were supposed to be caring for.

"Have you thought about college?" I changed the subject.

"Mom wants me to go, but I'm not sure I can leave them." Kye stared at Chloe. The two of them argued like cat and dog but he loved his sister something fierce.

She looked up, poking her tongue out at him.

"She's got trouble written all over her," I said.

"You're telling me. I'd lock her up and throw away the

key if I thought she wouldn't find a way out. At least you'll be around next year to keep an eye on her if I do decide to apply for college."

"Lucky me."

"Hey, maybe we could both take a year out and bus tables at Pizza Dash or work construction?"

"I've been thinking about looking for something more permanent." I picked up some work down at the mill on the edge of town sometimes, but between school and looking after Grams, it wasn't much.

"And quit school?"

"No way. Grams would kill me. But the shift manager, Morris, said he might be able to give me some more hours that fit around school."

"The graveyard shift? You'll be like the walking dead at school. Coach will never go for it."

"Football season is over soon. I could make it work." I didn't relish the idea of getting up at four a.m. every morning. But I'd do whatever's necessary to keep my grams comfortable.

"Have you talked to her about it?"

"The less she knows the better."

Miriam Washington was a stubborn old woman. As smart as a whip, and as quick as lightning. Her body might have been failing her, but her mind was as alert as ever.

But I knew it wouldn't always be that way, that eventually the MS would ravage her brain too.

"You could get a scholarship, Z. Talk to Coach

Farringdon. There's still time."

"Nah, we both know that's not in my future. There's no happy ending for me," I said, glancing over at Nix and Harleigh.

He'd found his salvation. His ticket out of this shithole. And he deserved it. He deserved all the good things. But I wasn't under any illusions that it was my turn. That there was something better out there for me.

Some kids escaped The Row, and some were left here to rot.

It's just how it was.

But so long as Grams was okay. So long as I did everything I could to make her life that little bit easier, I could accept my fate.

———

THE PARTY RAGED ON, but my mood only got worse. The girls had left the safety of our little circle and decided to dance over by the bonfire with Nix and Kye watching them like hawks.

"Having a little sister sucks," Kye complained as another drunken asshole tried to muscle in on Chloe.

She stood her ground though, giving him an earful and flipping him the bird as she whipped her hair around and carried on dancing with Harleigh and Celeste.

Celeste didn't look at me, and I didn't blame her. I was pissed and nothing good could come from verbally sparring with her.

"You going to sit there and sulk all night?" Nix chuckled.

"Fuck off, Wilder. You're lucky I stuck around at all when she showed up."

"Don't see why you would even care unless—"

"Do not finish that sentence," I growled.

"She's Harleigh's sister. She's Chloe's friend, Z. We can't just cut her out."

"She doesn't belong here."

"Has it ever occurred to you that maybe she doesn't belong there either?"

"What the fuck is that supposed to mean?"

"Nothing, forget it." He slouched down in his chair and blew out a long breath. "I'm just saying that her life might not be all sunshine and roses either."

"Yeah, well it's a damn sight easier than mine." I got up, blood rushing to my head. Shit, I'd drunk more than I thought.

"Where are you going?"

"To take a piss." I stalked off toward the tree line, slipping into the shadows to find somewhere quiet.

Nix's words bothered me.

What the fuck could Celeste have to complain about? She had the entire world at her feet thanks to her parents' wealth and status. They were two of the richest people in Hudson Valley. And she turned up here like she was one of us. Trying to escape her prim and perfect life.

Boo-fucking-hoo.

After I was done, I staggered back to the party,

drawing up short when I found her through the sea of people. Her blonde wavy hair taunted me, like a beacon in the night, as she lifted her arms high in the air, weaving them together. She laughed at something Chloe said, her whole face lighting up with joy.

It left a sour taste in my mouth.

I was about to make my way back over to Nix and Kye when someone approached her. Celeste smiled politely at him as he got all up in her space. But the guy—some asshole from our class—was persistent.

Before I could stop myself, I stormed over to them.

"Oh hey, man." He gave me a goofy grin. "I was just telling Blondie here that she's a long way from home."

"It's barely four miles, asshole. And I told you, I'm not interested."

"Now don't be shy, Blondie. We're all friends." He chuckled, moving closer to her. "I'll show you around, introduce you to some people."

"Get lost, Darren. She said she's not interested."

"Fuck off, Washington. I'm talking to the rich bitch."

"Take a walk, Daz," I said a little more forcefully.

"Ah, come on, man. Don't be like that. She's fair game." He started reaching for her. "Look at her, she's—"

Anger exploded from deep inside me and I shoved myself between them, glaring at him. "She said she's not interested, asshole."

"Yeah, yeah, okay." He flicked his gaze over my shoulder to Celeste and a low growl rumbled in my chest.

Darren stalked off, melting into the bodies. A few kids watched us, but most people were too high or wasted to notice.

"We had it handled, Zane." Chloe pinned me with an irritated look.

"Clo." Harleigh shook her head before turning her attention on me. "You good?"

"Darren Wellerman is an asshole."

"Maybe we should go," she said.

"You think?" My brow lifted. Harleigh should have sent Celeste packing the second she arrived.

"I'll go tell Nix we're leaving."

"I'll come with you," Chloe said, leaving me alone with Celeste.

I turned slowly, running a hand down my face as tension filled the space between us.

"Thanks for coming to my rescue." A shy smile tugged at her mouth.

She fucking smiled at me like I was her knight in shining armor.

"I didn't do it for you."

Hurt flickered in her gaze but she quickly steeled herself. "Well, thanks anyway. I didn't come here to cause any trouble."

"You don't get it, Einstein. You don't belong here with your designer clothes and flashy ride. You're an easy target and a reminder of everything we won't ever have."

"Zane, that's not—"

"Fair?" I sneered, and she blanched, the blood

draining from her face. "Look, I know Harleigh is your sister. I know you like Chloe. But if you want to do everyone a favor, stay on your own side of the res." *And the fuck out of our lives.*

"I'm a good person, you know." She lifted her chin, eyes glittering with defiance. "But you're too stubborn to even see it."

Fuck.

This girl.

She didn't know when the fuck to admit defeat.

I leaned in closer until I was breathing her air. Her scent. It messed with my head, the floral perfume she wore. Saturating my senses until I couldn't fucking think straight.

Her breath hitched, anticipation crackling in the air. But this wasn't going to be the heartfelt conversation I had no doubt she hoped for.

"I look at you," I drawled, "and all I see is a spoiled little rich girl who will never have to work for anything in her life. You and me, Einstein, you and them." I tipped my head over to where our friends were sitting. "We're not the same. So don't keep coming around here trying to pretend that we are."

Celeste recoiled, her throat bobbing as she swallowed. "I see." Pain shone in her eyes, but I didn't let it soften the jagged edges of my cruelty.

She didn't belong here, and the sooner she got that through her pretty little head, the better.

4

CELESTE

I TURNED AND WALKED AWAY FROM ZANE WITH MY HEAD held high.

His words cut deep. Deeper than he would ever realize. But it wasn't only the cruelty of them, it was the truth to them.

I *was* different to all the kids here. Even my own sister. I had been raised in a world of money and lavish dinner parties and exclusive country clubs. I didn't know the first thing about having to work for my allowance or next meal. But that didn't mean I thought I was better than them, not for a second. I enjoyed Chloe's company; we had a lot of things in common. I liked Kye's happy-go-lucky attitude and his lame jokes. I appreciated Harleigh and Nix's love for each other. Their unconditional acceptance of each other's strengths and weaknesses.

I even liked Zane.

Despite his barbed words and hateful glare, I liked the boy with a chip the size of the Hudson River on his shoulder.

But he didn't like me.

In fact, after his little outburst, hate seemed like a more accurate description for how he felt about me.

My heart sank in the pit of my stomach because for a split second, I'd foolishly thought that he was going to kiss me.

Chloe rushed over to me when she saw me approaching. "What's wrong?"

"Nothing." I forced my lips into a convincing smile. "My dad texted though. I need to go."

"Oh God, is everything okay? If you wait, I think we're going to lea—"

"It's fine, you don't need to leave on my account. I need to go though, he's asking questions."

"See you soon? Maybe you can come over one day after school and hang out at my house?"

"I'd like that," I said.

Chloe hugged me, then I went over to Nix, Harleigh, and Kye. "I'm going."

"Already? But the party is just getting started," Kye said.

"I'm sure you'll cope without me." Another smile. Another knot in my stomach.

"Where's Zane?" he added.

"Beats me."

"You'll be okay getting home?" Harleigh stood.

"Yeah, I think I can find my way. Talk tomorrow?"

"Sure." She hovered but didn't make any move to hug me.

"I'll walk you to your car," Nix offered, but I waved him off.

"Don't be silly. I can find it."

Besides, I needed a moment alone to catch my breath after Zane's verbal assault.

"Okay." He nodded. "Don't be a stranger. You're welcome at ours anytime."

The lie poured out so easily. Too easily, making my chest tighten.

"Thanks. Night." I gave everyone a small wave and doubled back toward my car. A few curious stares followed me, but no one approached me.

By the time I reached my car, some of the tears burning the backs of my eyes had slipped free, streaking down my cheeks. I inhaled a shuddering breath, trying hard not to let Zane's words affect me so much.

Maybe he was right.

Maybe I didn't belong here. But every part of my life was defined by expectation or unspoken rules. I was to carry on the family legacy. Uphold the longstanding line of Rowe's to graduate with honors and attend an Ivy League college. One day, my parents would introduce me to some wealthy ambitious guy they hoped I would marry.

My entire life was already decided for me. So was it really that misguided of me to want one thing that was truly mine. To rebel against the gilded cage that had always confined me.

I loved my parents. Sure, they didn't always get it right and they had made some downright bad decisions of late. But they were still my parents. They had provided me with a solid foundation to go out into the world. But they didn't want me to live a path of my own choosing, they wanted me to embrace the one laid out by their own design.

I got into my car and gripped the steering wheel, hanging my head in defeat as I inhaled another deep breath.

Cold, cruel, and callous, Zane Washington had been born and raised in The Row, and he was everything my parents would hate. He wasn't the kind of boy they would ever want me to date. I wasn't even sure Zane did date. But I wanted to find out.

I wanted to get to know him.

I wanted to find out what made the bad boy from across the res tick.

There was just one glaring problem.

He'd made it perfectly clear; he didn't want to get to know me.

THE HOUSE WAS quiet when I got home. Mom and Dad had said they might join the Vaughns for their annual Halloween dinner party. And my brother Max was nowhere to be seen.

Not that he was around much these days.

If I was sunshine, Max was thunder. A dark shadow hung over him lately.

I kicked off my pumps and hid them out of the way in the sideboard, then went into the kitchen in search of commiseration snacks. If there was ever a universal response to being cruelly rejected by a guy you harbored a secret crush on, it was eating your feelings.

I didn't head up to my bedroom, instead going to the roof terrace. Dropping my supplies on the small table, I grabbed a blanket and sat in the rattan egg chair, staring out at the view of Old Darling Hill in the distance.

I'd never really come up to the roof terrace before Harleigh moved in. But she'd loved it up here. And now she was gone, and it was the only place I still felt close to her.

A sister.

I had a sister.

It had been a shock last year, finding out that she was coming to live with us. Everything happened so fast, but I never resented her, not once. Not like Max who didn't take the news well at all.

I was just so grateful to have another girl in the house, someone to talk to and share things with. Little did I know, it wouldn't be anything like the picture-perfect scene I'd painted in my head.

But no matter what had happened over the last year, I loved Harleigh something fierce. I was so happy for her and Nix. That they got to have the life together they'd always dreamed of.

Even if I lost her again.

I refused to believe that would happen though. We were family. Sisters. That meant something. Something that not even space and distance could sever.

My cell vibrated and I smiled to myself. That was probably her now, checking to see if I'd made it home okay.

Except, when I opened my messages, it wasn't Harleigh at all.

Miles: I'm sorry I left. I'm confused, Celeste. I don't want to lose you, but I'm not sure I can pretend nothing happened either.

Ugh. Miles was… well, he was my best friend. The one person I'd always been able to count on. But somewhere the lines had blurred, and I'd convinced myself that maybe we could be more than friends. And now, there was every chance I was going to lose him too. The one constant in my life.

But I couldn't force myself to feel something that wasn't there.

I wouldn't.

It wasn't fair to him, or me.

Me: I get it, and I'm sorry too. You're my best friend, Miles. I don't want to lose you. But I can't pretend to feel something I don't. xo

He didn't reply, and really, I didn't blame him. Things had gotten messed up. We'd both said hurtful things. But maybe he was right. Maybe they both were.

Maybe I was the problem.

Maybe I should have been grateful for my life and all that came with it. Maybe I should have settled for the nice, safe boyfriend who didn't make my heart race or stomach flutter.

Maybe that was the life I was destined for.

A life of propriety and expectation.

But I wanted more.

I did.

I wanted to choose my own path. To make mistakes and get it wrong. To look back in ten years' time and have zero regrets. But going against the grain meant going against my parents...

Going against everything I'd ever known.

***

"WHAT HAPPENED TO YOU?" Max said when I entered the kitchen the next morning.

"I didn't sleep well," I murmured, making a beeline for the coffee machine. "You weren't in when I got home."

"I was out." He shrugged.

"At Buster's?" My brow arched, and he rolled his eyes.

"So what if I was?"

"Max…"

Buster's was a gym in Darling Row. The last place on earth my parents would want him hanging out. Which was probably why he hadn't told them about his new *hobby*.

"I don't want you to get hurt."

"Don't worry about me, Sis, I can look after myself. How's Mulligan?" He changed the subject. Not that I was in the mood to talk about Miles.

"It's complicated."

Awkward silence descended over us. Max and I had a strained relationship. He was sixteen going on twenty-one, and out of the two of us, he was the one who constantly rebelled against our parents' expectations.

He was moody, arrogant, and at times, downright cruel. But there was also something different about him the last few months. Something darker.

Maybe it was a good thing he was training at Buster's, keeping whatever demons haunted him at bay. But I wasn't so sure.

He was just a boy still.

My kid brother.

I didn't want him to lose himself completely. But if I'd learned anything over the last year, it was that you couldn't push people to see your point of view. You had to let them arrive at it in their own time.

"If it's any consolation, I didn't see the two of you going the distance anyway." He shrugged, and that was that.

"He's still my best friend, Max."

"Was… he *was* your best friend. But you dumped him and now he's your ex."

"That's not…" Oh, who was I kidding. That was entirely true.

I'd ruined one of the only friendships I valued, and now everything was a mess. Miles hated me. Harleigh had left Darling Academy and transferred back to Darling Hill High, and I spent long days at school all alone.

Zane had said I didn't belong in The Row, but part of me—the part of me who yearned for something more— didn't belong in Old Darling Hill either.

"Good morning," Dad breezed into the kitchen, looking immaculate in a charcoal suit. "How are we all?"

"Fine, Dad," Max grumbled, shoving another spoonful of cereal in his mouth.

"Celeste?"

"Morning, Dad," I said.

"How was last night with the girls?"

"It was fine." The half-lie rolled off my tongue.

"You know, you can invite them over anytime, sweetheart. I know things with your mother and

Harleigh are still strained"—understatement of the century—"but she's always welcome here."

Max shot me a skeptical look. He knew as well as I did that it wasn't that simple.

"I'll think about it, Dad," I said.

Because despite wanting to break free of his expectations and plans for *my* future, it was still hard to shake off the years of appeasing them and toeing the line.

I'd always been their golden child. The apple of my father's eye. *Capable of great things,* he'd told me growing up. And it had always been enough then—to be their pride and joy.

Their child genius.

But it wasn't enough anymore.

5

ZANE

"Zane, dear, can you come in here?"

I dragged myself out of bed and followed Grams' murmurs of frustration.

Peeking my head around her bedroom door, I found her struggling to put curlers in her graying hair. "What's up?

"Be a dear and help me out. My hands won't play nice this morning." She clenched a fist and slowly uncurled her fingers, frustration bleeding into her expression as she watched her hand quiver and tremble.

"Have you taken your meds?"

She tsked. "I am quite capable of remembering my meds, young man."

"I know, Grams. I know. Here, let me get in there." I went to her, taking hold of the difficult curler.

"Now remember to start at the ends and wrap it really tight."

If the guys could see me now, I'd never hear the end of it. But there wasn't much I wouldn't do for the woman who had raised me. Despite her ailing body, despite the fact my mom had left and never looked back, she had never once faltered.

And the truth was, no matter what her future looked like, no matter how hard things got down the line, I owed her.

"A little tighter," she instructed as I wound her thinning hair around the curler, securing it with a pin.

"You know, I'll never understand why you go to so much effort every day, Grams."

"Because it's not about how you look, it's about how something makes you feel. And looking my best just so happens to make me feel good about myself." She winked at me in the mirror. "How was the party last night?"

"Same old."

"Zane Thackeray Washington. Do I detect a trace of weariness in your voice?"

I glared at her, working through her hair as quickly as I could.

"No pretty girls to keep you entertained?"

"I am not talking about this with you."

"Oh, don't be ridiculous. Sex is the most natural thing in the world." She scoffed. "If we didn't have—"

"Grams, I am not doing this. So I suggest that if you want me to finish your hair, you stop."

It was her turn to glare at me. "I have to get my kicks somehow."

Well, it sure as fuck wasn't going to be over discussing my sex life.

I shuddered.

"You know I caught your mom and dad at it more than once. He was a horny thing, always feeling her up. No respect around me at all."

"Seriously, Grams, I don't want to hear about that shit."

I didn't want to hear anything about my parents, period. My sperm donor had skipped out on us before I'd been born and my mom... well, the less said about her, the better.

Grams was my family—the *only* family who mattered.

"Sorry, my sweet boy." She laid her hand over mine. "I know you don't like it when I talk about them."

"Whatever," I murmured under my breath, pulling away to finish adding the last of her curlers to her hair. "There, all done. Do you need anything else?"

"It's okay to talk about them, Zane. To remember."

"I'm going for a run."

She let out a heavy sigh. "Fine. I'll make a start on breakfast."

"I'll have cereal when I get back. You rest."

"Now enough of that. I will do what I can, while I can."

"Fine. I'll be back soon." I dropped a kiss on her head before getting the hell out of there.

My feet pounded on the sidewalk as I jogged through the streets beyond The Row. It was quiet out. The odd car whizzing past, the occasional dog walker out for a morning stroll.

Sweat rolled down my back despite the cool temperatures. Winter was fast approaching, the leaves turning brown and crisp. Decaying. Much like this side of town. From the derelict buildings and graffitied walls to the rust bucket cars abandoned on driveways. No wonder my mom had fled, chasing dreams of a better life.

She just hadn't cared enough to take me with her.

I'd spent years questioning what I did wrong. Why she didn't love me enough? But I never got any answers.

Grams had been bitter back then. Blaming my mother's own selfishness. Over the years she'd mellowed though. I think deep down, she missed her daughter. Hoped that one day, she might come back.

That was the last thing I wanted.

Isla Washington was dead to me.

Besides, you couldn't miss someone you barely remembered.

Adrenaline coursed through me as I cut across the street and headed toward the reservoir. The aftermath of the party lingered. Empty bottles of beer, red cups, and trash littered the whole area. I'd seen this sight plenty of times, but something felt different lately.

It was senior year. The most important year of our lives, or so Principal Marston would have us believe. But the truth was, for most of us it was just another reminder of everything we wouldn't achieve and would never have.

I followed the path around the reservoir to the other side. Technically, this was Old Darling Hill territory, but the res had always been neutral since it acted as the natural border between the two sides of town.

It was early still, so I didn't expect to see anyone down there. Least of all a familiar face.

"Washington, didn't expect to see you here." Nate Miller slid off the hood of his car and made his way toward me.

"The fuck are you doing down here?" I slowed to a walk, eyeing the blunt between his fingers, and lifted a brow. "Bad morning?"

"Couldn't sleep." He shrugged. "You want in?"

"Nah, I'm good."

"Suit yourself. Good time last night?" His gaze flicked over my shoulder across the res as if he could see the carnage left behind.

"You were here?"

"I came to get away," he said cryptically.

"You could have joined us."

Nate lived in Old Darling Hill and attended DA, but he was good people. There was something about him, a shadow that lingered in his eyes.

"And cramp your style?" His laughter was strained. "Maybe next time."

An awkward silence descended over us. I didn't know what to say, and I wasn't really looking to stick around and make small talk. He obviously sensed it, saying, "I should probably let you get back to it."

"Yeah. See you around, Miller."

Nate gave me a small nod, sucking on the end of his blunt like his life depended on it.

It was barely nine, too early to be getting buzzed, but what did I know? People had different ways of coping.

I ran right to the edge of Old Darling Hill, the big houses and perfect lawns visible in the distance. If I followed the street far enough, eventually, it would lead me right to Darling Academy.

Over the years, Nix, Kye, and I had enjoyed playing pranks on their football team, the Devils. Marc Denby, their captain, was a real asshole. They all were. They had everything we didn't: money, opportunity, and those blue blood genes that kept them out of trouble. But I guess, it occasionally worked in our favor.

Harleigh's dad had done a good thing for Nix and Jessa, I couldn't deny that. But he was the exception to the rule.

It's why I'd told Celeste to stay away. Why I'd looked her in the eye and crushed any hopes she had of having a bit of fun with a bad boy from the wrong side of the tracks.

Because I wasn't that guy.

And she sure as fuck wasn't that girl.

Celeste was nothing to me.

Nobody.

And it needed to stay that way.

***

"You're a cocky little shit, you know that?" Nix smirked at Max Rowe as the two of them danced around the sparring ring at Buster's Gym.

"Takes one to know one," he grinned back, throwing a hard right hook toward Nix. But Nix dodged it with ease, his padded fist flying into Max's stomach.

"Fuck," Kye whistled beside me. "That had to hurt."

I shrugged. "Something tells me the kid likes it."

Max was… unexpected. He'd shown up a few weeks ago, desperate to start fighting for Bryson. But he was only sixteen and even Brys knew better than to let a kid from Old Darling Hill go on his roster. He agreed to let him train with Nix though. Saw something in him apparently.

From his recent sparring sessions with Nix, I was inclined to agree. I liked to fight as much as the next guy here, but I didn't have a natural flair for it. It wasn't in my blood. Not the way it was in Nix's.

Max's too if the way he was swinging at my best friend was any indication.

"Holy shit," someone muttered as Max landed a powerful uppercut to Nix's jaw. He staggered back against the ropes, rubbing the tender spot.

"I'll let you have that one," Nix taunted, shaking it off.

But I saw the flash of surprise in his eyes at being bested by a kid two years his junior.

"Let me have it? I fucking got you good." Max smirked as he helped Nix off the ropes.

"Yeah, yeah, kid. Don't get too cocky. It was a lucky shot."

"Bullshit."

The two of them started pulling off their gloves and heading in our direction.

"How much longer do you think I'll have to train before he'll let me fight?" Max asked as he jumped down off the ring.

"So eager to get your ass handed to you?" I snorted.

"I'd take you any day of the week, Washington."

"Big words for a little kid."

He flipped me off, before grabbing his water bottle and chugging the thing dry. "You guys doing anything after this?" Max asked Nix.

"Jessa's away for the weekend, so we're going to hang out at my house," Nix said, his brows furrowing. "You want to come with us?"

Max shrugged. "Beats going home."

"Didn't realize this was the babysitters club now," I muttered, and Max flipped me off.

"My sister won't be there, right?" he quickly added.

"As far as I know Harleigh is home alone, studying."

"Good. I don't need Celeste riding my ass about this any more than she already is."

"Aw, is big sister giving you shit?" Kye hooked Max around his neck and ruffled his hair.

"Fuck off, Carter."

We all piled out of Buster's, heading for Nix's car.

"You guys feeling good about next Friday's game?" Max asked as we climbed inside.

"Hell yeah." Kye whooped. "One step closer to the playoffs. Although we'll have to make sure this one doesn't get injured now that he's headed for Albany U next year."

"Don't inflate his ego any more," I said. "Or his head won't fit in his helmet."

Max howled with laughter. "He's got a point."

"You're only jealous, assholes." Nix fired up his car and backed out of the parking spot. "Come next year, I'll be at college with my girl, and you'll be stuck in this miserable fucking town."

My stomach sank. It was a joke—he was joking. Except, it wasn't.

It was my reality.

I would still be here. Nix would be long gone, and fuck knows what Kye would be doing. Even if he stayed in The Row though, he'd make it work.

High school would be over.

And everything would change.

6

CELESTE

"CELESTE, CAN YOU COME DOWN HERE PLEASE," MOM called upstairs.

With a heavy sigh, I left my AP English homework, and went down. I peeked around the kitchen door. "Yes."

"I'd like to talk to you about something."

"Sure, Mom," I said, taking a seat at the breakfast counter. "What's up?"

"I've been asked to join the board of trustees for the Darling Hill Community Initiative, and I'd like you to get involved. I think it would really round out your college application, and I know Columbia appreciates their prospective students taking the initiative and engaging in philanthropy."

"What would it involve?" I asked.

I already had a full plate with the extra credit classes I was taking.

"Volunteering your time, but it's flexible. You can participate as much or as little as you'd like. The charity delivers several services. There are plenty of projects you could get involved with."

"I'm not sure, Mom. I'm taking five AP classes this year. My course load is stacked."

Disapproval shone in her eyes. "I talked to your father, Celeste, and he agreed this will really complement your application."

"I see." Everything inside me tensed and tightened. "So when you said you'd like me to get involved, what you really meant was, it's already been decided for me."

"Celeste, don't take that tone with me. This is a good thing, sweetheart. You've worked too hard not to give yourself the best possible chance you can of getting accepted into Columbia."

"Got it, Mom." I stood, unwilling to do this with her.

"Where are you going? I haven't finished telling you about the project."

"I've got an assignment to finish."

"Celeste, come—"

But I was gone, heading back upstairs and into the sanctuary of my bedroom.

It wasn't that I hated the idea of volunteering—I didn't. Mom had a point, I needed to work on rounding out my application.

Academically, I was a sure thing. I had a 4.0 GPA, I

was top in all of my classes, and I had an IQ of 132. It didn't get much better than that. But what I had in intelligence, I lacked in sociability.

The kids at school didn't want to get to know me; they never had. Right since fourth grade when it became increasingly apparent that my brain worked a little differently to everyone else's.

It had never really bothered me before. I had Miles, and the two of us spent days quite happily judging the rest of the DA student population. But I didn't have Miles anymore.

And with Harleigh gone, it meant I was all alone.

"It doesn't sound so bad," Max said as we drove into school. He still hadn't gotten his permit, so I was stuck driving him around.

But part of me was glad for the company. Usually, I rode in with Miles or Harleigh, but that wasn't going to happen again anytime soon, so it was either myself, or Max for company.

"I'm sure it's fine. But I wanted to choose my own extra-curricular."

"So choose one and tell Mom you can't do the initiative thing." He shrugged as if it was that simple.

But for him, I guess it was. Max had always struggled to toe the line where my parents were concerned, but something about him being the youngest and a boy meant that he usually got away with it with nothing more than a slapped wrist.

"You don't get it," I murmured, pulling into a parking spot. Kids milled around in their little cliques. The popular girls. The jocks. The nerds. But I didn't fit anywhere.

"Toby is here, so I'll see you later." Max shouldered the door and hopped out, heading for his best friend.

A group of tenth grader girls giggled, watching the two of them, and my expression dropped. I got it. Max was cute. In a he's-my-brother-so-it's-still-weird-to-think-of-him-as-cute way. But I couldn't help the stab of jealousy I felt at how easily he fit in with the masses.

It had never been hard for Max. People felt sorry for him living in my shadow and he embraced their sympathy. Their willingness to accept him as one of their own. Max was one of the most popular guys in school and he was only in tenth grade. While I could count my real friends on one hand.

Once I'd climbed out of the car, I found myself searching for Miles in the crowd. It was habit. One I needed to break considering his last message to me yesterday. I'd hurt him; it was only fair I gave him time to heal.

I'd been at this school for four years and not one single person greeted me as I made my way inside. *Lucky*, they said when they looked my way and whispered. My parents were so rich. I had such an impressive GPA. I was so smart. Going places just like my mother and father.

But I didn't feel so lucky.

Their comments didn't make my chest swell with pride.

They left me hollow.

Dejected.

And desperately lonely.

———

"MILES, THERE YOU—" The words died in my throat as I watched Marcy Gerard say something to him. He smiled down at her in a way I knew all too well.

Miles liked her.

My stomach sank as I stood there, rooted to the spot, prying on their conversation. I could barely hear them, but I didn't need to. It was obvious she was asking him out. Even more obvious that he was going to say yes.

I ducked out of the cafeteria and into the hall. I might not have wanted to be with Miles romantically, but I didn't want to see him with another girl so soon after our breakup.

Pulling out my cell phone, I sent our group chat a quick message.

Me: I'm freaking out. I just saw Miles and a girl in our class looking very cozy.

Chloe: How cozy are we talking? Making out? Hooking up?

Me: No, they were only talking, but I'm pretty sure she asked him out.

Chloe: Well, you don't want to be with him like that, right? So I guess you can't blame a guy for moving on. But it's a bit of a dickish move after he tried to persuade you to give him another chance. Maybe he's trying to make you jealous…

Me: Maybe. And I don't want to be with him. But he's still my best friend.

And that was the kicker. I'd thought we could go back to how things used to be. But we couldn't.

Chloe: I'm free tonight if you want to go out? Take your mind off him?

Me: Actually, that sounds kind of perfect. Thanks.

Chloe: Awesome, I'll text you later.

I felt marginally better when I pocketed my cell phone. Chloe had that way about her. Until I realized that Harleigh hadn't bothered to reply.

Deciding to avoid the cafeteria, I opted for the coffee

shop instead. But of course, the universe wasn't done screwing with me and the second I turned the corner, Miles called my name.

"Celeste, wait up."

My heart catapulted into my throat. I didn't want to do this, not here. But in true Celeste Rowe style, I pasted on a smile and whirled around to greet him.

"Hey, what's up?"

"I was hoping to talk to you."

"You were?" I played dumb.

"Yeah, uh… well, this is a little bit weird, but Marcy Gerard just asked me to Winter Formal." He gave me a strained smile.

"She did, wow. I don't—"

"I know it's totally out of left field, but since you and I won't be going anymore, I figured it wouldn't hurt to say yes."

"Oh, yeah. Of course." Dread pooled in my stomach. He was really doing it. Miles was going to Winter Formal with another girl.

It wasn't fair to be jealous or upset, but I'd always imagined we'd go together, even if we weren't dating. Because he was my best friend.

My *only* friend at school.

If he went with Marcy, I would have no one to go with and it was junior year. My first Winter Formal.

"Yeah?" His smile grew and I saw the relief in his eyes. He really wanted to go with her.

So much for being cut up about us.

"You don't mind?"

"No, of course not. She seems nice."

"She is. We have a couple of classes together and she said she's always wanted to ask me out but thought that we… well, you know."

"Yeah. Listen, Miles, I need to go. Have fun with Marcy."

I hurried down the hall and ducked in the girls bathroom with a sharp breath. God, that was awkward. But it was more than that. It was the fact Miles had moved on so quickly not only from our relationship but our friendship, apparently.

Max had warned me that things would never go back to how they were before, but I hadn't wanted to believe him.

Laughter sounded on the other side of the door, and I quickly slipped into a stall. The door swung open, and voices filled the bathroom.

"Oh God, can you believe he said yes?"

"Well, duh. You're ten times the girl Celeste Rowe is and so much prettier. I mean, she's so… weird."

"Amalie," Marcy laughed. "Don't be so cruel. She's his best friend."

"Was. She *was* his best friend. She ended things and now you get to help him move on."

Their laughter was like sharpened claws down my spine, and I pressed a hand over my mouth.

"I still can't believe it. I've crushed on him for years."

"It's your time to shine, babe. And by the end of the Winter Formal, it'll be like Celeste who."

They left the bathroom in a flurry of laughter, the door clicking shut behind them. But I didn't move. I couldn't. And the worst of it was, the one person I'd usually run to when something like this happened was no longer my person.

I pulled my phone out of my pocket again, opening up my text thread with Harleigh. But I stopped myself. She still hadn't responded in the group chat. Maybe she was busy... or maybe she just didn't have anything to say to me.

Chloe would though, she'd know exactly what to say to cheer me up. I switched to our chat thread.

Me: Can we get drunk tonight?

Chloe: Hells yes! I'll ask my friend to get us something from the store... what are you thinking? Vodka? Whiskey? Beer?

A small chuckle left my lips. I knew I could count on her.

Me: Nothing too strong. It's a school night.

Chloe: Fine, leave it with me. Meet at the gas station at six thirty?

Me: Where are we going?

Chloe: You'll see... I take it we're not inviting Harleigh?

I hesitated. I didn't want to deceive my sister, but things were different between us lately. She wouldn't understand.

Me: No. Let's keep this between us.

Chloe: Sounds good. See you later.

Chloe: And Celeste?

Me: Yeah?

Chloe: Don't let them get to you.

I didn't ask how she knew. But I was glad she did.
Because even though she wasn't here, it made me feel a little less alone.

7

ZANE

"LOOKING GOOD OUT THERE, SON," COACH FARRINGDON called as I held out my hand to help Warner Myson off the ground.

"Jesus, Washington, what the fuck did you have for breakfast?" he murmured.

"Sorry, I—"

"It's all good. Play like that Friday and the Terrapins won't know what's hit them."

He wandered toward Coach and the assistant coaches, but I lingered, giving myself a chance to catch my breath.

It had been a brutal practice, but only because I'd pushed myself so hard. I needed it though. Needed to expel all the restless energy zipping through me.

Kye spotted me and jogged over, dropping his arm

over my shoulder. "Shit, Z, man, I'm surprised Warner walked away from that."

"He can handle it," I said.

"We hanging tonight?"

"Yeah. I promised Grams I'd take her to this support group thing on Wednesday."

"Zane Washington, heart of the community, everyone."

"Fuck off, asshole. She thinks it'll be a good way to meet people in a similar situation."

"You or her?" He flashed me a sardonic glance.

"Haha, very funny."

"Relax, I'm only busting your balls. I think it's a good thing. Things are only going to get harder for her. Some support wouldn't hurt, for either of you."

We filed into the locker room and started stripping out of our sweaty uniforms.

"Where's Nix?"

"In with assistant coach Jameson. They're going over game tapes. Everyone's feeling tense going into Friday's game."

It was to be expected. A win would put us in the playoffs. Everyone had something to prove. My teammates. Coach and his staff. The school.

Being DA's poorer state-funded cousin meant we didn't have the best equipment or training facility. Our football stadium, if you could call it that, was old and tired. But what we lacked in resources, we made up for in grit and determination.

Kye unlaced his pants before reaching into his locker to grab his cell phone. His brows furrowed at whatever the text message said.

"Problem?"

"One word. My fucking sister."

"That was three words," I said.

"Asshole. She's asked me to cover for her tonight with Mom."

"Could be worse. She could bring a guy home and—"

"Whoa, whoa, whoa, Z. I do not need to be traumatized again."

"You think she's got a date?" I asked, and Kye's fingers flew over the screen.

A second later his phone bleeped. "No," he said. "She's hanging out with Celeste."

I tsked. "You need to discourage that shit."

"Got your panties in a twist over Harleigh's sister again?"

"Fuck off."

"Celeste is cool. I don't know why you—"

"She's not cool, she's one of them." My teeth ground together, irritation zipping down my spine. "She doesn't belong here."

"Yeah, I know. But she's Harleigh's sister. And we let Miller hang out with us sometimes and he's one of them too."

"That's different."

"Because he brings good weed?" Kye arched his brow, chuckling as he grabbed his towel and shower gel.

I shoved all my clothes into my bag and followed him into the showers.

"Yo, Z, man," Darius called from the end of the row. "Did I hear right that you turned down Freya at the party?"

"What of it?"

"A girl like that with a reputation like hers… you'd have to be an idiot to turn down—"

"And how is Cherri? Still wishing it was Nix's dick she was riding instead of yours?"

Kye let out a bark of laughter, but Darius only scowled.

"You're a real prick sometimes, you know that, right?"

"Yeah, yeah, tell it to someone who cares," I murmured, stepping under the spray.

Darius Hench needed to learn to shut the fuck up.

"He's not wrong," Kye murmured. "You need to lighten up… get laid." He smirked.

I grabbed my shower gel and threw it at his head. "You need to learn to shut the fuck up."

Kye's laughter filled the shower room. But I wasn't laughing.

Not even a little bit.

***

"HEY, MRS. CARTER," I said to Kye's mom.

"Zane, sweetheart." She grabbed my jacket and yanked me down so she could plant a kiss on my cheeks. "How many times do I need to tell you, it's Deb to you."

"Okay, Mrs. Carter." I smirked, and she swatted my chest.

"Boys. How was school today?"

"Riveting, Mom." Kye poked his head around her shoulder and kissed his mom's cheek. "But we survived."

"I don't suppose you know where that wayward sister of yours is going tonight?"

"Last I heard she's studying over at Brianne's."

"Hmm, that's what she told me too. But it's Chloe. I worry."

"So ground her *wayward* ass."

"Kye, you know I can't do that. She's almost seventeen. Besides, I never gave you a curfew once you got to junior year."

"That's because I'm your favorite." He grinned, foraging in the cabinet for snacks. He grabbed a box of Oreo's and slid them on the counter toward me. "Dig in."

"Does Coach Farringdon know that you live on a diet of cookies and soda?" Her brow arched as she watched Kye crack open a can of Coke. He guzzled it down in one, wiping his mouth with the back of his hand.

"But it tastes so good."

"You're a dork," I said with a huff of laughter.

"Is Nix with Harleigh?"

"Yep." Kye shot me a knowing look before sliding his gaze back to his mom. "But let's not go there."

"Ooh, do I sense a bit of tension brewing between my

three favorite boys?"

"They deserve to be happy," Kye said.

"You're right, sweetheart, they do. But we should never overlook our friends for love. Friends will be there to pick up the pieces when it all goes wrong."

An awkward tension descended over us, and Mrs. Carter got a faraway look in her eye.

"It's all good, Mom," Kye said, hooking his arm around her shoulder and squeezing. She jolted out of her reverie, giving him a sad smile.

"Excuse me. I think I'm going to lie down."

She left a different woman to the one who had greeted me. Kye let out a weary sigh, rubbing a hand over his face. "I thought we were making progress but it's like one step forward two back every fucking time. I don't understand how after all these years she's still so messed up from him."

"You're asking the wrong person," I said, glancing back to the hall.

"Want to get out of here?" A shadow lingered in Kye's eyes. He didn't let us see it much, always covering the truth with some lame-assed joke. But I knew what it was like to worry about someone you cared about. To wonder what would happen if you weren't there to look out for them.

"She'll be okay," I said as if it might help.

As if it might fix anything.

It wouldn't. But sometimes, a half-truth went a long way.

"She won't." He grimaced. "But it is what it is. Come on, let's go sit out back or something. I need to burn off some steam."

Code for he needed a smoke.

"Sure."

Unlike me and Nix, Kye lived in a prefab, one of the nicest places in The Row. They had a driveway and a proper backyard. But pretty things didn't mean much here. And Kye and Chloe had their own shit to deal with just like the rest of us.

We headed into the Carters' small yard and Kye dropped into one of the chairs, pulling a joint out of his pocket. "Fuck, I need this." He lit the end and inhaled deeply. "You want in?"

"I'm good."

"Shit, you feeling okay?"

"Someone's got to look after your sorry ass."

"Is it what you thought it'd be?"

"What?" My brows knitted.

"Senior year?"

"Never really gave it much thought." My shoulders lifted in a small shrug. "What about you?"

"Not much point in dreaming big when you know your chances of making it out are next to none." He stared off into the distance as if he could see his dreams on the horizon, taunting him. Daring him to go after them.

"If you could do anything, what would it be?" he asked.

"How the fuck should I know?"

"Come on, Z. We all want something." His expression guttered. "Something more than… this."

Sure I wanted things.

I wanted Grams to be cured, to not spend her days in chronic pain, wondering if her body would let her down again. I wanted to be able to pay her medical bills and get her the best care. I wanted to be able to provide for her and look out for her the way she had for me all these years.

I wanted—

"Fuck," I breathed, running a hand down the back of my neck. "You can't ask me that."

"I get it." He nodded. "You don't think I want to fix my mom? To give her everything she needs? But we're entitled to want something for ourselves too, Z. Otherwise, what's the fucking point?"

Silence filled the space between us. He made it sound easy—too fucking easy. I couldn't remember the last time I'd thought about my future, the one I might have had if I had a normal life with parents who loved me. Who wanted me around.

I'd learned long ago there was no point in wishing for things that would never come true. After my mom walked out, Grams told me that I waited weeks… weeks for her to come back. To say she'd made a mistake and that she couldn't bear the thought of being apart from me.

But she didn't.

She left without so much as a second glance. And it broke something inside my little kid heart, something that never fixed right. If you couldn't trust your mom, the woman who birthed you, the one woman on earth who was supposed to love you unconditionally, who the fuck could you trust?

Kye smoked the rest of his blunt, his eyes turning glassy as the drugs worked their way into his bloodstream. "This is some good shit," he murmured. "You sure you don't want some?"

"Nah, I'm good."

"Suit yourself." He pulled another joint from his pocket and lit it up. "It makes everything feel so much fucking better."

Yeah, for a little while.

Until you came back down to earth with a bang and realized everything was exactly the same as before.

"COACH IS GOING to shit a fucking brick when he sees the state of you at early practice," I hissed, trying to drag Kye's sorry ass into the house.

We'd been out here for hours, shooting the shit while he got high.

I'd abstained, determined to keep a clear head in case Grams needed me. Besides, practice with a hangover was no joke.

I managed to wrestle Kye into the kitchen, but his cell

phone started ringing.

"Get that, will you?" He slumped against the counter, chugging the glass of water I'd gotten him.

"Yeah?" I answered without even looking at the screen.

"K-Kye?"

"Clo? It's Zane. What's up?"

"Is Kye there?"

Glancing over at him, I grimaced. "He's... uh, he's unavailable right now."

"Shit, okay."

"Clo?" My spine straightened, not liking the trace of panic in her voice. "What's wrong?"

"It doesn't matter, I'll—"

"For fuck's sake Chloe, just tell—"

"Celesteisdrunkandidontknowwhattodo."

"Shit," I muttered. "How drunk are we talking?"

"She's pretty wasted. I got hold of some vodka and... she didn't handle it very well."

"Where are you?"

"At Maddox's house."

"Motherfucker."

"What?" Kye murmured.

I waved him off and stepped out of earshot. "No way Kye can come and get you. And I don't have a car."

"So borrow Mom's. You know she won't mind."

"Did you call Harleigh?" Celeste was her sister, she could deal with this.

"No. No way. You know things are weird between

them. Celeste just needed to cut loose."

"Stay put. I'll be there in ten minutes."

"Thanks. You're the best. And Zane?"

"Yeah?"

"Go easy on her."

I hung up, cussing Chloe under my breath. She couldn't just stay out of fucking trouble. And what the hell did she mean Celeste needed to cut loose? What could possibly be that wrong in her life of luxury that she needed to come to the other side of the res and get wasted with Chloe, and Maddox West?

"Who was that?" Kye was barely standing, his eyes two thin slits, bloodshot from all the weed.

"I need to borrow your mom's car."

"The fuck?" he slurred.

"Chloe—"

"Shit, she in trouble?"

"Don't worry about it, I'll handle it."

"Thanks, man. I think I need to lie down."

"Good plan. You think you can make it to your bedroom?"

"Sure, man." He moved sluggishly, using the wall to prop him up as he made his way down the hall toward his room.

I grabbed his mom's car keys off the sideboard and checked in on him. But Kye was already face down on the bed, snoring.

I hit his light switch, plunging the room into darkness and got the hell out of there.

8

CELESTE

THE ROOM WAS SPINNING.

Or I was spinning.

Either way, something was spinning, and I didn't feel so good.

I didn't feel—

"Celeste." Fingers snapped in front of my eyes. "Look at me."

"Clo Clo." I grinned but my face felt funny. "You're my friend. One of my ooooonly friends."

"Seriously, Clover," Chloe's friend glowered at me, and I hiccoughed.

"Two. I can see twoooo of you Maddog."

"It's Maddox."

"That's what I said, Maddog."

Jesus," he mumbled.

"I think I drank too much." I hiccoughed again.

"You think?" Chloe chuckled. "At least Zane is on his way."

"Z-Zane?" The air whooshed from my lungs. "No. Noooo. No. No. He can't see… me… like this."

"Kye couldn't come. My douchebag brother got too high to drive. So we're stuck with Zane, sorry."

This was the worst day ever.

First, I'd seen Miles with Marcy.

Then I'd overheard Marcy and her friends in the bathroom. Then Miles had acted like he'd all but forgotten about me. Throw in lots and lots of vodka, the room spinning, the wave of nausea rolling through me, and it was the perfect recipe for a pretty shitty day.

But Zane seeing me like this? I'd rather crawl into a dark hole and wait until morning.

Chloe's cell phone started ringing. "Oh. That's him." She answered. "Yeah? Yeah, okay. See you in a second."

"I am not ever never going with him. I won't do it."

"We don't have a choice. Maddox can't drive us, and you need to get back before your parents—"

"Oh my God. My parents." The pit of dread in my stomach sobered me a little.

"It's not that late. Zane can get you home before they even realize."

"Max. We should call Max. He can cover for me, he's good like that."

Chloe yanked me to my feet. "Okay?"

I nodded. Swaying a little. My head felt too heavy for my shoulders, bobbing on my neck.

"Text me when you're home," Maddog said.

"Thanks for all the vodka," I sang, leaning on Chloe. She curled her arm around my waist and led me out of the house, down the steps toward…

"Zane." My breath caught in my throat at the sight of him, standing there.

"A little help," Chloe snapped, and he stalked toward us, his expression hard.

"You came," I said, tripping on something. Chloe tried to grab me as I flung forward, but it was Zane who caught me.

"Fucking hell," he muttered, steadying me. I tried to burrow into his side, to get close to him. He was so strong, and he smelled good. Too good.

"How much did she drink?"

"Not as much as you would think given the state she's in."

"Help me get her in the car." Zane fisted the back of my jacket using it to steer me toward the door and the air whooshed from my lungs.

Chloe opened it. "You going to be okay in the back?"

"Me? I'm fine. Totally fined."

She snickered but Zane didn't laugh. He growled. A low rumble that made a shiver run down my spine.

"In you go, Einstein." He gave me a shove and I climbed albeit clumsily into the back. The door slammed shut and I inhaled a deep breath.

I didn't feel so good.

I didn't feel so good at all.

Chloe got in the front with Zane, the two of them talking about me like I wasn't there. But I could barely get my lips to work, to tell them that I could hear and that I was fine, as my head lolled to the side, and I closed my eyes.

"What's up with her anyway?" Zane asked Chloe and I felt his stare on me through the rearview mirror. Cold. Assessing… *Angry.*

I wanted to say something funny, to crack his hard exterior just a little bit, and make him smile. He deserved to smile.

Everybody did.

"Miles is going to Winter Formal with someone. I know she dumped him, but they were best friends. It's got to hurt."

"So she decided to drink her body weight in vodka?"

"I think there's more to it," Chloe said with a sigh. "But she didn't want to talk about it."

"Does it have to be you though, Clo? I know you like her, but she doesn't belong on our side of the res. She's not like us."

His words penetrated the drunken haze hovering over me. He didn't want me here. Zane didn't want me hanging out with his friends or being in his space.

Yet, he was here.

He came.

For Chloe, a sobering voice whispered. He came for Chloe because Kye couldn't.

Their voices became white noise, a distant rumble of vowels and consonants I couldn't quite distinguish. My stomach roiled, the liquor sloshing inside me like waves in an angry storm.

"I-I don't feel so good," I murmured.

"Do you need us to pull over?" Chloe asked.

"N-no, I think I'll be okay."

"Get her phone," Zane said.

"What?"

"Get her phone."

Chloe leaned between the seats, digging into my pocket.

"Wha—"

"Shh, just focus on deep breathing. In and out, okay?"

I nodded, my muscles lax and heavy all at the same time. The gruff cadence of Zane's voice filled the car, but I was too out of it to really hear the conversation.

When the car lurched to an abrupt stop, I jerked upright. Chloe and Zane climbed out, slamming their doors, and then my door was ripped open.

"Out you come, Einstein."

Zane.

My chest squeezed.

I hated how he called me that, wielding it as a weapon, as if my intelligence somehow defined me and all that I was. But it wasn't. I was so much more than mathematical equations, dictionary definitions, and test scores.

Strong, inked arms pulled me from the back of the car. My hands went to his biceps, bracing myself as he forced me onto my feet. "You good?" His eyes drilled into mine, but I couldn't look away.

"Why do you hate me?" The words spilled out.

His brows pinched, a flicker of surprise in his gaze. My heart galloped in my chest as the air turned thick, suffocating. Something electric crackling in the space between us. Or perhaps I imagined it as he turned me around and gently shoved me toward—

"Max?" I gasped.

"Fucking lightweight." My brother chuckled.

"I…" My gaze swung up to Zane. "You… you called Max?"

"Not sure daddy dearest would appreciate me marching you up to the door, Einstein."

Something passed between us again. My mind was too discombobulated to decipher it, but I felt it. A weird tingling inside me that seemed to spread from my stomach outward, making my skin vibrate.

"Zane, I—"

"Let's go, drunk girl." Max grabbed my arm and pulled me away from Zane. "Appreciate you looking out for her," he said.

His words filled me with a warm fuzzy feeling, but my blood quickly turned cold when Zane gritted out, "I didn't do it for her."

A small whimper escaped me and Max shot me a strange look.

"I think I'm going to puke." I slapped a hand over my mouth.

"Fuck's sake," my brother mumbled, dragging me toward the big imposing gates of our house.

"I'll text you tomorrow," Chloe called, and I waved a hand in the direction of her voice.

"Don't tell Mom and Dad," I murmured against my palm, trying to get air in and keep my stomach contents inside my stomach where they belonged.

"And here I thought I was the wild child." He slipped his arm around me and guided me through the gates and up to the house. "You're lucky Dad is trying to get back into Mom's graces. They went up to bed about an hour ago with a bottle of chardonnay and a box of chocolate-covered strawberries. Pretty sure he's going to try and sex his way back into her favor."

"Oh my God," I breathed, trying to block that mental image out of my head. "Why would you tell me that?"

"Because, dear sister, if I have to endure his lame attempt at romance, so do you." Max chuckled, the sound drowned out by the eerie silence of our huge house as we slipped inside.

"Kitchen? Bathroom? Or straight to bed?" he asked.

"Bed, definitely bed." Maybe with a trash can close by just in case all the vodka decided to make a reappearance.

Max helped me upstairs and into my room. I plopped

down on the bed and managed to wrestle out of my sweater.

"Celeste, seriously, I don't need to see that shit."

"Grow up, Max. They're only boobs."

He muttered something under his breath. "You want me to tell Mom and Dad you're sick in the morning?"

"I'll see how I feel." I pulled the cover over my head and curled into a ball, trying to breathe through the nausea rolling through me.

"Get some sleep."

"Mm-hmm."

But I didn't sink into a deep, dreamless sleep. I fell into a nightmare.

And the only person I wanted to save me was a boy who hated me and everything I was.

"CELESTE, WHAT ON EARTH HAPPENED?" Mom asked the second I dragged my hungover butt into the kitchen.

"I think I ate something." I clutched my stomach hoping she couldn't see through my lies.

"Sit, I'll make you my special smoothie. It'll fix you right up."

"Uh, sure, Mom." I didn't have the energy to fight.

"I already let school know you won't be in today."

"Thanks."

"Hopefully you'll be feeling better by tomorrow, I already told Mrs. Sinclair you'll be at the center."

"But, Mom—"

"Sweetheart, this is a great opportunity. The center works with a diverse group of people. I'm sure there'll be an opportunity to pick and choose the projects you get involved with. It'll really cement my position on the board."

And make her look good.

I bristled underneath my weak smile. "Sure, Mom. Whatever you think is best."

"Excellent. Now drink this." She shoved a glass of thick green sludge toward me.

"What *is* that?"

"It'll help, I promise."

I lowered my face to the glass and sniffed the contents. It smelled oddly sweet.

"It won't hurt. Go on."

I tested a small sip. It wasn't as bad as it looked, but I wasn't convinced it would settle my stomach.

Mom nodded her approval, leaning against the counter. She was so poised and perfect, not a hair out of place in her sleek, polished ponytail. Her makeup was subtle yet glowing. Sabrina Rowe-Delacorte oozed etiquette.

"You know, Celeste, the next two years are vital if you want to pursue a career in medicine. You can't afford any distractions, sweetheart."

"What is that supposed to mean?" I sat a little straighter, not liking the insinuation in her voice.

"Harleigh and her friends from across the

reservoir—"

"She's my sister."

She flinched at that, a flash of ire flitting across her impenitent expression. To Mom, Harleigh was a reminder that Dad wasn't perfect. That he'd had a life before her, before us. A dirty little secret that had almost ruined him.

But I didn't care that Harleigh's mom had escaped to The Row, that Harleigh had grown up there, barely surviving. She was my sister, my blood. Harleigh was my family. The rest meant nothing to me.

I just wished that Mom could see that. That she could put aside her misguided prejudice and see Harleigh for the amazing, strong, and brave girl she was.

But Sabrina Delacorte wasn't perfect either.

Even if she would never admit it.

She strived for perfection, to maintain her position among Darling Hill's elite. And part of me got it, I did. It was all she had ever known; it was imprinted on her DNA. But Mom lived in a world I hadn't asked to inhabit. A world that I both revered and resented.

I knew how lucky I was that this was my life. That things would come easy to me because of my name, my family's wealth and prominence in society. But I didn't want to exploit that, to rely on it so heavily that it became second nature to abuse it.

I wanted to earn people's trust, their friendship, and respect. I wanted someone to love me despite all that.

Not because of it.

9

———

ZANE

"You look like shit," I said, the second Kye's door swung open.

"Fuck, I'm sorry. I didn't know Clo would—"

"Relax, it's fine."

"She said you drove Celeste home and handed her off to Max."

"Yep."

"Anything else you want to say about it?"

"Nope."

"Glad we got that settled." His mouth twitched.

"How's your mom?"

"She's functioning, barely. Said we can borrow the car this morning, though you should probably drive." He threw the keys at me. "I still feel a little wired."

"Coach is going to kick your ass if you flake out of practice."

"I won't."

"Wait for me, assholes," Chloe called from somewhere inside the house.

"You have two minutes, Clo, and then we're out of here."

Kye grabbed his bag and followed me out to his mom's car. "Nix?"

"Don't ask," I murmured. He was riding in alone with Harleigh. Code for Jessa was home last night, and they were probably going to park somewhere before school and fuck like horny teenagers.

I loved the guy more than anything, but he'd turned into a fucking pussy.

"You know it won't be like this forever," Kye said as if he could hear my thoughts. "They're just in that honeymoon phase where you can't get enough of each other."

"Whatever." I yanked the door open and climbed inside, Kye's laughter grating on my last nerve.

"So." He got inside. "I know you said you didn't want to talk about it, but what was up with Celeste last night?"

"How the fuck should I know?"

"You gave her a ride home." He shrugged. "Figured you might have asked her what was up."

"Well, I didn't." The less said between us, the better.

But her words wouldn't get out of my head.

Why do you hate me?

Was she really that fucking clueless? She had everything. She had a family who had her back, more money than sense, and a future of her own choosing. Celeste Rowe was the poster child for the American dream, and Darling Row was nothing more than a living nightmare.

"She's really under your skin, isn't she?"

"Carter, I swear to fucking God, drop the shit with me and Celeste."

"Geez, relax. I'm just busting your balls. But if you're not going to hit that maybe you should consider saying yes to Freya. I swear, bro, a good fuck and you'll be feeling all kinds of better."

"You're an asshole."

"But I'm your asshole." He grinned. "Shit, I've got a meeting with Miss Kyrie. She's going to push for my decision on college applications."

"You should do it. Even if you apply and can't make it work, it might give you options."

"Yeah, I guess. But Mom is a fucking mess, and Chloe is a disaster waiting to happen."

"Don't be so hard on her, she's a good kid."

"Yeah, I know. I just worry. She's my kid sister. I want more for her, you know."

"More than Maddox West?" My brow quirked, and he snorted.

"Maddox knows to keep his hands off."

"You know she was at his place last night."

"I know. But she said nothing happened."

"I don't know how you do it," I said, gripping the wheel a little tighter as the car rumbled to life beneath us. "Worry about her and your mom."

I could barely handle looking after Grams, let alone a sister. But Kye didn't complain. Sure, he liked to get high occasionally or fuck away his problems. But he always did it with a smile and some lame ass joke.

"Hey, we all got shit to deal with, Z. It is what it is." He stared out of the window, watching Chloe burst out of the door and jog toward us.

"Yeah," I said. "You're not wrong there."

All you could do was try to survive too.

And hope it didn't drag you down with it.

"GRAMS, I'M HOME," I called the second I slipped into the trailer.

"I'll be right out."

I made a beeline for the refrigerator, helping myself to a carton of juice. Today had dragged. Practice was a shitshow. Nix and Darius got into it, twice. Kye was barely awake. And Coach Farringdon was like a bear with a sore head. Needless to say, we spent more time running suicides than we did actually practicing. My quads ached, my calves burned, and my mood was in the gutter. But I knew better than to complain to Grams.

Chugging down the juice, I surveyed the papers scattered on the table. It was usually a stack of bills that needed paying. But one letter snagged my attention. It was from the medical insurance company. I went to lift it off the pile when Grams shuffled into the room on her walking stick.

"Don't be worrying yourself with all that," she said, snatching it away from me. "Just another pointless letter. Waste of paper if you ask me. How was your day?"

"Same old."

"School is important, you know, Zane. If you don't graduate—"

"I'll graduate. Don't you worry about me, Grams." Ducking my head, I kissed her cheek. "What time do you want to leave?"

She had her new support group tonight.

"Are you sure we can borrow Nix's car?"

"He said we could." I'd double-checked today. He and Harleigh were having dinner with Jessa and her boyfriend, so Nix's beloved car was all ours. I really needed to invest in my own wheels, but money was tight and wouldn't stretch to a car. I'd started saving when I first started working at the mill. But every time I got close to having enough for a down payment, something would blow up, fall apart, or need replacing, and getting my own ride had to take a back seat again.

I watched Grams struggle as she cleaned off the counter. Today was a good day, she was managing to shuffle around on her own two feet. But it was getting less and less frequent.

We already had a wheelchair stowed away for her, but

the stubborn woman was refusing to use it until she absolutely needed it.

A cry of pain pierced the air, and I rushed over to her side. "Grams?"

"Just a spasm, dear." She inhaled a shaky breath, her skin pale and clammy. "Don't worry about me, I'll be fine."

"Do you need your meds?"

"No, no. It'll pass." She clenched and unclenched her fist, forcing her fingers flat against the counter as tremors of pain wracked through her.

I hated it.

Fucking hated that this degenerative disease was eating away at her, stripping away all her strength, and leaving her weak and vulnerable.

She took another deep breath, and I said, "Maybe I should call Doctor Hatfield."

"No. If it's still bad, I can speak to the nurse at the center."

"Fine."

Once she'd made her mind up about something, there was no changing it.

"Let me go load your wheelchair—"

"Zane Thackeray Washington, you will do no such thing… I am quite capable of walking with my stick."

"Whatever you say, Grams. Let me go freshen up and I'll bring the car around."

"Good idea." She managed to lift her hand and tap my cheek. "You're a good boy, Zane." Something passed over her, but I didn't have the courage to ask what she was thinking. Because I knew it wouldn't be anything good.

I went into my room and closed the door, giving myself a second to catch my breath. What I really wanted to do was kick the shit out of something. But I couldn't even do that, because I had to drive Grams to her support group. Besides, it would feel good for about a minute and then reality would come crashing down around me again.

Changing out of my Hawks hoodie, I slipped on a plain black hoodie and sprayed a couple of puffs of cheap cologne to hide the musty smell that came with poor ventilation and damp walls.

When I went back into the living room, Grams was trying to get her jacket on. Watching her struggle was just another knife to the fucking heart.

"Here," I said, helping pull it over her arms. "There, all set?"

She nodded and I helped her to the door before going to bring the car around. Grams couldn't quite manage the steps up to the trailer, so I'd installed a ramp over the summer that made things a little easier.

"Such a fancy car," she said as I helped her into the passenger seat.

"Don't let Nix hear you say that." I chuckled.

"You have the address for the center?"

It was a community center on the edge of town, right between Old Darling Hill and the neighboring town.

Thankfully, I could drive around rather than cutting through Celeste's neighborhood.

"It lasts for a couple of hours but I'm not sure I'll stay the whole time."

"It's okay, Grams. I can hang out in the cafeteria."

"Thank you, that's very kind of you."

"You're worth it." I flashed her a rare smile.

"One day, dear, you'll make a young woman very happy."

My brows crossed because surely, she wasn't going down this path again. The woman who had always drilled it into me that women couldn't be trusted, that love was a fool's game.

"I know you don't believe me, Zane. But you have so much love to give. You just need to find the right person."

I didn't reply, I couldn't.

Because I didn't want to disappoint her. I didn't want to break her heart.

"You know, I won't be around forever and the thought of you alone—"

"Don't." My voice cracked as I gripped the steering wheel tighter because I couldn't think about that.

I fucking couldn't.

She let out a small hum of disapproval. But Grams knew I didn't handle this shit well. Talking about my feelings, my emotions. I preferred to lock that shit down tight and bury my head in the sand.

We rode in thick silence, the quiet hum of the radio softening some of the tension. It was ironic really that she was trying to lecture me about life when she was one of the most stubborn people I'd ever met.

Finally, we reached the center. "Ooh, it's fancy," Grams stuttered over the words a little.

"You sure we shouldn't call Doc—"

"Stop fussing." She tsked. "I've been looking forward to this. Park close so I can walk in."

I rolled my eyes.

She was right, it was fancy. But it was hardly surprising given that it was on the edge of Old Darling Hill.

A couple of people entered the center ahead of us, and they looked normal enough.

"It's rude to stare, Zane Thackeray."

"I'm not... come on." I held out her stick and stuck close by in case she needed me. It was a slow process, her coordination weakened by the disease ravaging her body. But in true Grams style, she managed to walk inside with her head held high.

"And who do we have here?" A tall woman in a gaudy pink pantsuit greeted us.

"Mrs. Washington," Grams said.

"Ah, yes." She checked her clipboard. "It's so lovely to meet you. I'm Claudia Hancock. And you are?" Her assessing gaze swung to me.

"Zane."

"My grandson." Grams shot me a disapproving look.

"Will you be joining us?" she asked, and I shook my head.

"I was hoping there was a cafeteria where I could grab a drink or something?"

"There is, just down the hall. They make the best pie."

Pie. Great.

Schooling my bemusement, I gave Grams a kiss on the cheek. "Try and stay out of trouble. I'll see you in a bit."

"Shouldn't that be my line?" she murmured.

Claudia chuckled. "The youth of today. If you'd like to follow me, we can get you settled."

I watched Grams shuffle down the hall toward a set of double doors with a strange ache in my chest.

She needed this; I knew that. But it didn't make it any easier.

10

CELESTE

"Celeste, so lovely to meet you." Mrs. Sinclair motioned to the chair opposite her desk. "Please, take a seat."

"Thank you," I said, fighting off the urge to yawn.

The hangover from hell had lingered all day. It had been so bad that at one point I'd almost fallen asleep in math. Mr. Vance was not happy, but my classmates thought it was more than a little amusing.

Perfect little Celeste Rowe falling asleep in class, how scandalous.

"Your mother speaks very highly of you." I smiled unsure of how to answer that. "And we're excited to have you here for the rest of the year."

"Rest of the… yes." I swallowed over the lump in my throat. "Well, I'm excited to be here."

"Columbia is an excellent school. My grandson is due to go there next year. Maybe I could introduce the two of you? I'm sure he'll have some advice on how to win over the admissions board."

Oh, dear God. Was this all a setup? Mom's covert way of introducing me to a boy she thought worthy of my affections? I wouldn't put it past her. Or Dad for that matter.

They probably worried that Harleigh's penchant for bad boys from The Row would rub off on me and wanted to nip it in the bud sooner rather than later.

I suppressed a groan.

"Celeste?" Mrs. Sinclair's eyes crinkled with concern.

"I'm sure your grandson is very excited about starting at Columbia."

"Indeed. He's going to be a surgeon." She beamed. "Good with his brain, steady with his hands. Oh, listen to me, I sound like a bad dating ad." Her laughter turned a little strangled.

"I'm very much focused on my studies this year. It doesn't leave much time to have fun, I'm afraid."

"No, of course not. And now you'll be volunteering. But you know, my Cooper stops by now and again and helps out. Such a compassionate soul."

"That's… great."

And my worst nightmare. I didn't want to be set up with one of Mom's friend's sons.

"Once we figure out your schedule, I'll pass it onto Coop and see if he can make it."

"Oh no, you don't need to—"

"Nonsense, I think the two of you would have a lot to talk about. He's also an honors student."

I pursed my lips, hoping to end this line of discussion.

"Now, did your mom explain that we have a wide range of projects you can get involved with?" Mrs. Sinclair pushed a brochure toward me.

"She did."

"Good. Some of our projects are very well staffed. But others struggle to attract volunteers. I've marked a couple that might be of interest to you where we could really use the help."

"Great, thanks." I flicked through the brochure, pausing on the passages she'd highlighted. "MS support group, for people with multiple sclerosis?"

"That's correct. We have around twenty clients who access the group, and our focus is on support, advocacy, education, and wellness and healthy living. Attendees can also access any of the other services we run. Do you have a particular interest in this area?"

"I've been reading some papers on the impact of support groups on the overall quality of life for people across a range of diseases. MS sufferers were one of the sample groups."

The research demonstrated a significant impact in nearly all sample groups. It wasn't a perfect science, no intervention was. But if people had a safe space to share their experiences, seek and give support, and interact with people in a similar situation, their mental health generally improved which in turn usually reduced pain and symptoms.

"The group is actually meeting right now, if you'd like me to introduce you to Claudia, the project supervisor?"

"I'd like that."

"Great, I'll take you down and the two of you can have a chat. Then you can stop by and fill in the rest of these forms. How does that sound?"

"Sounds good."

I followed Mrs. Sinclair into the hall and down to the main meeting room. It was a big open-plan space with a kitchen hatch at one end and some clusters of tables. People milled about, talking and laughing. A couple were playing chess.

"Claudia." Mrs. Sinclair waved at a woman in a pale pink pantsuit. She reminded me a lot of Mom. Perfectly poised, not a hair out of place.

"Jeanine, is there a problem?" She looked me up and down. So much for the welcoming committee.

"This is Celeste Rowe. Sabrina's daughter."

"Nice to meet you." She smiled but I didn't miss the slight curl to her lips. "What can I help you with?"

"Celeste is going to be volunteering with us and she's interested in your group."

"I see."

"Be a doll and let her sit in on today's group. She can get a feel for things and meet some of the regulars. I'll see you back in the office in an hour." Mrs. Sinclair gave me a little clap on the shoulder and left me with Claudia.

"How old are you?"

"Seventeen."

She huffed, spinning on her heel and making a beeline for one of the tables. "You can keep Martha and Miriam company," she said, motioning for me to sit.

I slid onto a chair and smiled at the two elderly women. "Hello, I'm Celeste."

"I'm Martha. You're… very pretty," one of the women stuttered.

"Thank you." I blushed. "Have you been coming here long?"

"Al-almost a year."

I nodded and looked to the other woman.

"Miriam. It's my first day," she said.

"Then I guess we have something in common."

"Do you go to Darling Hill High?"

"Uh, no. I actually go to Darling Academy."

"Ah, I see." Miriam pursed her lips. "Born and raised in Darling Row myself."

"I have some friends who live in The Row."

"You do?" Surprise flared in her eyes. "Well, I guess we live in a different time to when I was a young girl growing up."

"The youth of today." Martha smiled. "Ah, what I w-wouldn't give." She took a deep breath. "To do it all again."

"It's not for me," Miriam huffed. "All that teenage angst and heartache."

"Oh, I don't know. It was exciting."

I listened to the two of them debate the impermanence of youth, smiling to myself. Here were two elderly women suffering with an awful disease, and yet, not once did they complain or gripe.

"What about you, Celeste?"

Both looked at me expectantly and I realize I'd zoned out of the conversation.

"Sorry, what?"

"What do you want to do when you're older?"

"I…" I hesitated.

Martha's question caught me off guard. It had been a long time since anyone asked me that. I had been planning to go to Columbia to study medicine for as long as I could remember. It was my destiny, decided by my parents the second I showed interest in playing doctors and nurses. It only grew from there. My natural affinity for caring. Add in the early signs of my impressive IQ and Mom and Dad had my future all mapped out for me.

Celeste Rowe, daughter of Michael Rowe and Sabrina Rowe-Delacorte, would make her mark on the world as a doctor.

"Dear?" Miriam said.

"A doctor. I want to be a doctor." The words sat heavy in my chest. It wasn't that I didn't want it. I just wasn't certain it was the path for me.

I wanted to help people, that I was certain about. But there were more ways than becoming a doctor to do that.

"A doctor, my, my. You must be very intelligent if you want to attend medical school."

"I do okay." A faint smile traced my lips.

"Ladies, how are we getting on over here?" Claudia laid her hand on Martha's shoulder.

"Celeste was just telling us about her dreams of becoming a doctor."

"Ah yes." Claudia's eye crinkled with disdain. "The future surgeon, was it?"

"I'm not sure what specialty I want to go into yet."

I'd never met this woman, but it was clear she had a personal issue with me—or my family name.

"We're going to all come together now to do our talking circle. You don't need to join us if—"

"Actually, I'd love to sit in, if that's okay?"

"Of course." She pursed her lips and spun on her heel, marching away.

Miriam whistled under her breath, and I glanced at her. "Someone feels threatened," she said quietly.

"Claudia is a good woman," Martha added. "But she's very precious about her groups. I've seen at least two volunteers leave this year because they didn't fit Claudia's vision."

"Oh." My stomach knotted.

Martha chuckled, laying a bony hand on mine. "Don't worry, doll. We'll look out for you."

Miriam nodded, a conspiratorial smile on her face but all I could think was...

What had I gotten myself into?

IT WASN'T easy listening to everyone share their stories in the talking circle. More than one person got upset, sharing how much of a burden they felt to their family, how much pressure it put on the people around them.

For as unwelcome as Claudia had made me feel, it was impossible to deny how good she was at her job. She gave everyone space to talk, reassuring them, offering them words of advice and practical tips. But she didn't steal the show. She encouraged everyone to pitch in, to share the little things that made living with MS easier for them.

It was humbling to see the strength among the small group of people who face a daily struggle of chronic pain and fear for what the future might hold for them.

At the end of the session, Claudia offered one-to-one counsel, as did a local nurse with experience in pain management. But Miriam made a beeline for Mr. Clarkson, the center's advisor on financial aid and support. I watched as she pulled a letter from her purse and showed him the contents.

"It's likely to be the insurance company refusing to cover all the medical bills," Mrs. Sinclair said over my shoulder, startling me.

"I… that happens a lot?"

"More often than you would think. A lot of our attendees have Medicare. It works when it works, but when it doesn't… things can be very tough for those families."

My heart sank. I didn't ask what would happen. I was

well versed on the flaws of the healthcare system. But I'd never witnessed firsthand the impact of it.

She motioned for me to follow her down the hall. "Did you enjoy the session?"

"Very much. Although Claudia didn't seem to approve of my presence."

"Claudia is one of our best managers. She cares a great deal about her groups and attendees. But she can be... precious." We reached some sunny yellow double doors. "This is our cafeteria. It's open daily and offers a range of light lunches and snacks. Staff and volunteers get a discount. And I've heard the lemon cake is particularly good." She winked, pulling the door open.

I slipped inside, my stomach rumbling at the burst of smells. But the feeling quickly passed as dread flooded me.

For sitting in the corner, with a scowl on his face, was Zane.

11

ZANE

THE UNIVERSE ENJOYED FUCKING ME OVER.

That was the only explanation for the fact Celeste Rowe was standing by the door, looking like a fish out of water.

"Celeste?" The woman commanded her attention, and Celeste blinked up at her, forcing a smile.

"I could use some coffee."

I snorted. She followed the woman to the service counter, and the two of them ordered, paying me no attention.

There were a few other people in the cafeteria. Nobody had bothered me while I'd been here, waiting. But I was used to people giving me a wide berth. The residents this side of the reservoir usually took one look at my tattoos, my piercings, and black hoodie, and deemed me suspect.

Once they had their drinks and cake, the woman led Celeste to a table within earshot of mine. I could have gotten up and left, waited outside in the car. I could have gone to the restroom or even waited in the hall.

But I didn't.

Because despite hating the fact that she was here, inserting herself into yet another part of my life, I was curious about why the fuck she was here.

"Your mother said you could commit to three sessions a week? Is that correct?"

"Yes, I should be able to do two evenings after school and some hours over the weekend. But my course load is pretty heavy since I'm taking a lot of AP courses, so I don't want to overcommit."

"Of course not."

I fought the urge to tsk. Little Miss Einstein was quite something.

Her eyes flicked to mine as if she heard my thoughts, and instead of looking away, I held her stare with a glower of my own. Her cheeks flushed as her breath caught at the strange crackle of tension that rippled between us.

Hatred. That's all it was.

I hated everything she represented.

Celeste broke first, ducking her head as she pushed the piece of cake around her plate.

If she was going to be volunteering here, I'd need to

find out when so I could avoid her. The last thing I wanted was to cross paths with her any more than I already had to, given that Chloe seemed insistent on keeping her around as a friend.

"That's great," the woman said. "It's so exciting for us to have Sabrina's daughter joining our team of volunteers. We're very lucky and grateful to have her on the board this year."

My fist curled against my thigh. These people, the world they lived in. I knew the center relied on and benefited greatly from donations such as the ones I'm sure Celeste's parents made on the regular. But it seemed so unjust, so fucking unfair, that they had enough money to give to charity like they were handing out candy, when some families in The Row couldn't afford to put a hot meal on the table.

I shot up and stalked toward the door. I needed some air.

"Excuse me, young man," the woman's voice stopped me.

"Yeah?" I glanced back.

"Are you… attending one of our groups?"

"What's it to you?"

She blanched, and for a second I felt an ounce of guilt. But fuck her and this place and fuck Celeste Rowe for sitting there, pity shining in her eyes.

"I meant no offense." The woman's expression softened. "You seemed troubled is all."

"I'm waiting for someone. The group leader said I could hang out here."

"Of course. We welcome everyone—"

"I gotta go." I stormed out of there, the jaws of shame nipping at my heels.

———

I FOUND Grams talking with a white-haired woman with skin as wrinkled as dried grapes.

"Here he is now, my Zane Thackeray." Grams beamed, reaching for me.

"I hope you didn't get into too much trouble," I said.

"Who, me?" She winked. "This is Martha."

"Hi."

"They sure didn't make 'em like you in my day. You look like one of them sexy rock gods—"

"Martha, don't embarrass the boy."

"Okay, Grams. Why don't we get you to the car." I took her elbow trying to steer her away.

"Such a good boy," Martha cooed. "I'll see you next week, Miriam. I'm sure Mr. Clarkson will come up with a solution by then."

"Mr. Clarkson?"

"Nothing for you to worry about," she rushed out, shooting her new friend an irritated look. Martha clapped a hand over her mouth with a small gasp.

"What is—"

"Let's go, dear." Grams started shuffling away, leaving me to follow.

"What aren't you telling me?" I hissed, remembering the letter she'd left out on the counter.

"It's just some insurance claptrap. Like I said, dear, it's nothing you need to worry about."

But I couldn't let it go, and the second I got her situated in the car, I twisted to look at her. "Grams, whatever it is, you can tell me."

"Zane…"

"Grams…"

The air turned thick around us. It wasn't uncommon for the two of us to butt heads. I could be as stubborn as she was, and I refused to let this go.

"You don't need to protect me. Whatever it is, I can help. I can—"

"The insurance won't pay out for the new treatment."

"Okay." Dread sluiced through me, making my blood run cold. "What does that mean exactly?"

"It means, sweetheart, that I can't afford it."

"But that's bullshit. Doctor Hatfield said the infusion therapy could help, right? Especially since your flare ups are getting more regular."

"I know, sweet boy." She released a weary sigh. "I know."

"How much short will you be a month?"

"About eight hundred bucks."

"Fuck."

"Zane, it'll be fine." She laid a trembling hand on my arm. "I'll be fine, dear. I always am."

"But you need the treatment. The doctor said—" Fear coiled around my lungs, squeezing the air from them.

If she couldn't have the treatment her symptoms would get worse. She would need more help. Specialized care I couldn't give her.

"Shh, now. We'll figure it out. Mr. Clarkson is going to make some calls on my behalf. I'm sure there are other options."

Her voice was drowned out against the roar of blood in my ears. What use was I if I couldn't even take care of her? After everything she'd done for me, the sacrifices she'd made. I had to figure out a way to raise some cash and fast.

"Zane Thackeray."

"Y-yeah. Okay." I fired up the engine when something caught my eye.

Celeste.

My jaw clenched as I glared at her.

"Sweet little thing," Grams said, and I frowned over at her.

"What?"

"The blonde. Celeste. She's going to be volunteering at the support group. I like her, she's…"

More white noise filled my mind, pulsing inside me like a violent storm on the horizon. Celeste was going to be here weekly, helping out at the group my grams was attending?

Fuck. That.

I couldn't deal with her every week, befriending Grams and filling her head with her entitled, privileged ideals.

"Zane, dear? We're not moving."

"I… what?"

"The car. We're not moving."

With a grumble, I backed out of the parking space and hit the gas.

"What on earth has gotten into you?"

"Nothing."

"Nothing my ass. It was her, wasn't it? The girl."

"Nope. I have no idea what you're talking about."

"Really?" She scoffed. "Because you're acting like a damn fool."

"Sorry, I can't hear you." I turned up the radio and ignored her protests.

It was childish, yes. But there was no way in hell I was going to talk about Celeste with my grams.

No fucking way.

"WHO KICKED YOUR PUPPY?" Kye asked me the next morning as we walked the short distance to Nix's place.

Harleigh had an appointment in Albany with her therapist but much to his annoyance, Jessa had offered to take her.

"Don't ask," I murmured, kicking a stone with my boot.

"But I am asking."

"I took my grams to that support group yesterday."

"Oh yeah. How did it go?"

I hesitated, the words teetering on the top of my tongue. But I'd barely digested Grams' confession about the insurance. I'd spent half the night lying awake, trying to come up with a plan for raising the money that didn't end up with me in jail or worse.

"Celeste was there," I said.

"At a support group for MS? What was she doing there?"

"Volunteering apparently. Star student clearly isn't enough for her, so she needs to be Little Miss Goody Two-shoes as well."

Kye's brows furrowed. "Did something happen?"

"Nope. We ignored each other."

"Very mature of you."

"I have nothing to say to her."

"Say to who?" Nix appeared in the doorway.

"Celeste is volunteering at Grams' new support group."

"She is?"

"Harleigh didn't mention it?" I asked.

"No. She hasn't said much about Celeste, Max, or her dad."

"Yeah, what's up with that?" Kye said as we piled into Nix's car.

"I think she's finding it hard being Harleigh from The Row *and* Michael Rowe's daughter."

"Yeah, the two don't exactly go hand-in-hand."

"Hopefully her therapist can help her work through some stuff, because I feel like every time I try to talk to her, she clams up." Nix gripped the wheel with both hands before jamming the key in the ignition.

"Going back to Celeste… did you talk to her?"

"No, why the fuck would I do that?"

He shrugged. "After last night—"

"Give it a rest, Wilder. I had enough of Grams quizzing me all night on her new friend."

"No shit, she met Celeste?" Kye's eyes glittered with amusement.

"Why are the two of you so obsessed about Celeste all of a sudden? Didn't think so," I added when neither of them answered.

"What's the plan for the weekend? Away game, baby." Kye rubbed his hands together. "You know what that means?"

"A long ass bus ride?"

He shook his head with a grin. "Fresh pussy."

"One day, your dick will rot and fall off," Nix said.

"Says the guy who's settled for one pussy for the rest of his life."

"Let's not talk about B's pussy." Nix glowered. "Chloe and Harleigh are riding with Jessa. Something about a girls' road trip."

"Nice," Kye said.

"Please tell me Celeste isn't going."

"Would it be a problem if she was?" Kye smirked. "Since you obviously don't give a shit about her and all."

"Fuck you." I grabbed a half-empty water bottle and threw it at his head.

"You're not fooling anyone, Z, man. You want her."

"Like fuck I do. She's one of the most stuck-up, annoying girls I've ever met."

"Kye," Nix warned. "Don't bait him. It never ends well."

"Worried he might corrupt your girl's sister?"

Nix glanced at me and cast me a scathing look. "That's exactly what I'm worried about."

"Trust me, I will never touch Celeste Rowe, even if she was the last girl on the fucking planet."

Kye pinned me with an amused look, and I glowered, "What?"

"Famous last words, Z. Famous. Last. Words."

12

CELESTE

"So how did it go?" Mom asked as we ate breakfast. It was unusual for her to be home. Usually, she and Dad were long gone in the morning.

"It was fine," I said, pushing eggs around my plate.

I just wasn't hungry. And it had nothing to do with Mom's question, or Claudia's icy reception, and everything to do with Zane Washington.

He was the last person I'd expected to see at the center. And I still couldn't figure out for the life of me what he was doing there.

Not that I'd asked Harleigh or Chloe. I couldn't—they would have too many questions. Besides, I didn't want to make trouble for him if they didn't know.

"Really, Celeste, would it hurt to sound a little more enthusiastic? This is a great opportunity for—"

"You, Mom. It's a great opportunity for you."

"And what is that supposed to mean, young lady?" She glared at me, shock glittering in her eyes.

I rarely talked back to her. It wasn't worth it. Sabrina Delacorte was a formidable woman, and although she was my mother, I'd been raised to respect my elders. Especially her.

"Nothing, it means nothing. I'm just tired and cranky. Mrs. Sinclair seemed really nice. But Claudia was—"

"You helped with her MS support group? I thought you'd be more interested in the brain injury group?"

"Actually, I enjoyed it."

"Claudia is a snake, Celeste. I don't want you anywhere near that woman."

"Well, maybe you should have thought about that before you volunteered my time there."

"You know, darling, I haven't wanted to say anything because quite frankly, this family is fractured enough, but I'm worried about you, Celeste. Ever since Harleigh—"

"Save it, Mom." I bolted off the stool. "Harleigh is my sister. She will always be my sister. Nothing you do or say will change that."

"That's exactly what I'm worried about," she said sharply.

"Mom!" I gasped.

"Well, she's not a good influence. Her and those… those boys she insists on hanging around with." Her face screwed up in blatant disgust.

"And what about Chloe? She's my friend." Frustration coursed through me. Mom was so narrow-minded, unwilling to look past her position of money and privilege to recognize that just because someone didn't have the kind of life we had, didn't make them a bad person.

"Yes, well. I would prefer it if you didn't."

"I can't believe you just said that." I winced, trying to disguise the hurt I felt. "Do you have any idea how hard it is to make friends at school? How lonely it can be?"

"You have Miles."

I had Miles. I swallowed the words. She didn't get it. Friendship wasn't important to Mom, success was. Station in society was. Friends—true friends, people you could trust—were few and far between in our world.

No, not my world, her world.

I hadn't asked for this life. And although I was grateful for it, for the opportunities it gave me, happiness was more important. A sense of self-worth and acceptance was more important. To know that the people around you cared because they wanted to, not because they thought they could use you to their own ends.

When I'd started Darling Academy in seventh grade, I'd made my first real girlfriend. At least, I'd thought she was. Turned out Jolie Radley's parents had pushed her to befriend me in hopes of getting close to my parents. For five months, they welcomed me into their family, treated me like their own, only to drop me like a sack of bricks when my mom publicly embarrassed Mrs. Radley at a school event.

I gave up trying to make friends after that. If my intelligence didn't intimidate them, my parents did.

Emotion swelled inside me, and I blinked away the tears building.

"Celeste, really," Mom scolded. So hard faced and cold hearted. Max had been made in her image, but me… sometimes, I wondered where the hell I'd come from.

"I'm going to brush my teeth." I hurried out of there, steeling my spine.

But when I reached my room and slipped inside, the door clicking shut behind me, the dreadful weight of loneliness felt insurmountable.

I was Celeste Rowe. The perfect student, the perfect daughter, the perfect college applicant.

I had the perfect life.

But perfection had a price.

One that was costing me my own happiness.

BY THE TIME Friday afternoon rolled around, I was miserable. Miles was ignoring me, in favor of hanging out with Marcy and her friends. Harleigh was still avoiding me. And things at home were more strained than ever.

So when Nate Miller stopped me dead in the hall, I snapped, "What do you want?"

"Geez," he said. "Is that any way to greet a friend?"

"And where have you been all week, *friend*?" My brow lifted.

We'd hung around a few times with Miles and Harleigh. It didn't make us friends. It made us acquaintances at best. But he had been there for Harleigh at the beginning of the semester. I guess I owed him that much.

"I was thinking of heading to the Hawks game in Teller Valley tonight. Want to tag along?"

"You're inviting me to a football game? A Hawks game?"

"Pretty sure that's what I said."

"Why?"

"Because it'll be less weird if I turn up with you since you're practically family."

"I… what?"

Nate studied me, waiting for it to click. When it did, a strange pang of something went through me. "They didn't invite you."

"Did they invite you?"

"I… no." My heart clenched. Chloe had told me about the game. About how her and Harleigh were riding with Jessa. But she hadn't invited me.

Harleigh hadn't even mentioned it.

"So let's gatecrash."

"Why would you want to do that?"

"Because it's fun?" He shrugged. "Because it beats sitting at home in my room wondering why I don't fit in with the kids at DA. Because I want to make life happen, not sit around waiting for it to happen."

"Teller Valley is hours away. We'd have to leave now if we wanted to make it." A quiver of anticipation zipped through me.

Nate flashed me a devious smile. "Ever cut class before, Rowe?"

I shook my head.

"There's a first time for everything."

Mom and Dad would kill me. But that only spurred me on. I never broke the rules. I always colored inside the lines. Always played it safe.

But Nate was right. You couldn't sit around waiting for life to happen. You had to live for the moment.

"Let's do it."

"Atta girl."

I glanced down the hall as if I half-expected Principal Diego to appear, ready to reprimand me. Max had cut class more times than I could count. But I'd never wanted to tarnish my attendance record.

In this moment though, doing something for me—something completely unexpected of me—was more important than any punishment.

Besides, Nix and Kye were my friends too. Cheering them on so close to the playoffs was a normal thing to want to do.

"This way." Nate nodded toward the fire exit.

"Wait, isn't that—"

He slammed his shoulder into it, and it swung open. "The mechanism is broken. I've been using it for years."

"You... oh."

He chuckled. "Don't look so worried. I know all DA's little secrets. Including the blind spots in the cameras."

Nate pointed to the security camera on the corner of the building. "When I say run. Run."

"What—"

"Run!" Nate took off, running toward the parking lot. I darted after him, adrenaline coursing through my bloodstream.

"Your car or mine?" he called.

"Yours?"

Nate zigged and zagged around the rows of vehicles, coming to a stop in front of his car. He pulled open the passenger door. "Your ride, madam."

"Please, never call me that again." I rolled my eyes, glancing back up at the building again. Surely, someone would burst out any second and drag me back inside before calling my parents.

But nothing happened.

Not a damn thing.

Nate went around the driver's side and climbed in. "You're really living on the edge, huh."

"Just drive," I murmured, my heart galloping in my chest. "Before I change my mind."

"No backing out now, Rowe." He pressed the ignition and the car purred to life.

"Fine. Just... don't make me regret this."

"It's probably a terrible idea. But all the best ones are." He winked, put the car into reverse and backed out of the parking space.

And then we were driving out of school and headed for Teller Valley.

FOUR HOURS. It took four hours, one rest stop, and a whole heap of awkward conversation to get there.

The crowd was already amassing. Hawks fans in magenta and black dotted around a much bigger home crowd in their white and green. Nate found a parking spot and cut the engine, grabbing his cell phone off the console before climbing out.

"Should I text them?" he asked as I joined him at the hood of his car.

"I don't know. This was your great idea." But now we were here, the rush of adrenaline I'd felt earlier had melted away, replaced with trepidation.

What if they didn't want us here?

Zane definitely wouldn't.

"Oh no, Rowe. I don't like that look. You can't back out now unless you plan on sitting in the car all night."

"I don't. I just…"

"Come on. Let's go see if we can get tickets."

"You mean we don't have any?" I shrieked.

"No, I don't have any." He gawked at me. "What do

you think I did, drove all the way here, bought the tickets and drove back?"

"I don't know. I thought—"

"Relax. These games never sell out."

He hoped.

Otherwise, this entire journey was a waste of time. Not that I was even sure we should stay. When—if—the others saw us here, it might be awkward. It might—

"Rowe, let's go." Nate nodded at the line of people moving toward the small stadium.

"Celeste?" someone called, and my stomach tumbled as I spotted Chloe up ahead. She started moving through the crowd to get to us.

"What are you doing here… with Nate?" She cast him a wary look.

"So, funny story. We thought we'd come and surpri—"

"Wanted to come and support the guys," Nate said with a shrug.

"Oh." Her gaze moved to me. "And the two of you came together?"

"Celeste?" Harleigh appeared, frowning. "What the hell are you doing here?"

"Maguire," Nate smirked. "It's good to see you."

"What is going on?"

"They came to support the guys," Chloe explained, suspicion glittering in her eyes. Surely, she didn't think there was something more going on between me and Nate Miller.

"Let me guess," Harleigh sighed, pinning Nate with a hard look. "This was your idea."

"What can I say, Maguire, I am nothing if not predictable."

"You shouldn't have—"

"Harleigh," Chloe said, shooting me an apologetic glance.

My heart sank.

"Fine. Fine." She conceded. "Just… try to stay out of trouble."

Nate dragged a finger over his chest. "Cross my heart."

"Come on, you can line up with us." She stormed off, clearly annoyed. Nate shrugged again, taking off after her. I couldn't figure him out. He acted like he didn't care what anyone thought about him, but if that was true, he wouldn't be here.

"I'm sorry we didn't invite you," Chloe said, breaking the awkward silence.

"Why didn't you?" I lifted my chin in defiance.

Things were complicated, yes, but we were still friends.

At least, I thought we were.

"I… Harleigh thought…"

"She didn't want me to come," I said quietly.

The truth hurt, but I'd expected it. Ever since moving out, Harleigh had started to pull away. She'd promised me it wouldn't happen, but deep down, I knew it would.

It was ironic really, that my brother, the boy who had

been so mean to her in the past, was now part of their circle more than I was.

But as my gaze flickered past Chloe and beyond the cross to the football stadium beyond, I had to wonder if a certain boy inside also had something to do with their sudden cold shoulder.

13

ZANE

"Holy shit," Kye said, something in the crowd catching his eye.

"What is— no, no fucking way." Fiery anger ignited inside me as I found her in the crowd.

The girl who refused to stay away.

"How the fuck did she get here?"

"If I had to guess, I would say that Miller probably brought her."

"He's here?" I searched the crowd, a new flurry of anger rising in me when my eyes landed on Nate Miller.

What the fuck were they doing together?

"That wouldn't be a flash of jealousy in your eyes, would it?"

I barely heard Kye's taunt over the roar of blood in my ears.

I wasn't jealous. I was fucking confused. She didn't belong here. Neither of them did.

Sure, Nate was decent enough, but this was a Hawk game four hours away from Darling Hill.

It didn't make any sense.

"Okay, ladies, gather in," Coach boomed, steering Nix toward our crudely formed circle. "This is it, if we win tonight, we're guaranteed a spot in the playoffs. The Terrapins will be gunning for you. Keep your eyes open and your tempers in check. You're not only representing yourselves tonight, but you're also representing each other, this team, and the school. Let them talk shit as much as they want, we'll show them what we're about on the scoreboard.

"Okay, Nix. The stage is yours."

"Coach is right. We hit them where it hurts, the only place it hurts. On the scoreboard. Hawks on three."

We all gathered in, piling our hands into the circle. I shot Nix an amused smirk, mouthing, "Nice speech."

"Fuck you," he mouthed back, and Kye snorted.

Despite leading the team for the last three years, motivational speeches weren't exactly Nix's forte. But the guys didn't need a pep talk, they knew the deal. They knew we had a lot to prove. To show these assholes and everyone else watching that we had what it took to go all the way. That despite our underfunded school and shitty lives, we could still play football with the best of them. To send a clear message that when you stepped out on that field, it didn't matter where you came from.

At least, that's what I might have been thinking if it wasn't for the very unwelcome distraction sitting in the bleachers.

Fuck. I still couldn't believe she was here—with Nate, no less.

It was a four-hour ride. What the fuck had they talked about for four hours?

"Z, earth to Z?"

"Huh?"

"It's time to do that thing, you know, where we play football." Kye stared at me expectantly.

"You're an asshole."

"So you like to keep telling me. You okay? You were completely zoned out then. I know things with your grams are—"

"Not the time or place." I shook my head. If I let myself think about that, there was every chance I would lose my shit the first time a Terrapin player so much as breathed in the wrong direction.

A lick of anticipation ran down my spine. I needed this. Forty-eight minutes of running off some of the overwhelming sense of hopelessness I felt at Grams' situation. Because beyond trying to steal from a bank, I knew my options were slim. I could quit school and take on more hours at the mill, but she would never forgive me. I'd do it if I had to, but I was hoping to save her the disappointment of having a high school dropout for a grandson.

Nix finished up his final pep talk with Coach and

jogged over to us. "You good?" he asked me, and I nodded. "Don't worry about me, worry about yourself. Their defense are giants."

"They gotta catch him first." Kye held out his fist but neither of us bumped it. "Oh, it's like that, huh? Now you're both shacked up, you're going to leave—"

"Knock it off," I grumbled.

"Get serious, both of you." Nix pulled on his helmet and jogged toward the referee and the Terrapins captain.

"You think Miller has a boner for her?"

"What the fuck?" I spat. "Why would you say that?" Now I was thinking about things I definitely did not want to be thinking about. Mostly Celeste, in various stages of undress.

"Well, she's a free agent, and he's a free agent..."

"If you have something to say, just say it."

"Nah, I'm just busting your balls, Z, man."

"You're an asshole."

"So you keep telling me." He grinned and jogged onto the field while I moved off to the sidelines with the rest of the defensive players.

He was wrong. Little Miss Goody Two-shoes wouldn't like someone like Miller, no fucking way. But even if she did...

He was welcome to her.

CRACK.

My shoulder rammed into one of the Terrapins players and we both went down, hitting the ground with the thud. Our small section of the crowd roared, the noise reverberating through me, feeding the adrenaline coursing through me.

"Too bad, princess," I drawled, rolling onto all fours and clambering to my feet.

The Hawks were on fire. A force to be reckoned with, we'd already put five touchdowns on the scoreboard by the fourth quarter. Their defense was sloppy, and their offense couldn't break through our lines.

It was a good feeling, to be winning, to be annihilating them. Every time I crashed into one of their players, a little bit of tension ebbed away. But then I remembered *she* was in the bleachers, determined to push her way into my life no matter how many times I told her to stay the fuck out of it.

It was desperate really.

She was fucking desperate.

I jogged off field and headed for the water table while our offense took over.

"You're looking good out there, Washington," Coach Farringdon called. "You sure I can't convince you to talk to some colleges?"

"It's not for me, Coach."

A strange pang went through me. But I couldn't go to college. I couldn't leave Darling Hill, Grams, my responsibilities. She needed me. Besides, I didn't have a good enough GPA, or any money set aside for such things. Every penny I scraped together went into the bills, and the occasional smoke or beer. College wasn't in my future. A life out of The Row wasn't in my future. Not while Grams was still alive and needed me.

I shoved *those* thoughts down.

He gave me a long assessing look, one that had me turning my back on him. Part of me got it, got why he tried to encourage us all so much. To instill a sense of worth and confidence.

Most of the guys on the team didn't have a positive male role model at home, and if they did, they usually had some other shit going on.

I tried to stay focused on the game. Nix commanded the team like any good quarterback, delivering the perfect pass to one of his wide receivers and straight into the end zone.

"Touchdoooooown," the announcer roared over the PA system, sending our supporters into yet another frenzy.

A flicker of a smile braved my lips. It was hard not to get sucked up into the atmosphere, the thrill of the win. But it never truly penetrated the layers of ice around my heart.

Nothing did.

Because for as much as I loved being out here with my team, this was as good as it was ever going to get. A bittersweet ride toward an end I knew was inevitably coming.

My hard gaze moved past the huddle of Hawks players

toward our section of the bleachers, the sea of magenta and black. And among them a girl who didn't belong.

A face I didn't want to see.

But someone I couldn't stop thinking about.

I hated her.

Hated Celeste Rowe in a way that made me seethe.

Yet, Kye was right. Somehow, some fucking way, she had burrowed herself under my skin. And there was only one thing for it.

I needed to dig her the fuck out.

WE WON BY A LANDSLIDE, and when we filed out of the field house our fans greeted us with a loud round of applause. Nix made a beeline for Harleigh and Jessa, pulling them both into a big hug, while Kye threw his arm around Chloe's shoulder and ruffled her hair before fist bumping Nate, and saying hey to Celeste.

She hovered awkwardly on the periphery. Miller clearly didn't give a shit he'd turned up uninvited, congratulating Nix on a good game before teasing Harleigh about something.

Without thinking about it, I inched closer to Celeste, noting the way her breath hitched at my proximity.

She was so fucking obvious.

"You're a long way from home," I murmured, as the rest of them chatted, too wrapped up in the high of the win and what it meant for the team to worry about me and Celeste.

"I… It's a long story."

"You fuck him?"

"Excuse me?" Her eyes flashed to mine full of fire and ice.

"You heard me, Einstein. Couldn't get on my dick, so you jumped on Miller's? He fancies himself as a bit of a bad boy, doesn't he? But at least he's from the right side of the tracks. I bet Mommy and Daddy will love—"

"Stop, Zane." The heat in her gaze guttered out. "Just… stop."

"Z, man. Get the fuck over here," Kye said, completely oblivious to the tension.

Chloe narrowed her eyes though, noticing Celeste quiet and still beside me.

"Good game, Zane," Nate said.

"Didn't expect to see you here."

"Figured we'd come support you guys."

"Miller felt left out we didn't invite him, isn't that right?" Kye chuckled, and Nate ran a hand down the back of his neck.

"Well, I'm glad they came." Chloe glanced over at Nate. "Now I don't have to ride back with Harleigh, Nix, and Jessa. No offense, Jessa."

"None taken." Nix's stepmom smiled.

"You got Coach's blessing to ride home with them? That's some bullshit."

"Unlike you, Z, Coach actually likes my ass." Nix smirked, and I flipped him off.

"He's made a reservation at some diner on the route home. Everyone's invited."

"Sounds good to me, I'm starving," Kye said, clapping Nix on the back. "See you all there."

He headed for the bus where some of the players were already waiting. Celeste went over to Harleigh, Nix, and Jessa.

"Would you like to ride with us, Celeste?" Jessa asked. It sounded pretty genuine, but Harleigh failed to hide her annoyance at the request, and Celeste noticed, her expression dropping.

"No, it's okay," she said. "I'll ride with Nate and Chloe."

She didn't wait for them, walking toward the parking lot.

"I fucked up, didn't I?" Nate said.

"No, it's… complicated."

Nix tucked Harleigh into his side.

"She's had a shitty week at school so I thought this would cheer her up."

"What do you mean?" Chloe asked Nate.

"Miles has been all over the girl he's taking to Winter Formal. And it isn't like she has any other friends."

"Bullshit," Kye snorted. "Of course she has friends."

"No, she had Miles and Harleigh."

"But that's not possible. She's hot and rich and her

dad is Michael Rowe. I don't get it," Kye went on. "Celeste is good people."

"Maybe that's the problem." Nate shot Harleigh a strange look, but she didn't take the bait.

"Hawks, let's go. We've got a long night ahead of us," Coach boomed.

"He's not fucking wrong," I murmured, my cold stare sliding to Celeste.

Nate had it all wrong. He must have. Because the idea that Little Miss Perfect's life wasn't so perfect after all, rattled me.

And I didn't fucking like it.

14

CELESTE

"You could have rode up front," Chloe said from Nate's passenger seat.

"It's fine." I watched the Darling Hill High school bus disappear in the distance, my stomach churning still at Zane's cruel words—his accusation.

I wanted to believe it was jealousy, and maybe there was an element of truth to that. But even if he was jealous, it only made him hate me more.

"I know things are messed up with Harleigh." She twisted around to look at me. "But I think that she's just worried about making life difficult for you with your parents."

"Yeah." I didn't meet her eyes. I couldn't. Or else the tears caught in my throat might overwhelm me.

"Hey, Rowe," Nate said, and I met his gaze in the

rearview mirror. "Make life happen, remember." He winked, but it was lost on me.

I'd thought maybe by coming here, things would be different. That maybe Harleigh would be excited to see me. Impressed, even. But it had backfired spectacularly and only served to make Zane angrier than usual.

And now I had to survive dinner with them all, pretending that everything was okay.

That I was okay.

They were all so quick to judge the kids in Darling Academy—and sure, maybe most of the time it was warranted—but loneliness didn't discriminate. You could be in a room full of people, attend the biggest parties, the most expensive restaurants, and still feel completely alone.

I thought Harleigh of all people, understood that. But she was so distant lately. It was hard to believe we'd spent months living as sisters, sharing our lives.

We felt like strangers now. Old friends who no longer had anything in common.

I hated it.

I was beginning to hate most things in my life.

Chloe and Nate chatted as we followed the small convoy of Hawks fans out of Teller Valley, but I barely heard them, too lost in my own thoughts. By the time Nate pulled up outside the roadside diner, along with the other cars, the team had already moved inside.

"Does this usually happen?" I asked Chloe as we headed inside.

"Sometimes after a big win or if the ride is a few hours, Coach takes the team for dinner. It's never anything fancy but it builds morale and gives the guys a chance to celebrate and eat something decent."

I didn't know what to say to that, so I gave her a small nod.

"Come on, it's fun. You'll see."

"Don't need to ask me twice, I could eat a small cow," Nate said, looking inside.

Chloe let out a small sigh. "He's so freaking hot." Her gaze turned sad. "Why are the hot ones always off-limits or not interested?"

"He might be—"

"He's not. Besides, my brother would have something to say about it."

"At least you can't get into trouble here," I said.

"Oh, I don't know about that." Her lips twitched. "You know I don't care what they all think. I'm glad you came. And I am sorry I didn't invite you."

"It's okay."

"It's not. But I'll find a way to make it up to you. Now let's go give the guys something to moan about." Chloe winked and pulled me inside.

It was chaos. Hawks players and their friends and families crammed into the small diner. Someone had loaded the old jukebox in the corner and some 1970's music drowned out the conversations and chatter.

"Over here," Kye called, scooching up to let us in. But

there wasn't room, so I grabbed a chair and sat awkwardly at the end.

"I'm getting one of everything," he said, scanning the menu underneath the clear tabletop.

"Ten-dollar budget per person, remember, asshole."

"Relax, I got it." He waved Nix off, reeling off all his options.

"What do you want?" Chloe asked.

"Oh, I'm okay."

I wasn't sure I could eat.

"You should eat," Nate said. "It's been hours since we left school and you haven't eaten a thing."

It was true. They'd all had corn dogs from the concession stand, but I hadn't wanted anything then either. The knot in my stomach had only grown worse every passing hour. A bitter reminder that I didn't belong here.

That I wasn't *wanted* here.

Harleigh caught my eye and said, "He's right, you should eat something. We're still at least two-and-a-half hours away from home."

Home.

The word clanged through me.

Old Darling Hill had never been her home, but it would always be mine. It would always be the thing driving a wedge between us.

Just then Mom chose to call me again. She'd been calling ever since she found out I'd skipped out on last period. Her last voicemail had been a shrill diatribe about how irresponsible and reckless I was behaving.

I'd deleted it and ignored her next three calls. She probably thought I was acting up because of the volunteer gig at the center. Either way, she wouldn't want to hear the truth.

"Who's that?" Chloe whispered, and I glanced up at her.

"No one." I shoved my cell back in my pocket. "I'm going to find the bathroom."

"Want me to come?"

I gave her a wry smile. "I think I can manage."

A couple of people gave me a strange look as I headed for the counter.

"Excuse me, where are the restrooms?"

"Down the hall, last door on the left," the waitress said.

"Thanks."

"Watch your step. The lights can be temperamental."

I nodded, taking off down the hall as the celebration went on behind me.

Coach Farringdon did this for his team and the few fans who had made the journey out. He gave them something a lot of them didn't have—family. And it made me ashamed to sit there, probably with more money in my trust fund than the entirety of everyone's bank accounts sitting around me.

I peed quickly and washed up, avoiding my gaze in the mirror. Overhead, the lights began to flicker, dropping in and out and sending my heart into overdrive. Hurrying back into the hall, I didn't expect to run straight into someone.

Not just anyone.

Zane.

"Watch it," he said, glowering at me, his demeanor as cold as ice.

"Sorry, I'm going." I went to move around him, but he stepped in front of me, blocking my path.

"Are you crying?" he sneered.

"No, I'm not—"

His hand snapped out, cupping my face, his thumb brushing a single tear off my cheek. "Poor little Einstein. Must be such a hard life for you living in your Ivory Tower with your endless trust fund and everything handed to you on a silver platter."

"I get it, okay. You hate me. You hate everything about me." I inhaled a shuddering breath as I went to shove him away, but Zane stepped closer, crowding me against the wall.

The hall was empty, nothing but the gentle whir of the faulty strip light and the frantic beat of my heart filling the space around us. He leaned in, glaring down at me with such intensity my breath caught in my throat.

"Z-Zane?" I choked out when he didn't say anything, just stood there looking at me.

"I—"

"Shh." His finger slid to my mouth, dragging over my bottom lip. "You're fucking under my skin, Einstein. And

I don't like it. I don't… fuck." His hand collided with the wall beside my head, making me flinch.

"We should go." Panic flooded me because Zane looked at me like he either wanted to murder me with his bare hands… or fuck me right out from under his skin.

"You need to move." I gently shoved at his chest, but he caught my wrists, pinning my hands in one of his and anchoring them above my head. "What are you doing?" My voice quivered.

"I need to try something."

"Wh—"

His mouth crashed down on mine, hard and unyielding. It wasn't a kiss; it was total annihilation. I couldn't think about anything except how amazing his lips felt moving against mine, his tongue plunging into my mouth in greedy, forceful licks.

I pressed closer, curling my fingers into his t-shirt. God, the boy could kiss. My head swam with desire; strange, unfamiliar sensations igniting a wildfire inside me. Until I was burning from the inside out.

Miles and I had fooled around, spent a lot of time kissing and learning each other's bodies. But it had never been like this. Like I might explode right out of my skin if I didn't get more. More… *More.*

"Zane," I whispered, hitching my thigh around his waist, needing to be closer.

Needing more.

"Fuck," he breathed, curving his hand around my throat to slow the kiss. Control it.

Control me.

He licked deep into my mouth again, punching his hips forward.

"Oh God," I cried, gripping him tighter, but laughter at the end of the hall startled me and like the spell was broken, he shoved me away.

"Fuck." He punched the wall again. Not hard enough to break skin… but hard enough to make another dent in my heart.

"What was that?" I blinked up at him, my heart crashing violently against my rib cage.

"That… was a fucking mistake."

His words landed like bullets, tearing through my chest.

"Go," he growled. "You should—"

"Wait, we can talk about it." I made the fatal mistake of reaching for him, but he jerked away. Physically repelled by me.

Dejection sank into me, extinguishing the flames inside me, making my lungs squeeze. But I couldn't accept that it was nothing—that it meant nothing. "You kissed me…"

"Yeah, and I won't ever do it again." Disgust washed over him.

He meant it.

Zane meant every word.

It was a mistake; one he wouldn't make again.

Refusing to let him see how much he'd hurt me, I slipped past him and walked away with my head held high.

Even if my heart was in tatters.

"CELESTE, COME OVER HERE."

Chloe had moved seats when I returned, sitting with some guys I didn't recognize. I hesitated, glancing over at Harleigh. But she didn't look up. Kye scowled at his sister, and she flipped him off, much to her new friend's amusement.

Zane was nowhere to be seen.

With a heavy sigh, I decided to trade one shitshow for another.

"Hey," I said, reaching Chloe.

"Guys this is Celeste. Celeste, meet the guys. Greg and Warner."

"Hi." Lifting my hand in a small wave, I slid in next to Chloe.

"You're Harleigh Wren's sister, right?"

"That's me."

"Cool. So is it true you're like so rich your dad owns a private jet, because I heard—"

"Dude, not cool." The other guy elbowed his friend with the verbal diarrhea.

"What? It's just a question."

"You'll have to excuse Warner," he added, and I deduced he was Greg. "He doesn't get out much."

"Fuck you, man. I was only—"

"It's fine." I gave them a tight smile. "But no, he doesn't own a private jet."

"Too bad." Warner frowned. "How come you decided to come cheer for the Hawks? Unless you're here as a double agent. I wouldn't put it past the Devils to send in a—"

"Seriously, asshole." Greg shot me an apologetic look. "If it's any consolation for this idiot, I think it's cool you came to support your sister's guy and his friends."

"Thanks, and congrats on the win."

"Hells yeah. We're in the playoffs baby." Warner banged his fists on the table, making Chloe shriek.

"You really are an idiot."

"A good-looking one though, right?" He waggled his brows, and she gave him a playful smirk.

"The jury is still out," she said.

"I'm sure I can win you over."

Greg rolled his eyes, casting his gaze over to where my sister was sitting. "You might have to win over big bro too, if the death stare he's giving you is any indicator. And who's the other guy? I don't recognize him."

I glanced over, surprised to find Nate glaring in this direction too.

Interesting.

I caught Chloe's eye and arched a brow.

What are you playing at?

Boys. So fickle. Her eyes seemed to say.

It might backfire. I narrowed my gaze, and her lips curved with amusement.

"Warner is cute," she mouthed, giving a little shrug as he looked at something on his phone.

Greg snorted, having noticed our exchange. "You're really pretty," he said, changing the subject.

"Uh, thanks." My cheeks flushed at his brazen compliment.

"Maybe we—" He stopped, his eyes flickering with confusion.

"What's wrong?" I turned slowly, instantly regretting it.

Zane was back at his table, staring right at me. No, not me… Greg.

And he looked furious.

15

ZANE

My jaw clenched as I watched Celeste talk and laugh with Greg Selcott.

"You're going to crack a tooth," Kye said around a mouthful of cheese and bacon fries.

"I'll crack your face in a minute if you don't shut the fuck up."

That only made him smirk harder.

Asshole.

"Shouldn't you be pulling your overprotective big brother bullshit? Chloe and Warner look pretty close."

"Nah, he knows if he so much as looks at her, I'll break his legs."

"He's looking," Nix said.

"The fuck he is. They're talking."

"Talking, right. About all the freaky, wild sex they're going to be hav—"

"Nix." Harleigh gave him a disapproving look.

"What?" He shrugged. "Asshole deserves it. What do you think, Miller? You think he's got that look in his eye?"

It was a dick thing to say. Especially since we'd all picked up on some tension between him and Chloe. But Nate had played it down. I didn't know whether it was because Chloe was more interested in him than he was her, or because he didn't want to overstep with Kye.

"I think she can talk to whoever the hell she wants," he replied a little too harshly.

Oh, he cared all right. He just didn't want Kye to know.

"Okay, kids." Coach Farringdon stood, and the room hushed into silence. "First things first, you played a good game tonight. Represented yourselves and the team with the professionalism and pride I know you all possess. It doesn't matter if football is in your future, what matters is you play the season out in a way so that win or lose, you can hold your heads high. And you did it, you put this team—our team—in the playoffs."

Everyone began stamping their feet and banging their fists on the tables, chanting, 'Hawks, Hawks, Hawks'.

"Okay, okay, quiet down." Coach whipped off his ball cap and ran a hand through his hair. "Finish up your food, go use the John and grab a drink for the road.

Twenty minutes, I want you all back on the bus or your sorry ass will get left behind."

"Thank fuck. I need some sleep," I said, glancing over at Celeste again.

An unfamiliar sensation surged inside of me as I watched Greg casually drape his arm over the back of the booth of where she was sitting.

"You know, if she keeps coming around, one the guys will make a move—"

"Carter," I growled.

"Yeah, yeah, you don't care. Already got that memo." He stuffed the last couple of fries in his mouth and got out of the booth. "I drank too much soda." He stalked off toward the hall leading to the restrooms.

The hall where I'd intercepted Celeste. Where I'd made the colossal fucking mistake of putting my mouth on hers.

But I'd thought… shit, I don't know what I'd thought. She was just looking at me with those big blue eyes of hers, staring at me like I was worth something.

Fucking idiot.

I needed to get a grip.

Girls like Celeste only fooled around with guys like me to get their kicks. Their taste of the bad boy before they were swept off their feet by some pretentious entitled douchebag.

It wasn't in my plan to ever be anyone's dirty little secret.

"I'm going to ask Coach if I can ride back with you and Jessa," Nix said.

"Seriously?" My brow arched.

"Fuck off, Z. You don't get it."

"No, I really don't."

They couldn't even go a couple of hours without seeing each other. It was fucking embarrassing.

"You should ride with the team," Harleigh said, kissing the corner of his mouth. "You get to sleep with me all night."

"Damn right, I do."

"I should probably ask Celeste if she wants to ride with us."

"It's fine, she can ride with me," Nate said, and my eyes snapped to his, a strange crackle going through the air.

"Relax, man. I'm not into her like that."

"None of my business if you are." I got up. "I'll be outside."

I walked straight out of the diner, ignoring the calls of my teammates. The air was frigid, my breath turning to fog as I exhaled.

Pulling out my cell phone, I dialed Grams.

"Zane Thackeray. You're late."

"Sorry, we stopped at a diner. Coach treated us to dinner. I would have called soon—"

"Hush now. You called, that's all that matters."

"How are you feeling?"

"I'm okay. I-I was hoping you'd take me to the center

again tomorrow. Mr. Clarkson called. He might have some information for me."

"On a Saturday?"

"He's very committed to his job."

"Sounds like he needs to get laid if you ask me." My mouth twitched.

"Well, I didn't. And don't be so crude. He seems like a very nice man."

"I'm sure he is." The smile dropped off my face as I added, "You'll be okay until I get home?"

"I'll be fine. Nothing's changed yet."

But it would if she couldn't get the treatment.

The hollow pit inside me yawned wide open.

"Okay, bye."

She said goodbye and hung up, leaving me cold and angry.

It was bullshit.

She'd been a hardworking woman all her life. Busted her ass to raise me and give me the best life she could. We didn't have much, but what we did have, she'd worked for. All she had was some meager savings and the trailer we lived in. She relied on the insurance to help pay for her medication and treatment. If it didn't, there wasn't a magic pot of gold at the end of a rainbow.

I ran a hand through my hair, tugging on the ends in frustration. I needed to do something. I needed to fix it. To save her, the way she'd saved me when my mom abandoned me.

The door to the diner swung open and laughter

spilled out, dragging me from my thoughts. I straightened and watched my teammates pour out, heading for the bus. High on the win and a full stomach thanks to Coach's generosity. The school board didn't give him the funds to take us all out to dinner. He paid out of his own pocket because he was that kind of man.

The kind of man so many of us could have done with as a role model growing up in The Row.

"You ready to roll?" Kye sauntered over.

"Yeah."

We waited for Nix, but it was a mistake. Because Celeste, Chloe, Warner, and Greg appeared first.

Chloe and Warner were huddled close, looking at something on his cell phone while Celeste and Greg chatted. My gaze cut to Nate, but he barely looked at Chloe.

Before I knew what I was doing, I stepped toward them.

"So maybe I could get your number," Greg said.

"Oh, I—"

"Take a walk, Selcott," I said. "She's too fucking good for the likes of you."

Somewhere behind me, Kye snorted. I ignored him then, focused on the sliver of space between Celeste and Greg.

Walk away, asshole. Walk the fuck away.

He looked ready to argue, but his argument dried on his tongue, and he sighed, "Maybe I'll see you around,

Celeste." He gave her a small wave and headed for the bus.

Anger and embarrassment swirled in her blue depths. "What was that?" Her voice shook.

I stepped up to her, glaring down at her. "Couldn't have me so you moved onto one of my teammates? Are you really that desperate for some dick from The Row?"

Crack.

Her hand landed against my cheek with a fiery sting.

"You hit me." Surprise coated my words.

"Z-Zane, I—"

"You fucking hit me."

Rolling back her shoulders, her expression hardened. "Yes, well, you're an asshole."

"Z, man. Let's go," Kye called, and I was vaguely aware of our friends watching us. But I couldn't make myself move.

She'd hit me.

I was furious. But there was also something else beneath the fury burning through me. My dick was hard behind my jeans. Rock fucking solid.

"If I want to go out with Greg, I will. He's nice and kind and *he* won't treat me like nothing more than dirt on the bottom of his boot."

Pushing my face into hers, I sneered, "Stay the fuck away from him. And stay the fuck away from me."

I spun away and headed for the bus. I needed to get away from her before I did something really fucking stupid…

Like kiss her again.

———

THE SECOND THE bus pulled off, Greg asked Kye to switch seats. The guy had balls, I'd give him that. He was a junior. Not too cocky or full of himself. But he wasn't a friend. No one was outside of Nix and Kye.

"Hey, can I talk to you?" he said.

"Doesn't look like I have a choice. Thanks for that, traitorous asshole," I spat at Kye.

He grinned. "You're welcome."

"So… you and Celeste, what's going on there?" Greg kept his voice low since some of the guys were already sleeping.

"Nothing." I huffed, kicking up my foot against the seat in front.

"For real? Because I sensed some tension."

"You really want to go there?" I asked. "With a girl like her?"

"What's that supposed to mean?"

"She's not like us, Selcott. She's rich and spoiled and when she's had her fun, she'll settle down with a pretentious asshole from across the res."

"I'm not looking to marry the girl. But she's cool and funny and she—"

I cut him with a hard look.

"You want her," he said.

"That's not—"

"Yeah, I think it is. You want her and you hate yourself for it."

"You don't know what the fuck you're talking about."

A knowing smile tugged at his mouth. "Then you won't mind if I get her number off of Harleigh."

Irritation rolled through me. Irritation and something I refused to acknowledge. Because I wasn't jealous, I wasn't.

"Harleigh doesn't want her getting tangled up with anyone on the team," I said.

His smug expression dropped. "Oh."

"Yeah. So do yourself a favor and forget about her."

Because fuck knows, it was what I planned to do.

"Yeah, okay." He got up and walked away and I should have felt relieved. Should have felt a small kernel of smug satisfaction that I wouldn't have to witness them together.

But the only thing I felt was confusion. Because he was right—I did want her.

And I did fucking hate myself for it.

"So, what did moon eyes want?" Kye slid back into his seat beside me.

"Moon eyes?" I balked.

"Yeah, you saw the way he was looking at Celeste, with those big ol' moon eyes. The guy is in love."

"Fuck off." I folded my arms over my chest and closed my eyes. "I'm going to sleep."

"To dream about Cel—"

I elbowed him hard in the ribs and Kye choked out. "Celery, I was going to say celery."

"Fucking idiot," I murmured, hoping to get some shut-eye.

Because Celeste already haunted my life, I didn't need her haunting my dreams too.

16

CELESTE

I woke to the sound of knocking at my door.

"Come in," I murmured, trying to force my eyes open. They were bleary with sleep, my muscles tired and achy.

I'd barely slept after Nate dropped me home and I snuck into the house only to find it empty. Max was nowhere to be seen as usual, and my parents were at some dinner party.

"Good morning, sweetheart," Dad said, poking his head inside.

"Hey."

"Can we talk?"

"Did Mom send you?"

"I may be here to run interference, yes." He sat on the end of my bed.

"At least you're honest," I said.

"She's worried."

"Because I cut class."

"Because you're acting out." His brows pinched. "This isn't you, sweetheart."

"Maybe it is." I shrugged. "Maybe I'm finally acting like the girl I'm supposed to be."

His frown deepened. "Whatever do you mean?"

"It's too much, Dad. The constant pressure. The looming weight of the future. I'm seventeen. What if I don't know what I want to be yet or what I want to do? I feel like life is passing me by and I haven't lived yet."

"Celeste, sweetheart." He chuckled softly. "You're seventeen. You're not supposed to have all the answers."

"But Mom does. Both of you have always made it perfectly clear what you expect from me."

"You're right, we have." His expression turned wistful. "Because your intelligence is a rare gift that will let you do great things one day. But greatness comes in many forms."

"Who are you and what have you done with my dad?"

"I admit, I've had my eyes opened a lot lately."

"Because of Harleigh." The words caught on the lump in my throat.

He had changed for her.

Not for me or Max, or because he realized how suffocating his expectations were of us. He's changed because he'd almost lost Harleigh again.

I didn't know what to do with that.

I loved my sister so much, and I hated that she'd

grown up with so much pain and uncertainty. But it had been easier to defend and believe in our relationship when she lived here.

Now everything felt wrong.

She was keeping me at arm's length, and some part of me wondered if it was because she thought I was like them. Like my mother and father and the rest of the Old Darling Hill elite.

"I made a lot of mistakes where your sister is concerned, some I fear I will never be able to rectify. But I am determined to keep her in my life. I am determined to show your mother that Harleigh Wren can be a part of our family, in her own way.

"I can love you and Max and your mom, and love Harleigh. It isn't a scenario where I have to choose."

"Does Mom know that?"

His expression tightened. "She'll come around eventually. But what would really help my case is if you weren't running off with Nate Miller and cutting class to go across the reservoir—"

"He's my friend. They all are."

But my voice had lost its usual conviction where Harleigh and her friends were concerned. After all, you couldn't be the only person to fight for a friendship. If one of you started to let go, it left the other drifting. Clutching at air.

"You can invite them here," he said. "I've told you more than once Harleigh and Chloe can come here and hang out."

"So I can be friends with them but only if it's under your roof?"

"Celeste, that's not—" He let out a weary sigh. "I'm just saying, sweetheart, that things are a little tense right now. Max is… well, he's Max. He'll do whatever the hell he wants whether we tell him he can or not. But you're different, sweetheart.

"It would mean a lot to me if you could try and appease your mother a little. She only wants the best for you. We both do."

Pressing my lips together, I gave him a tight smile. "Got it, Dad. Maybe Chloe will want to hang out here."

I don't know why I said the words. She wouldn't come here. Just like Harleigh wouldn't. And I couldn't blame them. But I also couldn't keep trying to explain my side of things to my parents only to have them ignore me.

Dad was only worried about appeasing my mother and not losing the fragile relationship he had with Harleigh. Mom was only worried about impressing her friends and boosting her own reputation around town. And my brother… well, who knew what he worried about, but he certainly wasn't confiding in me.

"That sounds great, sweetheart." He smiled. "And please, don't cut class again. Your mother almost had a heart attack when she got the call from Principal Diego." He stood.

"I won't, Dad."

Dad gave me a small smile and left me alone. I

grabbed a pillow and hugged it to my chest. I didn't regret cutting class, not for a second. But I did regret letting Nate talk me into going to the game. Because now everything was only more confusing.

Zane had said some horrible, vile things to me. But then he'd kissed me.

He'd kissed me like he couldn't help himself. And I'd loved it—I'd *drowned* in him, ready to cross all kinds of lines that would only end in my ruin. Until he'd pushed me away like he hated me, and my heart had sunk. But just when I'd started to lose hope, to think that maybe I'd imagined all the tension between us, he had warned Greg off me like he was jealous. Like he couldn't stand the idea of another guy wanting me.

I could only assume he wanted me. He just didn't *want* to want me.

And I didn't know which was worse.

That he wouldn't allow himself to cross whatever imaginary line he'd drawn between us.

Or that he even had the willpower to stop.

"CELESTE, so nice to see you again." Mrs. Sinclair beckoned me into her office.

"I had a few hours to spare so figured I'd drop by."

The truth was, I couldn't bear to stay at home with Mom and Dad there. She'd collared me at breakfast, outlining her disappointment over bacon and eggs. I'd barely touched my plate, a potent mix of guilt and bitterness churning in my stomach.

My whole life, I'd followed the rules. Stuck to the rigid expectations bestowed on me by my parents. Any teen would crumble eventually. Fall prey to the whims of impulsivity and opportunity. Adults—*parents*—were foolish if they truly believed their kids weren't getting up to no good on a weekend. The student population at DA had access to money, and money could buy all kinds of vices. Statistics suggested that nearly one out of every ten alcoholic drinks purchased in the country was consumed illegally. In a place like Old Darling Hill, that figure was probably a lot higher. The only difference was, the adults, the people in authority, turned a blind eye to the parties and scandals so long as it didn't tarnish the reputation of the elite families in the town. Money talked, and when you had enough of it, you could bury any indiscretion deep enough to wipe it out of existence.

"How was your Friday evening?"

"I… uh, it was fine, thank you." I flushed, thinking of Zane and how he'd kissed me.

How I'd kissed him back.

It was all I could think about.

I needed to get a grip.

"It's usually pretty quiet on a Saturday. But Mr. Clarkson runs a financial support and advice clinic, and the cafeteria stays open all day though. We offer free hot drinks and cake. I'm sure Lewis could use an extra pair of hands."

"Sounds good."

"Excellent. I'll take you down there and make the introductions and leave you to it, if that's okay?"

"Of course." I nodded.

"Great." She got up and I followed her into the hall.

"You know, Celeste. We really are very lucky to have you with us." A burst of pride swelled inside me. "Such a bright young girl. You really are a credit to your mother—"

The pride popped like a balloon, deflating inside my chest until it felt hollow.

Of course, it always came back to my mom.

"In fact, we were talking last night and discussing a possible press release to raise the center's profile."

"Press release?" I balked.

"Nothing excessive or gaudy, of course. But with the Rowe-Delacorte name behind us, we could draw some new major donors. Isn't that exciting?"

Exciting?

"Sure," I murmured, a sickly feeling spreading through me.

"I'll get something organized and hopefully you and Sabrina can both be involved. Maybe I can invite Cooper too, make it a real family affair."

"Great."

Not.

I couldn't think of anything worse, but how could I tell Mrs. Sinclair? Especially when I had really enjoyed helping out the other day.

We reached the cafeteria, and I was surprised to see so many people filling the tables.

"The bus from Darling Row and the next town over stops right outside, so we get a lot of foot traffic. Especially when the weather turns. The offer of a hot drink and warm place to sit for a few hours is worth the bus fare. Lewis," she called as we reached the service hatch. "Celeste would like to help out."

A head popped up and the man I assumed to be Lewis smiled. "I'll never refuse the offer of help from a pretty girl."

There was nothing seedy about his remark. In fact, the old man reminded me of Grandpa Rowe.

"How do you feel about dish washing?"

"I think I can handle it."

"Excellent, come on around and I'll get you an apron."

"I'll leave you in Lewis's capable hands." Mrs. Sinclair gave me an encouraging nod and went to greet some people in the line.

Despite her obvious position of power, she was kind and gentle, offering a hand to everyone and engaging them with a warm smile. Her heart was in the right place, even if what she'd said earlier about the press release idea had rankled me.

I liked it here though. I felt good being here. Like I could make a real difference somehow. And not because I was Sabrina Delacorte's daughter. But because I genuinely cared and wanted to help.

Even if I was washing the dishes.

I'm pretty sure when Mom signed me up for this, she didn't anticipate that I'd be in an apron, doing my bit to help.

A smile tugged at my mouth.

It felt like a small rebellion somehow.

A secret 'fuck you' to my mother.

LEWIS WAS one of the most interesting men I'd ever met. A war veteran, he'd done tours of Iraq, Bosnia, and Afghanistan, until he'd been medically discharged after a nasty shrapnel incident. But he talked fondly of his life in the military, and it was clear that he had a deep sense of community from the way he talked and joked with the many people making the most of the free hot drinks and cake.

"Celeste, be a sweetheart and go grab some empties. We're almost out of coffee mugs," he said, pulling a freshly baked tray of cakes from the oven.

"Sure thing." I wiped my brow with the back of my hand.

It was fast-paced in the kitchen, a constant stream of tasks that needed completing to keep up with the endless flow of people. I didn't have a chance to chat with many people since I wasn't serving out front, but I overheard some of their stories. It seemed that people from all walks of life came here. People struggling to make ends meet, older people looking for a hot drink and some company, war veterans like Lewis who had no one else to share their lives with.

It was heartwarming to see how despite their personal circumstances and experiences, people came together over something as simple as a mug of coffee and a slice of cake.

I dried my hands and grabbed a tray, taking it out front.

"Ah, Celeste," a familiar voice said, and I turned to find Miriam smiling at me. "Don't you have anything better to be doing on a Saturday?" Humor twinkled in her eyes.

"Actually, I don't. Can I help you to a table?" I asked, noticing how frail she looked on her walking stick.

"No, it's fine." She waved me off with a defiant look. "My grandson will be here any— oh, here he is now." Her eyes went over my shoulder, and I glanced back, almost dropping the tray.

Because the only person standing at the door was the last person I expected to see.

Zane.

ZANE

CELESTE GAWKED AT ME, HER MOUTH DROPPING OPEN AND closed, once... twice... three times, as if she couldn't quite figure out what to say.

"Celeste, dear, whatever is the matter?" Grams asked, her eyes crinkling with concern and a slight hint of amusement.

Shit.

This was a clusterfuck. Grams already suspected Celeste and I knew each other, but if she picked up on the strange tension between us, I'd never hear the end of it.

I narrowed my eyes at Celeste.

Don't say anything. Don't fucking say—

"I didn't realize you were Zane's grandma." She gave

Grams a big smile, but I saw the strain in her eyes. The confusion.

The last thing I wanted was Celeste to know our business. But I hadn't known she was going to be here today? How could I?

Fuck.

"You'll have to excuse my grandson's manners. Zane Thackeray is what we old folk refer to as brooding. But then I suppose you already know that if you two know each other."

Celeste smirked a little at that, and I bristled.

"Grams, I am not—"

"Oh, hush now. You know damn well how you can be. At least now you won't have to wait alone while I meet with Mr. Clarkson. Celeste can keep you company." A knowing smile played on her mouth.

"Actually, I thought I'd come with you."

"You will do no such thing, dear. I am quite capable of attending a meeting about my personal business." She turned to Celeste. "Now, be a doll and sit with Zane, will you? I'll be back as soon as possible."

She backtracked toward the double doors, her movements slow and jerky, but in true Miriam Washington style, she kept her head held high and her expression poised.

"So Miriam is your grandma," Celeste said. "I would never have made the connection."

"What the fuck is that supposed to mean?" I sneered.

"Well, she's so sharp and witty… and you're… well, not."

"What the—" Celeste's smirk grew and the anger inside me deflated a little. "You're joking."

She gave me a small nod. "I didn't make the connection, but I can kind of see it now I've seen the two of you together."

I didn't realize we'd moved toward an empty table until Celeste glanced at the two seats. She was doing that weird thing again, sucking me into her orbit.

"I'm not staying," I bit out.

"Oh. But I thought your grandma said—"

"What are you doing, Einstein?"

"W-what?" Celeste balked.

"This. Us." I wagged a finger between us. "We're not friends."

"I know. I just thought after last night…" She inhaled a sharp breath. "You know what? Forget it. I have to get back to work."

She spun on her heel and walked off. And I didn't like it.

I didn't like that she'd turned her back on me.

Fuck.

She was making my head spin.

But I didn't want to sit around and talk about my feelings either. Especially not with her.

I needed to get out of there, to put some distance between us. I couldn't trust Celeste. And I definitely couldn't trust myself around her.

I didn't leave though.

I slid right into one of the seats and watched her as she collected people's empty mugs and plates, adding them to her tray. Celeste had a smile for each and every one of them, stopping to talk to the occasional person. I couldn't hear what they were saying, but I could see the effect she had on people. She was like a ray of sunshine, lighting them up, making them beam. Even the miserable looking bastard in the corner sat a little straighter when she moved past his table. She said something to him, and he laughed, a look of disbelief washing over his face as if he couldn't quite believe he'd done it. They all soaked up her warmth, her infectious smile, and soft laughter. As if her volunteering here somehow made her one of them.

Un-fucking-likely.

I wondered what they would have to say if they knew that she drove home to a gated estate in a car worth more than the average income in the country.

Celeste could pretend all she liked. She could volunteer and hang out with her friends in Darling Row. She could cut class and kiss bad boys up from across the reservoir and play the lonely little rich girl. But the truth was, she would never know what it was like.

She would graduate high school, go to some Ivy League School, and fall in love with some pretentious asshole with a stick the same of the Hudson River up his ass.

That was her destiny.

So the why the fuck couldn't I stop thinking about

her? Why couldn't I stop replaying that kiss over in my head? Why couldn't I stop imagining what it might feel like to get Little Miss Perfect underneath me?

Her eyes snapped to mine across the cafeteria. She didn't look away. Not when I narrowed my gaze and not when I curled my fist on the table. Celeste stared back at me with as much intensity as I glared at her.

Something had shifted between us. But I refused to walk that road again.

One kiss was a mistake.

But two…

Well, that would be downright stupidity.

"Zane?" A woman I didn't recognize loomed over me.

"Yeah?"

"It's your grandma. She had a little incident. She's—"

"What?" I shot out my seat. "Where is she?"

"She passed out in Mr. Clarkson's office. She's okay now. If you'd like to follow me, I can take you to her."

I followed the woman out of the cafeteria, my heart racing a mile a minute.

"What the fuck happened?"

"I believe she got up after meeting with Mr. Clarkson and felt a bit dizzy. He managed to get her situated again right before she passed out."

"Shit." I ran a hand over my face, inhaling a shaky breath. "But she's okay?"

"She appears to be, but we've called the emergency services just to be safe."

"She'll love that."

"I suspected as much. She's quite the woman." She gave me a warm smile.

We rounded the corner right as Celeste was coming out of the staff bathroom.

"Zane?" Her brows furrowed. "What's wrong?"

"Nothing. I've got to go." I kept walking, desperate to get to Grams.

"You know Celeste?" the woman asked.

"Something like that."

"She seems nice. A real hit with our Saturday regulars."

Didn't I know it? I'd spent the best part of forty minutes watching her bewitch the cafeteria with her warm smile and friendly conversation. But I hadn't found it in myself to leave. To put myself out of my misery.

A bolt of guilt went through me. I'd been watching Celeste like some creepy stalker while Grams was fainting.

Brilliant fucking grandson I was.

"She's just in here." The woman pushed open a door and stepped aside for me to enter.

"Grams—"

"Now, now, dear. Don't go freaking out. I'm fine. Tell him, Hal, tell him I'm fine."

The man seated beside her smiled. "Your grandma has quite the stubborn streak."

"Tell me about it," I murmured.

"I already told them I don't need to be checked over. It was nothing more than a little light-headedness."

"It's center policy, Miriam. Just in case."

Grams scoffed. "Fine."

I crouched in front of her. "How are you feeling, really?"

"Zane Thackeray," she sighed, but I saw the weariness in her eyes. Grams struggled with her speech sometimes, and her motor skills were growing increasingly uncooperative, but she'd never passed out in public before.

"You'd tell me, right? If something felt different."

"I got a little light-headed is all."

"The EMTs are here," the woman said.

"Miriam?" The EMT came inside.

"That'll be me."

"Why don't you tell me what happened while I take a look at you?"

I moved aside to let him work.

"I was meeting with Mr. Clarkson." She hesitated, drawing in a small breath. "When I stood up, I got a little light-headed."

"Any dizziness?"

She glanced at me.

"Grams," I warned.

"Fine." She gave a little huff. "A little dizziness."

"Any spots in your vision? Double vision? That kind of thing?"

"I…" I shot her another scathing look and she added, "A little."

"What are you thinking?" I asked him.

"It's not uncommon for people with MS to develop orthostatic intolerance. Has this happened before?" He glanced at me, and I shook my head.

"Not that I'm aware. Grams?"

Guilt etched into her expression. "I get dizzy sometimes."

"But you didn't think to tell me?"

"I didn't want to worry you."

"That's bullshit and you know it. You have to tell me these things. I can't help you if you—"

"Zane, was it?" Mr. Clarkson stood. "Why don't you and I go and get some fresh air? Your grandmother is in good hands."

"Fine." I stormed out of the room, ignoring her pleas.

How the fuck was I supposed to help her if she kept lying to me?

"Come on." He followed me. "Some fresh air will do you good."

Mr. Clarkson led me out of a side exit, the air a welcome reprieve from the anger and frustration burning in my chest.

"Your grandmother tells me you're a senior at Darling Hill High."

"Yeah, so?"

"Look, Zane, I get it. You want to protect her. And she wants to protect you. But it's okay to ask for help, son. It's—"

"Don't call me that."

"I'm sorry." He held up his hands. "Your grandmother's disease is advancing. Soon she will need specialized care. Care you might not be in a position to give her."

"You think I don't know that?" I spat. "You think I don't spend every minute of my life worrying about the day when I can no longer take care of her?"

"You're young, Zane. Too young to shoulder such a big responsibility. There are care facilities—"

"No, it's not what she wants. Not yet."

"And I understand that, I do. But eventually, the time might come where you have to make some difficult decisions for her."

Did he honestly think I didn't know that?

I agonized over it. Every day of my life I asked myself these questions over and over. But the answer was always the same.

Not yet.

Not while I could still take care of her.

But he had a point. It was easy to become complacent now, while she still had most of her faculties. Easy to tell myself—each other—that we could manage. That we would be okay.

But what if she started falling more? Passing out? I had school. A job. The team. I couldn't be home twenty-four seven, and even if I could, she wouldn't want me there.

Hopelessness sat heavy in my chest, crushing my lungs. I leaned up against the wall, dropping my head back and inhaling a deep breath, letting it roll through me. Calm me a little.

"I want to connect you with a social worker—"

"We don't need that," I said.

"You might think that now. But what happens when your grandmother becomes unable to independently dress herself? Toilet, bathe? I know these are all things you'd rather not think about, Zane, but the fact of the matter is, her health is declining. It's only going to continue to decline. Add in Miriam's age and that increases the chance of other health-related issues. There are people and organizations out there who can help, but you've got to be willing to ask."

"I…" I slid down the wall, dropping onto my ass, not caring that the ground was hard and cold. This was the reality I'd been putting off for as long as I could. Burying my head in the sand in hopes that we would be handed a miracle.

But the grim truth was, Grams wasn't getting better—she was getting worse.

And the bottom line was there would come a day, where I wouldn't be able to look after her on my own.

18

CELESTE

Something was wrong.

I'd watched Zane rush down the hall and disappear into one of the rooms, but I hadn't lingered. It felt rude to pry.

As I helped Lewis wipe down the kitchen counters and equipment, I couldn't help but wonder if everything was okay. Zane's grandmother was sick, and although I didn't know much about how advanced her MS was, I still couldn't imagine what it was like for him.

I knew from Harleigh and Chloe that there was only Zane and his grandmother. I didn't know the whole story about his parents, but by all accounts, his dad was never on the scene and his mom had abandoned him when he was just a young boy. Miriam had raised him in their stead.

"Thanks for today," Lewis said, pulling me from my thoughts. "You did well today. Same time next week?"

"Maybe." I smiled.

"Fair enough." He chuckled. "Go on, get out of here. And don't forget to take your box of cake."

Lewis let the volunteers divide any leftovers to take home. It was a sweet gesture. One I'm sure Mom would frown upon.

I pulled the apron off and added it to the pile of dirty towels before heading to the staff room to grab my purse and jacket. When I slipped back in the hall, I spotted Zane outside, sitting on the cold hard ground.

My heart ached at the sight of him out there all alone. He looked so lost and lonely.

Before I could talk myself out of it, I headed for the door. He looked up as I stepped outside.

"What do you want?"

"You look like you could use a friend."

"I thought we already established, we're not friends."

An exasperated breath left my lips. "You don't make it easy, do you?"

He craned his neck, looking right up at me. The hopelessness in his expression my chest squeeze. "Am I supposed to know what you're talking about?"

God, he was so infuriating at times. But I ignored the urge to throw the box of cake at him and shook it gently in front of him. "Hungry?"

"Not really."

"It's leftover cake. Everyone is hungry for cake. Here."

I handed him the box and sat down on the bench opposite.

He lifted the lid a fraction and peered inside. But to my disappointment, he let it close again and placed the box down on the ground at his feet.

"Is your grandma okay?" I asked, sensing the warring emotions rippling off him.

Anger. Sadness. Regret. Hopelessness. It was intense being in his orbit, feeling so much from one person at once.

"Honestly? I don't know," he replied, surprising me.

"Do you want to talk about it?"

"No, I really fucking don't."

"Okay."

"Why did you come out here, Einstein?"

"Because despite what you think"—*and how you treat me*—"I care."

He snorted at that.

"Is something funny?"

"Yeah, you. What are you doing here, Celeste? In this place? Trying to fix the world one coffee mug at a time? It's fucking pathetic."

"Are you done?" I fumed.

"You're still here, so apparently not." His eyes were darker than night, cutting into my skin like a thousand blades.

"What happened to you, Zane? What made you this way?"

Because he was so cruel. Acting out like a child who hadn't learned to express his emotions.

It occurred to me, maybe he hadn't.

He pressed the back of his head into the wall, his eyes boring into mine. Daring me. Challenging me. But I wasn't so easily broken now. Because every time he hurt me, my skin grew a little thicker. And every time I learned another piece of the Zane Washington puzzle, my heart grew a little wiser.

"Is it so wrong that I care? That I want to be your friend?"

"Friend?" he practically spat the words. "Do you think I look at you and see a friend?"

"Okay, so what do you see when you look at me?"

His lip curled with devious intention. "I really don't think you want to know the answer to that."

There was something in his gravelly voice that made my insides quiver and tighten. This boy was completely under my skin, but I was under his too.

"You think you know me, know what my life's like. But you're wrong, Zane. And you're too stubborn to see that. To even consider that maybe I'm a good person. That maybe life isn't so rosy for me either."

I don't know why it mattered what he thought about me, but it did. I wanted him to give me a chance, I wanted to prove him wrong. Maybe it was the perfectionist in me, the girl raised to believe she could be anything, do anything. But I'd met my match in Zane Washington. He was the one problem I couldn't solve.

And he frustrated me to no end.

Silence hung between us. Thick and suffocating. But he watched me. He watched me like he couldn't take his eyes off me.

I only wished he would talk to me. To let me in.

To let me help.

We were different, sure. Our lives, our experiences, our views on the world. But that didn't make us enemies. It didn't—

"How would you help me?" he said, surprising me. "What would you do to make it all better?"

"I… w-what?"

"You keep telling me you care, that you want to help. So I'm asking you how?" A wicked glint shone in his eyes, and it felt like a trap.

"You can… you can talk to me." I swallowed, my throat dry, my heart crashing inside my chest.

"Talk… I don't need to talk, Celeste. I have Nix and Kye for that." He dragged his thumb over his bottom lip, the intensity of his eyes stealing the air from my lungs. "So maybe you should tell me just exactly how you plan on helping me?"

Zane's stare turned hard, smug even. He knew he had me. He knew he'd won this round. Because he wasn't talking about me being his friend at all. He was talking about something else entirely, something I wasn't sure I wanted to entertain.

"Yeah." A resigned huff left him. "Didn't think so." He

climbed to his feet and gave me one last cold look. "Go home, Celeste."

Zane stalked back inside, pausing at the door. For a second, I thought he might turn around and say something else, but he didn't. It was almost as if he was disappointed.

Disappointed in me.

I couldn't help but think I'd failed some kind of test.

And if there was one thing I hated more than anything, it was failing.

I FOUND out that Miriam had passed out during her meeting with Mr. Clarkson. The EMTs had been leaving as I walked to my car, and I overheard them discussing it.

It didn't take much to deduce they were talking about Miriam.

I couldn't stop thinking about Zane—how terrified he'd looked storming down the hall, how defeated he'd sounded underneath his cruel taunts when we'd sat outside.

He was hurting. And something told me that underneath all those layers of ice, Zane was lost and afraid and he didn't know how to handle that.

Nix had Harleigh, Kye had Chloe. But Zane... Zane only had his grandma.

Deciding to throw caution to the wind, I left a note for my parents telling them I'd be back later, grabbed my keys, and got in my car. It was a risk. Going to The Row to see them. But I liked Miriam and I wanted to make sure she was okay.

That they were both okay.

I could take some flowers, maybe some dinner so it was one less thing they had to think about. A smile tugged at my lips. It was perfect. I was just a girl who cared about a woman and her grandson and wanted to check in on them.

There was nothing wrong with that.

It didn't stop the butterflies wreaking havoc in my chest though as I drove to the store and bought a beautiful bouquet of wildflowers—because Miriam seemed like the kind of woman who appreciated the beauty in chaos—and a freshly baked baguette and a lasagna. Because who didn't love lasagna. And an apple pie for dessert.

Maybe it was a tad over the top, but I'd committed now.

But as I crossed the boundary lines into Darling Row, a frisson of trepidation went through me. I couldn't just pull up outside his trailer. It would cause ripples. Someone might see. Someone like Harleigh and Nix. Or Chloe and Kye.

Ugh.

What was I doing? Turning up uninvited like some weird stalker.

No, I was doing this. I was determined to prove to him that I wasn't the girl he thought.

Realizing I couldn't drive into The Row, I parked at the gas station on the stretch of road leading to the trailer park and called a cab. I didn't know Zane's exact address, but I knew where his trailer was, so I directed the driver there.

God, I felt nauseous. My stomach churning as I climbed out and walked the short distance up to his door. It was dusk out. The sun long disappeared behind the tree line in the distance.

I took a deep breath and knocked. A light came on followed by muffled voices and then the door swung open, and Zane stood there, glaring at me.

"What the fuck are you doing here?"

"I came to see if you're both okay. I brought flowers." I thrust the bouquet toward him, and he gawked at me like I'd lost my mind.

Maybe I had.

"They're for Miriam, not you. Obviously." The words tumbled out, my nerves getting the better of me. "I also brought some dinner because I thought you—"

"Let me get this straight. You brought us flowers and dinner?"

"Well, like I said already, the flowers are for your grandma, but yes."

"You're so fucking weird." He shook his head.

"Who is it?" Miriam called, and Zane murmured something under his breath.

"No one, Grams."

"Oh." Disappointment welled inside of me. "I thought—"

"You thought you'd turn up here like Suzy Homemaker and I'd what? Let you in and we'd all hang out? Yeah, never going to happen, Einstein. She'll appreciate the flowers and food, but you should probably get out of here before anyone sees you."

"No."

"No?" He glowered at me, his expression as cold as ice. "What the fuck do you mean, *no*?"

"I came to check on Miriam and I'm not leaving until—"

"What's going on out here?" Miriam appeared behind Zane. "Celeste, dear, is that you?"

"Hi, Mrs. Washington. I came to check if you were okay. I heard about what happened."

Zane practically had steam coming out of his ears, but I ignored his heavy stare as I focused on the frail woman behind him.

"Zane Thackeray, have you completely forgotten your manners?" She tsked. "Invite the girl in."

"Celeste can't stay, Grams. She was just delivering some flowers and dinner for you."

"That's so sweet." She flashed me a warm smile. "We haven't eaten yet. Would you like to join us?"

Zane stiffened; his jaw clenched so tight it looked painful. "Celeste needs to go."

"Actually, I'd love to stay." I flashed him a sickly-sweet smile earning me a low growl.

But I wasn't going to be so easily intimidated by him this time.

"Zane, let the girl pass."

"Yes, Grams," he murmured, reluctantly stepping aside to let me in.

"And be a dear and put those beautiful flowers in some water. I think there's a vase in the cabinet under the sink."

He closed the door, slamming it a little harder than necessary, but I shoved down the awkwardness. Miriam wanted me here, even if Zane didn't.

I could work with that.

19

ZANE

ONE MINUTE CELESTE WAS STANDING AT THE DOOR WITH A bouquet of flowers in her hands, the next, she was sitting at my table, eating the lasagna she'd brought for me and Grams.

What the fuck was happening?

I was in hell.

That was the only explanation.

I was in some living version of hell. Watching as she and Grams talked and laughed like they were old fucking friends.

"Zane Thackeray," Grams snapped. "Stop being so damn rude and offer our guest a fresh drink."

"Oh, it's okay, Miriam. I can get one." Celeste got up and went to the kitchenette, helping herself to another glass of water. "Anyone else?" She glanced at me.

"No."

"No, thank you, dear. This bread is delicious. Where did you get it from?"

"My favorite store in town. They bake everything fresh. So good." Celeste noticed my scowl and her smile dropped. "I thought it would go nice with the lasagna."

"Perfect," Grams replied. "It goes just perfect. What do you think, dear?" She patted my hand, and I blinked over at her.

"Uh, what?"

"The bread?" Grams raised a brow at me.

"The bread is… fine."

"Boys." She rolled her eyes. "No appreciation of good food."

"I love what you've done with the place," Celeste said.

Was she for real?

She lived in a goddamn mansion while me and Grams lived in a single trailer that had seen better days. Sure, we kept it clean and tidy, but there was no disguising the old paint jobs and peeling wallpaper.

"That's very kind of you, dear. Zane is a great help with maintaining the place."

"I'm going for a smoke." I went to get up, but she pinned me with a hard look.

"You'll do no such thing. I believe Celeste brought pie."

"I did."

"Zane, show Celeste where the bowls are."

"But—"

"Zane Thackeray!"

Celeste fought a smile, only making the anger churning inside me rise higher.

"Come on," I said, not bothering to wait for her as I moved to the kitchenette. Reaching up, I grabbed three bowls from the cabinet. "Here you—" I turned, practically bumping into her.

"God, sorry. I'm such a klutz," she said, grabbing my arm to steady herself.

The air crackled again as my gaze dropped to where she held me. "S-sorry." She snatched her hand away, tucking some hair behind her ear. It drew my eyes to the slope of her neck, the creamy skin there.

Fuck.

She was too close. All up in my space, infecting my thoughts. Poisoning my common sense. Because I wanted to kiss her again. I wanted to push her up against the wall and lose myself in her sweet, needy kisses. The soft curves of her body.

It wasn't supposed to be like this.

I hated her.

I did.

But I also wanted her. I wanted to corrupt her.

Ruin her. To dirty up her squeaky-clean image.

I wanted to knock the rich little princess off her pedestal.

"Zane?"

I blinked, dragging my eyes to hers. Instantly regretting it. Lust swirled in her inky blue depths.

"What are you thinking about?" I drawled, unable to resist the urge to toy with her.

"I… nothing."

"Liar." I leaned around her, pretending to reach for something behind her. "You're thinking bad things, aren't you? Dirty things."

"Zane, your grandma—"

"Can't hear us." She was too busy humming along to the radio in her favorite seat at the table facing the television.

I slid my other hand to the counter, caging Celeste in, my mouth right next to her ear. "Are you wet for me, Einstein? If I touched you right here." I pushed my hand between our bodies and cupped her pussy. "What would I find?"

"I-I…" Celeste bit back a whimper and I pressed the heel of my palm against her. "Oh God," she breathed.

"Not God, sweetheart. The devil, and I'll ruin you given half the chance."

She jerked back to stare me in the eyes. "What are—"

"How's that pie looking?" Grams called, and I staggered back, the spell broken.

Jesus, she reeled me in so easily.

I realized then, I liked toying with her. I liked watching her eyes glaze over with desire as I whispered cruel dirty words to her.

"It smells great," Celeste answered, her voice a small croak. I smirked and she scowled, mouthing, "Go away."

"I'm helping, remember?" I moved beside her,

running a finger down her spine. A shudder went through her as she grabbed the edge of the counter.

Oh yeah, this game was fun.

Watching the princess squirm every time I got close to her.

"Just… stop doing that."

"Doing what?" I leaned closer again or maybe she was pulling me in. Like gravity.

Yeah, that sounded about right.

"Touching me."

"Trust me, Einstein. If I was touching you, you'd know about it." I grabbed two of the bowls of pie she'd prepared and stalked off, hoping like hell neither Celeste nor Grams would notice how fucking hard I was.

"I'M GOING to call it a night," Grams said sometime later.

We'd demolished the pie, the two of them talking about anything and everything. School. Celeste's plans for the future. How much Grams liked the group at the center. But conversation never veered toward the fact that Celeste was from Old Darling Hill or the fact that Grams was deteriorating. I had to give it to Celeste, she didn't pry, and she didn't fuss when Grams had a bad spasm. She simply asked what she could do to help and did it.

I didn't know what to make of it. Her here, in my space. I didn't like it. I didn't like her knowing our business. But Grams seemed to enjoy her company, and that was a big fucking problem. Because this couldn't become a regular thing. I couldn't have her coming around here. Not when all I could think about was making good on my words from earlier.

I wasn't usually a foreplay kind of guy. Sex was a means to an end. A way to release some tension. I didn't do sleepovers and I rarely went back for seconds. Girls became too clingy after sex. They wanted to cuddle and talk and all that girly bullshit I didn't have time or the inclination for.

But this game I'd started with Celeste had me eager. Eager for more. Eager to see how far I could push her. How far I could corrupt her.

Harleigh and Nix would likely kick my ass if I touched her, but they didn't need to know. Besides, something told me Little Miss Perfect wasn't advertising the fact she was chasing me.

Whether she admitted it or not, Celeste was finding more and more ways to be around me. Because she wanted a taste of something bad.

Something rotten to the core.

"Do you need some help?" Celeste asked, getting up to help Grams with her stick.

"No, no, I can manage. Zane will help me get my pills."

I got up too, going over to the kitchen drawer where Grams kept all her meds.

"I should probably head home myself. It's later than I

thought."

"If you wait a few minutes Zane will walk you back to your car."

"Oh no, that's okay. I can call a cab."

"Nonsense. Zane will walk you, won't you, dear?"

Celeste gnawed the end of her thumb, watching me expectantly.

"Where did you park?" Because I hadn't seen her car outside when I'd found her standing at the door earlier.

"I, uh… I left it at the gas station and got a cab here."

Smart girl. I swallowed the words.

"Give me ten minutes and I'm all yours."

It wasn't until the words spilled out that I realized how they sounded. But interest, and a little bit of surprise, flared in Celeste's eyes.

"Don't be a stranger, dear," Grams said, waving her off as she shuffled down the hall.

I glanced back at her, holding her gaze for a second and then went after Grams.

"Such a sweet girl," she said, the second I entered her room.

"Grams," I warned.

"What? It's just a simple observation."

"Hmm," I murmured, helping her lay out her night clothes. Sometimes she needed my help undressing. It wasn't a problem yet—she could still do enough to retain some dignity—but eventually, probably sooner rather than later, she would need somebody to dress her.

No sixty-nine-year-old woman wanted her eighteen-year-old grandson to have to do that. She was going to need in-home care which cost money. Even if the insurance covered part of it, there would still be the co-payment.

"How are you feeling, really?" I asked with my back to her to give her some privacy.

"I enjoyed Celeste's company tonight. It was nice to have another female around. Maybe she can stop by again…"

"Not going to happen."

"And why not? Okay, all done."

I turned around and helped her into bed, offering her a drink and pills.

"Because… it isn't."

"You like her." Mischief danced in her eyes.

"I don't like anyone."

"Oh, I don't know. I think I saw something between the two of you over dinner."

"Promise me, you won't try to play matchmaker. Celeste is all kinds of wrong for me, Grams. Not that I'm looking for a girl, I'm not."

"Zane Thackeray, my sweet boy." She reached for my cheek. "Sometimes, I worry I was too harsh about—"

"Don't." I sighed, gently pulling her hand away and tucking it beside her. "There's only room for one woman in my life—you."

"Oh, hush now. Go and make sure Celeste gets to her car in one piece."

"I will." I pressed a kiss to her forehead. "If you need me—"

"I know. I'm fine, stop fussing." She gave me a smile, but it didn't reach her eyes.

We hadn't talked much about what happened earlier at the center. But we needed to. We needed to have the hard conversations and make some hard choices.

I turned off the main light and headed back to the kitchen where I found Celeste washing the dishes.

"You don't need to do that," I said.

"It's okay, I want to help."

She kept saying that.

Dangling the words in front of me as if anything she could do would make things better.

I moved closer, pushing my body up against hers as she dipped the plate in the soapy water. Celeste's breath caught as I slid my hand around her waist and buried my nose in the back of her hair, breathing her in.

She smelled so fucking good. My hand trailed up her stomach and over her tits until I cupped her jaw, forcing her to twist her head a little.

"Zane," she breathed, her eyelashes fluttered as we stared at each other.

"You want to help, Einstein?"

"I…" She nodded.

Fuck it.

I smashed my mouth down on hers, plunging my tongue into her mouth as she gasped. She managed to turn, twisting her fingers into my hoodie and anchoring us together. I poured every ounce of frustration and anger and hatred into the kiss, punishing her with my mouth and tongue and teeth. But she gave it back just as good.

"Fuck, you're a hot little thing." My hands were all over her body, mapping her curves, slipping underneath her sweater so I could feel the heat of her skin.

"Wait," she whispered.

I pulled back, arching a brow. My mouth twisted. "You having second thoughts?"

"No." She shook her head, pressing a soft kiss to my lips. "But not here, not like this while your grandma is down the hall."

I glared at her. I didn't like that she'd stopped me. I didn't want to talk or hang out or share stories.

I wanted to drown.

Preferably in her sweet kisses and soft curves.

That's all I needed from her.

A distraction.

That's all she could ever be.

"Zane," she said again when I dove in to kiss her.

I blew out a frustrated breath, feeling the lust inside me ebb away a little.

"Come on," I said, grabbing her hand. "I know a place we can go."

20

CELESTE

"IT'S BEAUTIFUL OUT HERE," I SIGHED, FLICKING MY EYES to Zane who was staring out of the window.

After he'd walked me to my car, he'd climbed in beside me and directed me to drive to a concealed spot down by the reservoir. It was stunning, the moonlight reflecting off the vast body of water which glittered like diamonds were sprinkled upon it.

But the heat between us earlier had cooled somewhat, and now, I didn't know what to say.

When Zane kissed me, I felt alive. For the first time in my life, I felt like more than the girl everyone around me believed me to be.

It sounded silly, I knew that. Girls didn't need a guy's attention to feel worthy. But it wasn't about his attention so much as it was about how I felt around him.

Like for the first time, I was choosing something for myself and not the expectations pressed upon me.

I wanted him.

Plain and simple.

It didn't matter who he was or where he came from. It didn't matter that my parents wouldn't approve, or the elite families of Old Darling Hill would be scandalized by such behavior. I wanted him.

And I wanted him… no, I *needed* him to want me back.

"Your grandma seemed happy enough. How is she doing, really?" I asked, desperate to lighten the thick tension hanging between us.

"Come here," he said, reaching for me.

"W-what?"

My stomach curled at the intensity in his eyes. How he seemed to look right through me.

"I didn't bring you out here to talk about my grams or to look at the view." He said drolly, pulling me onto his lap, pushing my thighs apart so that I straddled him. My arms linked around the back of his neck as my heart galloped in my chest.

Zane smirked up at me, his eyes glinting with mischief.

God, I was in trouble.

So. Much. Trouble.

But I didn't care, because when he looked at me like that, I wanted to give him everything. I wanted to hand over my heart and let him do whatever he wanted with it. Because this feeling, this wild, reckless rush I got around him, it was worth the risk.

"I hate how beautiful you are." He slid his hand along the side of my neck, pushing the hair out of my face and over my shoulder.

"I hate how fucking smart you are, how easily people fall for your smile." His eyes grew hooded as he stroked his thumb back and forth over my pulse point, sending my heart and certain parts of my body into overdrive. "Fuck, I hate your smile."

"Zane..." I didn't like hearing him say those things.

He wasn't supposed to hate me.

Not here. Not while we were like this.

Not ever.

Emotion welled inside me as I trembled at his cruel, confusing words. Because he was saying one thing, but he was doing another thing entirely.

"I hate everything you are," he said in a low pained whisper. "But most of all I hate that I want you so fucking much."

He guided my face down to his, our lips almost touching.

"Wait," I said, panic clawing up my throat. Maybe this was a bad idea. Maybe it meant something different to him than it did to me.

Maybe I'd completely misread the signs.

"You said you wanted to help, Einstein. So help me." He kissed me hard, rendering me breathless.

I felt his hatred in every stroke of his tongue, every

graze of his teeth. His fingers flexed around my neck, taking control of the angle, how deep he licked into my mouth.

It was unlike anything I'd ever experienced. The way he commanded me to his every whim.

His hand dropped to the curve of my ass, pressing me down on him, the thick ridge in his jeans. "See what you do to me?" he taunted, thrusting up a little, making me moan. "You get me so fucking hot. And I hate it. I hate—"

"Shh." I slid a finger to his lip, kissing around it, running my tongue over the seam of his lips.

I didn't want to hear how he hated me.

I only wanted to feel *this*. His body, hard and strong beneath mine. The way his hands mapped my curves, encouraging me to rock above him.

I ran a hand through his hair, pushing it back off his face and staring into his eyes as I rocked faster, harder. Letting him hit just the right spot over and over.

"It feels so good," I murmured between kisses.

"Not as good as it'll feel when you're riding my dick," he ground out.

"Oh God... *God*," I cried, burying my face in his shoulder as intense waves of pleasure began to rise inside me.

But Zane stopped abruptly, his hand on my hip forcing me to stop too.

"W-what—"

He pushed his hand into my pants and underwear,

sliding two fingers into me without warning. "Use me to get off," he said, his voice a cracked demand.

I leaned in to kiss him, but he held back, curling his fingers deep inside me as I rode his hand, chasing the ebbing waves once again.

"More," I cried. "I need more."

Zane smirked, rolling his thumb over my clit. "If everyone could see you now. Letting me finger fuck you in your fancy car. Bet Daddy Rowe would be so proud of his little princess."

I stilled, his words landing like a blow to the stomach. "What did you say?"

"You heard me, Einstein." Zane sneered, his fingers still moving inside me.

"Z-Zane, stop. I-I…" His thumb pressed harder, and I sucked in a shaky breath.

"Feels good, doesn't it? Slumming it with the bad boy." He leaned in, running his nose along my jaw to kiss the corner of my mouth.

"Please…"

I didn't know what I was begging for. For him to stop or for him to finish. But he didn't let up, working me with his fingers until I was a boneless, breathless mess above him.

"Jack me off," he ordered, guiding one of my hands to his zipper. Together, we lowered it and took out his thick erection.

I wrapped my fingers around him and started

pumping up and down. Zane sank back against the chair with a low groan. "Yeah," he drawled, "just like that."

It was hard to concentrate. My senses unraveling with every stroke of his fingers. But I tried to maintain focus. To make it as good for him as it was for me.

Because by God, it felt good. Even when he was spewing hateful, spiteful words at me, my body wanted more. Demanded it.

"Shit, babe. That feels… fuck," he choked out when I twisted my hand on the upstroke, sliding my thumb over the tip. "*Fuck*."

He wasn't the only one with the power—I had some too.

I had the power to make *him* lose control.

"Again," he murmured, both of us chasing our releases. Racing toward the finish line.

I got there first, crying his name as my thighs tightened around his hand. But he was right behind me, coming all over my hand and sweater with a rumbling groan.

We stared at each other, trying to catch our breath, and I couldn't stop the faint smile tracing my lips. "That was a—"

"Fuck, I even hate how prettily you come." He spat the words, cutting me off, and driving a knife right through my heart. "But you make it so easy."

I scrambled away from him, smoothing down my clothes and hair as I slid back into my seat.

"Mmm, you even taste expensive." He licked his

fingers clean. It should have been hot watching him do that, but I only felt cheap.

"I… I think you should go." Dejection roiled in my stomach.

This was a mistake.

Thinking I could play by his rules was a mistake.

A dark chuckle rumbled in his chest. "See you around, Einstein. Thanks for the ride." He climbed out without so much as a backward glance and disappeared into the shadows.

While I sat there trying to catch my breath…

And soothe my bruised heart.

"What happened to you?" Max said the second I entered the kitchen.

"Nothing, why?"

"You look… different."

"I'm fine." I ducked behind the refrigerator door to grab a carton of juice. "Where have you been tonight?"

"Shouldn't I be asking you that question?" He arched a brow as I leaned against the counter.

"I was out with some friends."

"What friends? Last time I checked you had Harleigh and Miles, and Harleigh left and Miles—"

"You're an ass."

"What? I'm just stating facts. I know you weren't with Miles because I heard Marcy Gerard telling everyone they had a date. And Nix was with Harleigh because he texted me to—"

"Nix texted you?"

"Yeah, so?"

"I didn't realize the two of you were friends now."

Max shrugged. "He mainly texts about training, but we talk occasionally. It's not a big deal."

To him.

It wasn't a big deal to him.

But to me, it was just more evidence that Max was more involved in their lives than I was.

Strangely, I was more bothered about that than hearing Miles was on a date with Marcy.

"Were you with Chloe? I won't tell if you were."

"No, actually." I let out a heavy sigh. "It's kind of lame but I went to the movies on my own." The lie soured on my tongue, but it wasn't like I could tell him the truth.

"That is lame. Jesus, Sis," he chuckled, "you need to get out more."

I leveled him with a hard look. "We can't all be social butterflies like you."

He shrugged again. "What can I say? People dig the Maxmeister."

"Maxmeister, really?" I scoffed.

"You're only jealous I have a social life and you... well, don't."

My expression dropped.

He was right, I was jealous. It had always come so easy to him. Making friends. Being the life and soul of the party. It wasn't that I didn't enjoy having fun. I did. But I found it difficult to connect with people. Miles had been my people.

And now I didn't even have him.

"I'm going to bed," I said, taking off toward the hall.

"Hey, come on. I didn't mean it like that. I'm a dick. I say the wrong thing all the time. It's like my…"

I kept going, ignoring his apology.

I'd been so sure going to see Zane and Miriam was the right thing to do, but it had only left me feeling worse than ever.

Zane wanted me, I didn't doubt that. But I wasn't sure he would ever see past our differences to truly accept me.

I couldn't win.

I was a good person. Kind and compassionate, if not a little overbearing at times. I loved hard and stood up for what was right. Sure, maybe my brain processed things a little differently to the average teen, but I didn't flaunt my intelligence or use it against people. If anything, sometimes I wished I wasn't so smart. It had only ever brought me crushing disappointment and the heavy weight of my parents' expectations.

Graduating with honors, getting accepted to Columbia, and pursuing a career as a doctor was their dream.

Not mine.

I just didn't know how to make them see that.

21

ZANE

"Grams, you okay in there?" I rapped my knuckles on her door.

"I'm okay," she called, but there was a distinct lull in her voice.

"I'm coming in." I waited a second or two before gently pushing the door open. "What's wrong?"

She was sitting up in bed, staring at nothing, her eyes slightly glazed over.

"Oh, I'm just tired." Her smile was tight, failing to hide the truth.

"Dizzy? Light-headed?"

"No, dear. Come, sit." She patted the edge of the bed, and I went to her. "Tell me about last night. Did… did Celeste get… home okay?"

I tensed at the mention of her.

"I walked her to her car and then I assume she went straight home."

Things had gotten out of hand. I'd meant to toy with her a little. Maybe get her off and add new material to my spank bank. I hadn't anticipated that the second I pulled her onto my lap that things would go from zero to sixty. If she hadn't frozen up when I got a little too mouthy, I would have ended up deep inside her. I had no doubt about that.

Only, I couldn't decide whether that was a good thing or a bad thing.

"You didn't check?"

"She's seventeen, Grams. Pretty sure she's capable of getting home."

"Zane Thackeray, I know I raised you better than that. I might not have been a shining example of trusting people when you were younger, but Celeste is a beautiful young woman, and that makes her an easy target."

"Relax, Grams, I'm sure she's fine."

But now she'd planted a little seed of doubt that let a trickle of guilt in.

I'd gone too far saying all that shit to her. But it was the only way I could control the situation. The only fucking way I could remind myself that I hated her. That she was everything that was wrong with the world.

"I thought maybe you'd cell phone message her."

"You mean text her."

"That's what I said."

"No, it isn't." I smirked.

"To-may-to. Tom-ah-to." She winked, the cloud over her expression melting away a little.

"You know Grams, you need to tell me when you don't feel right."

"Oh hush, I am quite cap—"

"This is important. I don't want you to fall and hurt yourself."

"I am not a complete invalid yet, dear."

"I know that. But we can't pretend your symptoms aren't getting worse." I took her hand in mine, hating how frail it felt beneath my fingers. Sometimes it was hard to remember she wasn't even seventy yet.

"What did Mr. Clarkson say? You never did tell me yesterday."

"Because..." She inhaled a shuddering breath. "I don't want you to worry."

"It's my job to worry about you. Now, tell me."

"The insurance isn't going to pay for the new treatment. There's a couple of options but I'll still need to find a percentage of the cost."

"You mean we. We'll need to fi—"

"Zane Thackeray, you listen to me, and you listen good. This is my problem, my sweet boy. I won't have you worrying about it or doing anything stupid to try and help. I need you to focus on school and graduate. You hear me?"

"Grams, I can—"

"No, Zane. I... I did not bust my ass raising you so that you could throw away your high school diploma."

She inhaled a ragged breath. "It's important to me that you graduate, and it should be important to you too."

"I don't need a diploma to work down at the mill, Grams."

"And that is exactly why you need to graduate. Because you are worth more than that."

She said the words, but I didn't feel them. I couldn't. I wasn't blessed with the smarts like Celeste or the football skill to go all the way like Nix. Even if I went to college—and it was a big if—I had no idea what I would study. Because I didn't look into the future and dream.

This was my hand. Looking after Grams and working some dead-end job.

She lifted a shaky hand and laid it on my cheek. "My stubborn headed, strong boy. What am I going to do with you?" Her eyes crinkled with sadness.

"Don't worry about me, Grams. I'll be okay."

I always was.

Me: I need a favor.

Chloe texted straight back.

Chloe: What do you need?

Me: Celeste's number.

Chloe: Dare I ask why?

Me: She's volunteering at the support group my grams goes to and I need to ask her something.

Chloe: Did that actually sound like a plausible excuse in your head?

Me: Do you have her number or not?

She forwarded me Celeste's number, and another text came through.

Chloe: I'm guessing you want this to stay between the two of us?

Me: Yep.

Chloe: It'll cost you. I'm going out with Warner later. If Kye asks I'm with Brianne.

Me: You're playing with fire. If he finds out you're seeing someone from the team...

Chloe: Yeah, yeah. I know the risks. We won't get caught.

Me: You know you're too good for the likes of Warner, Clo, right?

She was always dating assholes who didn't treat her right. I didn't get it. But what did I know about girls?

Nothing, apparently.

Chloe: Thanks for your concern, Dad. But why don't you leave my love life to me, and I'll leave your love life to you.

She added a winky emoji for effect.

Me: Brat.

Chloe: Yeah, yeah. Tell it to someone who cares. And Zane... hurt Celeste and I will fuck you up!

My lips curved. She was something all right, and I didn't envy Kye having to deal with her as she got older. But despite all the headaches she gave him, they were lucky to have one another. To always know that they had someone who had their back.

Storing Celeste's number, I opened a new message thread.

Me: Did you get home okay?

Einstein: Who is this?

Me: Really, you're going to act that dumb?

I'd sent it before I could stop myself. But there was just something about her that pushed my buttons.

Einstein: How did you get my number?

Me: I have my ways. Now answer the question... did you get home okay?

Einstein: Since I'm texting you back in complete sentences, I think you can assume I am not being held hostage by some psychopath.

Before I could text her back, she sent another message.

Einstein: Although I'm surprised you care. Unless...

Me: Go on.

Einstein: Unless your grandma put you up to this.

Fuck.
This girl.
This fucking girl.

Einstein: She did, didn't she?

Me: Does it matter?

Einstein: No, I guess not.

Me: What are you up to?

Why?

Why the fuck did I ask her that?

It didn't matter though because she didn't reply.

Celeste didn't reply and she left me sitting there, clutching my phone, willing it to vibrate like a fool.

It was all Grams' fault. Acting like I should care about Celeste. Reminding me what a good, kind soul she was.

She wasn't good, she was a nuisance. An interfering, busybody who had nothing better to do than stick her nose where it didn't belong.

My cell bleeped again, and I smirked. I knew she wouldn't be able to resist replying now she had my message.

But when I opened the text, it was Chloe, not Celeste.

**Chloe: Kye mentioned Grams isn't doing so good...
you know I'm always here for you both too, right?**

A lump clogged my throat.

Me: Yeah, Clo, I know.

But nobody could help me raise the money she needed. I would never ask that of my friends.

No, that fell squarely on my shoulders. And I needed to figure out something.

Fast.

AFTER I MADE sure Grams was okay, I ended up at Buster's to burn off some steam.

I hadn't invited Nix and Kye. I needed some time to think, to weigh up my limited options. Grams needed that treatment, so I needed to find a way to raise some cash. I'd already spoken to Morris, the shift manager at the mill, and he'd offered me a few extra hours here and there, but it wasn't permanent, and it wasn't guaranteed. If the orders dried up, the work did too.

I hit the bag harder, grunting as my knuckles cracked, sending a lick of pain up my arm. Sweat trickled down my back but the exertion was good. It helped clear my head and focus. For those few minutes, it let me forget about the crushing weight of responsibility I carried on my shoulders.

Grams said it wasn't my place to worry. But if I didn't, who would?

No one, that's who.

Sure, she could attend the support group, make friends with people in a similar situation. There were counselors she could talk to and charities she could get some help from. But ultimately, nobody was going to hand her a check and send her on her way to the hospital.

I hit the bag harder. *One. Two. One. Two.* This was the kind of shit parents were supposed to handle. Not grandkids. But my mom had up and quit a long time ago. I'd always thought that she had abandoned me, but I realized now, she'd abandoned Grams too.

Grams had raised me, despite me being a constant reminder of the daughter she'd lost. Despite losing a part of herself the day Mom walked out.

Fuck.

I fell against the bag, my chest heaving as I fought to catch my breath. Blood whooshed in my ears, adrenaline coursing through my bloodstream. But it wasn't enough.

It was never enough.

That's why I didn't get in the ring like Nix did when he needed to burn off steam. Because part of me feared I would never stop. That it would *never* be enough.

Grabbing my towel, I wiped my face and the back of my neck and headed over to the bench where I'd dumped my stuff. Bryson spotted me, and came over, handing me a bottle of water.

"That was some workout," he said. "What's eating at you, kid?"

"Just got some shit going on." I unwrapped my hands, clenching a fist and relishing in the sting of tender skin tightening over bruised bone.

"You need to talk, I'm here." He folded his arms over his chest.

I wasn't close to Bryson like Nix was. He was a dangerous man. And he never gave up his time or resources without wanting something in return. A trap I'd managed to avoid so far.

But I was desperate.

"Actually, you might be able to help me."

"I'm listening." His brow cocked.

"Can we… uh"—I glanced around the gym—"go somewhere private?"

"Sure, kid. Follow me." He turned and stalked toward the door leading to his private office.

It was a bad idea.

The worst.

But if anyone could help me, it was Bryson Shaw.

And I was all out of other options.

22

CELESTE

I'M NOT GOING," MAX SAID, EARNING HIM A HUFF OF disapproval from Mom.

"For once in your life, you will do as you're told, Maximilian."

"Why? So we can pretend we're the perfect happy family in front of all your stuck up friends? I'm good thanks, Mom."

"Michael, will you please say something?" Mom pinned Dad with a hard look.

It had been like this since I'd finally dragged myself downstairs. Mom wanted us all to go to Mrs. Sinclair's for afternoon tea. She'd invited us to celebrate Mom's new position on the board.

It sounded like the worst kind of hell, but she was digging in her heels.

"Your mom is right, Max. It wouldn't hurt you to come this once. The center is important to your mother. We should support that. It's only for a couple of hours, then you and Celeste can escape."

"Michael!"

"Sabrina," he implored, "I'm trying to find the middle ground here. Let them come, show their faces, and then they can leave."

"Or we can stick around and drink all the free champagne if you'd prefer that?" Max smirked and I found myself resisting the urge to chuckle.

Max liked to antagonize our parents—especially Mom. But it was worse than usual lately, the two of them butting heads over anything and everything. Usually, she let him win. Let him avoid anything business related. At least, that way, he wouldn't show her up. But it seemed today she had decided we would present a united front.

"You really are incorrigible."

"I have no idea what that means," he snorted.

"Adjective. Not able to be changed or reformed," I said.

"That is not normal." He rolled his eyes. "You really need to get out more."

I stuck my tongue out at him. Not the most mature response but I was too exhausted to verbally spar with him.

Zane had texted me earlier out of the blue. Of course, his grandma had put him up to it. Which is precisely why I'd left him hanging when he asked me what I was up to.

But the fact he'd asked someone for my number—most likely Chloe since I didn't think he would ask Harleigh or Nix—was still confusing.

I was trying not to read too much into it. It was difficult though when all I could think about was how it felt to have his mouth on mine while his fingers made me come apart.

Why couldn't I have just liked Miles the way I liked Zane?

Miles was good and nice… and safe. Miles wouldn't hurt me or say cruel, wicked things.

But I'd tried good and nice and safe, and it didn't make my stomach flutter like a swarm of butterflies were soaring inside me.

Everyone deserved to feel that trickle of anticipation, the heart-stopping rush every time you were close to the object of your desires. And even though the best friend in me found it hard that he'd moved on so quickly, part of me hoped Miles had found that with Marcy. He deserved it. They both did.

"This is non-negotiable," Mom said. "I want us to go as a family and we will. We leave at five. If you decide not to follow these simple instructions, Max, you can expect to be grounded until you can act like a reasonable adult."

"Bullshit. You haven't grounded me since I was thirteen."

"Yes, well, I'm beginning to think we've gone too easy on you." She pinned him with a scathing look. "Your attitude lately is reprehensible."

"Again, with the big words, Mom. I have no—"

"Adjective. Deserving censure or condemn—"

"Thank you, Professor Merriam-Webster." Max rolled his eyes.

"Wow, I'm surprised you even know what that is."

"I'm surprised you have any friends," he said. "Oh wait, you don't."

"Max!" Dad chided but it was too late. My brother's thoughtless taunt had landed its blow, punching me straight in the stomach.

"I'm going to take a shower," I said.

"Come on, Sis, I didn't mean it. I'm just stressed because Mom is clearly on the rag and—"

"Maximilian Rowe-Delacorte, you will not…"

Their raised voices became inaudible rumbles as I rushed upstairs to my room. Max was an insensitive ass at times, but I wouldn't hold it against him too much. Something was going on with him, something he'd yet to confide in me. If he ever did. Knowing my brother, he would rather take his secrets to the grave than actually trust me to keep them.

The second I slipped into my room, my cell phone vibrated, my heart doing a silly little flip at the sight of Zane's name again.

Zane: Ignoring me, Einstein? That's not very neighborly of you. Grams will be disappointed.

I flopped down on my bed and kicked my legs up behind me as I pondered what—*if*—to reply.

The straight and simplest answer was to ignore him. But Max had hit a vulnerable spot and Zane made me feel good.

Even when he was saying mean things, he still made me light up inside.

Me: Using your grandma to pull me into the conversation... now that doesn't seem very neighborly to me.

Zane: Worked though, didn't it?

Me: Maybe.

Zane: What are you doing?

Me: What are you doing?

Zane: That's for me to know, Einstein.

Me: That is quite possibly the least sexy nickname ever...

Zane: It's not supposed to be a compliment.

Damn him. He was good at this. At maintaining the upper hand, always making me feel one step behind.

Me: Don't worry, Zane Thackeray. I know what I am and what I'm not.

Zane: What the fuck does that mean?

Me: Nothing. It means nothing.

His next reply was slow coming. Probably because he didn't understand my vague message. But it was true. I knew most guys didn't find girls like me attractive.

Whoever said intelligence was sexy had lied, because in my experience if a female was too smart, she was intimidating. Most of the guys I knew didn't want girls who knew more than they did. They wanted girls who laughed at their jokes and nodded at their stories. Girls who didn't think too much on their own.

They certainly didn't want a girl who knew the dictionary definition of words like incorrigible and reprehensible.

Zane: Meet me tonight?

Me: What? No! Why would you even suggest that?

Zane: You're right, it's a bad idea.

Me: The worst.

I threw my phone down like it was contaminated with an infectious disease.

He couldn't seriously want to meet me? Not after last night?

Snatching it back up, my fingers flew over the screen.

Me: Is this a game?

Zane: Why? Do you want to play?

My head screamed at me not to engage. But my heart —my foolish, fickle heart—liked Zane's attention.

Me: How can I play if I don't know the rules?

Zane: You're the genius... figure it out.

Me: I have a thing tonight.

Zane: What thing?

Me: A family thing...

I bit my lip, my stomach vibrating with a heady mix of anticipation and excitement.

This... this is what I craved. Zane wasn't a good guy, and he definitely wasn't a parent-approved guy, but he wasn't a bad guy either.

He was just doing his best to survive.

And after seeing how he was with his grandma, how protective and caring he was with her, it was hard not to be sucked into his orbit. Even when I knew he would probably eat me alive.

Zane: Pretty sure you'll have more fun with me than at some lame family thing.

Me: I can't get out of it.

If Mom and Dad ever found out about me and Zane, I could kiss any freedom I had goodbye. Dad was only in my corner because he wanted to rebuild his relationship with Harleigh. But if he knew I'd been intimate with Zane, that would all change.

Zane: Your loss then.

Maybe so.

But something told me if I did meet him, I'd stand to lose a hell of a lot more.

THE SINCLAIRS LIVED in a big Craftsman Ranch on the outskirts of town. It was stunning with its low-pitched gable roof and overhanging eaves, patterned windowpanes, and covered front porch. Stunning and expensive if the gated access and surrounding land were any indicator.

"I hope they have good champagne," Max murmured under his breath, toying with the collar on his polo shirt. Mom had wanted him to wear a dress shirt, but Dad stepped in before an argument ensued.

At Mom's suggestion, I'd opted for a simple dress that tapered in at my waist and fell to my knees, pairing it with some heeled pumps. My hair was curled at the ends and gathered on one shoulder in a loose ponytail.

"Sabrina, so good to see you," Mrs. Sinclair greeted us at the door. "And Celeste, my, don't you look beautiful."

"You have a lovely home," I said, smiling.

"Thank you. We love it out here. Michael, welcome." She leaned up to press a kiss to both of his cheeks, before turning her attention to my brother. "And you must be Max," she said.

"Hi."

"Your mom has told me all about you."

"Only good things I hope." Max flashed her a cheeky smile and she chuckled.

"Oh, I like you. Come in, please. Hannah is just laying out tea."

"Hannah?" Dad asked.

"Hannah is our housekeeper turned cook, and a most excellent one at that. I hope you're all hungry, she's put on quite the spread."

Max shot me a bemused look as we followed Mrs. Sinclair into the reception area.

"Joseph, our final guests are here."

"Final?" Dad asked.

"Sabrina didn't tell you? I invited my son and his family. Cooper is just dying to meet you." She winked at me, and the ground went from underneath me.

"Cooper?" Max asked.

"Yes, my grandson. He'll be attending Columbia next year. I know your mom is very keen for him and Celeste to meet."

"I bet she is." Max grimaced.

"Shall we?" Mrs. Sinclair motioned down the hall.

But Dad took Mom's elbow, holding her back a little as our host waltzed off.

"A little heads-up might have been nice," he said in a hushed voice.

"It's just an introduction. I'm not expecting her to marry the boy."

"Come on, Sis, let's go find the champagne. Something tells me you're going to need it." Max laced his arm through mine and steered me down the hall, leaving Mom and Dad to their tense conversation.

"It's a setup. She set me up," I murmured in disbelief. Not that I should have been surprised.

"She knows I'll never continue her legacy, so that burden falls solely on your shoulders. Sorry about that." Max gave me a tight smile.

"I don't want to spend all evening making small talk with some guy I've never met just because mom and his grandma think we're compatible."

"It could always be worse."

"How? How could this possibly be worse?" I glowered at him.

"You could have walked in on Mom and Dad doing it up against their bedroom wall."

Strangled laughter spilled out of me. "Oh my God, you can't say that."

"Just did, Sis. Just did. Now I don't know about you, but I intend on drinking this place dry. Wish me luck."

"Max," I warned. "Don't do anything stupid."

"Who, me?" He grinned. "Wouldn't dream of it."

23

ZANE

I STARED INTO THE FIRE, FIXATED ON THE WAY THE FLAMES danced together. The sun had long disappeared, sinking into the horizon, leaving behind a cold, starless night.

I was drunk.

But it was better than acknowledging the events of the day. Meeting with Bryson's contact. Stupidly texting Celeste. Asking her to meet me.

But I needed it to stop. I needed everything to just. Fucking. Stop.

Fuck.

I kicked my boot against the dirt, sending a spray of dust into the air. It wasn't enough. Didn't even begin to temper the storm raging inside me.

How has life gotten to this point? Where I was

making deals with the devil just to be able to pay for my grams' treatment?

She'd have questions, no doubt. And all I would have was a bunch of lies to feed her. But as long as she got what she needed, so long as she was okay… that's all that mattered.

My cell phone vibrated, and I pulled it out. It wasn't the name I wanted to see though.

Kye: Where you at?

Me: Needed some space. Things got heavy with Grams.

Kye: She good?

Me: She will be.

Kye: What did you do?

Me: You don't need to worry. I handled it.

Kye: Why do I not like the sound of that?

He texted again.

Kye: Want to hang out? I got hold of some premium weed. We can smoke all our troubles away.

It sounded tempting but getting high with Kye would

mean talking to him. Or avoiding his questions. So I gave him an excuse.

Me: Can't. Headed home soon. See you at school tomorrow.

Kye: It'll all work out, Z. You know that, right?

Me: Yeah.

The lie snaked through me, the heavy weight of dread settling in the pit of my stomach. Everything was fucked.

But I had the money—that's all that mattered. I'd figure out the rest.

I drained my beer and cracked open another. It barely touched the tension radiating through me though.

After meeting Bryson's contact, I'd returned home and eaten an awkward meal with Grams. I couldn't tell her the truth, not yet. Maybe not ever. So I'd gotten her comfortable in front of the TV, kissed her on the head, and told her I was meeting the guys for a bit.

I hated lying to her; my mom had done enough of that over the years. But this wasn't to harm her, it was to help her.

"Fuck," I breathed, bringing the bottle to my lips.

I needed something else to take the edge off. Something that no buzz or high could give me.

Without overthinking it, I opened my chat history with Celeste and sent her another message.

Me: How's the family thing?

To my surprise she texted straight back.

Einstein: I'm hiding out in one of the reception rooms with their dog Pippa.

My mouth twisted, picturing her in some huge lavish room with a rich people dog around her feet.

Me: That bad, huh?

Einstein: We're going to escape soon.

Me: We?

Einstein: Me and Max.

Me: Come meet me...

I waited. And waited. She'd blown me off so easily earlier, and I didn't like it. Because I'd grown used to her attention—her blatant interest. Even if I hated it.

Einstein: Where are you?

That's my girl. My lips twitched. Fuck. I wasn't supposed to be thinking like that. But this was fun. A distraction. And for as much as I wished it were different, feeling Celeste pressed up against me was addictive. A false high I never thought I'd chase.

Me: Down by the res.

Einstein: At a party?

I hit her number and waited.

"Z-Zane?" she whispered. "I can't talk, someone might—"

"Meet me here."

"I can't get there. I don't have my car."

Shit. That was a problem.

"Meet me on your side of the res then. At the water tower."

"I… It's dark. It's getting la—"

"I need you, Einstein," I breathed, feeling the words roll through me. The truth of them. "I fucking need you, okay?"

"Zane, what happened?"

Fuck.

Fuck. Fuck. *Fuck*.

"It's been a rough day. I'm wired. Can you meet me or not?" My tone was harsh, and I heard her suck in a sharp breath.

"I… yeah, okay. Give me an hour."

"Thirty minutes."

"Forty."

"Done. And Einstein, don't let me down."

SHE WAS LATE.

And my mood was in the fucking gutter.

I'd finished off the six-pack of beer and walked around the res to the water tower. I rarely came out here. It was DA territory, and usually, we stayed on our side and they stayed on theirs. But desperate times called for desperate measures, and I was about as desperate as I could get.

Headlights cut through the night sky and Celeste's Range Rover came into view. She cut the engine and hopped out.

"I went home to get my car."

"What the fuck are you wearing?" The words tumbled out.

"What's wrong with it?" Her cheeks flushed.

"Nothing's wrong with it…" My gaze dropped down her body, lingering on the swell of her hips, her mouthwatering curves.

Shit. Nothing was wrong with it, but the dress hugged the lines of her body, taunting me with what lay underneath, and her legs… fuck me, she wasn't wearing any stockings.

"Aren't you cold?"

She shrugged, wrapping her arms around her midriff. "I'll live."

"I can warm you up." I stalked toward her, crowding her against the side of the car.

"Zane, wait—"

"Don't wanna talk, Einstein." I nuzzled her neck, breathing in her sweet scent. My lips latched onto the skin beneath her ear and sucked greedily.

Celeste whimpered, clutching my hoodie. "Oh God," she moaned.

"Already told you, babe. Not God." I lifted my head to find her watching me, her eyes glittering with wariness. "What?"

"I thought…"

"You thought what?" Irritation crept in. "That I invited you here to talk? I don't want to fucking talk, Celeste. And I don't think you do either."

Dipping my head, I brushed my lips over hers. Soft and slow, giving her time to warm up to me. Her fingers tightened in my hoodie, dragging me closer until my body fell against hers, pressing her into the side of the car.

She opened for me, and I swept my tongue into her mouth, loving how responsive she was. Usually, I fucked a girl, got my kicks, and moved on. But Celeste was different. I found myself imagining all the ways I could make her come apart, make her scream. I wanted to lay her out and take my time, completely lose myself in her.

It was unnerving.

She unnerved me.

But rather than walk away and forget all about the pretty girl from the other side of town, I kept pulling her back in. It was supposed to be a game. A distraction. A bit of fun. But the rules were changing.

"I haven't stopped thinking about how good you tasted on my fingers." I slipped a hand between us, grabbing her bare thigh and sliding my hand up, up, up.

"Z-Zane," she choked out as I pressed the heel of my palm against her.

It wasn't enough. I needed to feel her. Lose myself in between her soft thighs. Hooking Celeste's panties to the side, I dipped two fingers inside her.

"Maybe we should get in the car," she murmured, her words thick with desire.

"I don't think so. I think it gets you hot knowing anyone could see us. See the Darling Hill princess letting the boy from The Row dirty her up."

"Oh God…" she cried, trying to bury her face in my shoulder. But I crashed my mouth down on hers, swallowing her moans.

It still wasn't enough though. I needed more.

"I need to fuck you."

The words landed between us like a bomb. Celeste blinked at me, her expression unreadable. But then her eyes softened as she leaned in, brushing her lips over mine.

"Okay."

Okay? Was she for real?

She wasn't supposed to say okay. She was supposed to put a stop to this. To end this. Because I wasn't thinking straight. I was a fucking mess and I just needed it to stop.

I needed the constant pressure inside me to disappear. So that I could breathe, just for a little while.

"Zane, it's okay." She cupped my face, kissing me. "I want you."

Thank fuck.

I hitched her leg around my waist, curling my fingers deeper.

Celeste's moans filled the air, her body trembling as I pushed her closer, rolling my thumb over her clit how I knew she liked it.

Fuck, this girl.

I was in so much trouble.

Because how could something you hated so much feel so fucking good?

Maybe that was the allure though. Maybe knowing I was corrupting a princess from Old Darling Hill was my way of saying a giant 'fuck you' to them and everything they stood for.

"Zane... it's..." She came hard and fast, crying my name over and over as I wrung out every ounce of pleasure from her. Leaning around her, I yanked open the back door and nudged her inside. "Scooch back into the seat."

Celeste hopped up on the seat and laid back, gazing up at me like I was everything she ever wanted.

I wasn't.

I'd destroy her. Piece by little piece I would dirty up her soul until the light radiating inside her winked out.

I snapped my belt and pushed my jeans down my hips a little. "Condom?" I drawled, barely in control.

She nodded, a flare of panic in her eyes.

"You want this, right? You want me?"

I was an asshole, sure. But I wasn't *that* asshole.

Celeste licked her lips nervously and gave me a little nod.

I sheathed up and crawled over her. We didn't have much room to work with, but I didn't need it, letting her thighs cradle my hips as I slid my hand under her leg and lifted it a little.

"Put me inside you," I said, staring down at her, my body trembling with unrestrained need.

Celeste took me in her hand, guiding me to her entrance. Her heat enveloped me, and I groaned. This, this was what I needed. That blissed out moment sex provided.

I didn't wait, thrusting into her in one smooth stroke. She cried out, wrapping an arm around my shoulder.

"You good?" I asked, realizing she'd gone deathly still.

"Mm-hmm," she murmured.

"You feel so fucking tight." I pulled out slowly and glided back in, slower this time, reveling in the way she rippled around me.

"God, Zane…" Her fingers dug into my shoulders, her breath catching as she arched beneath me. "It's so intense."

She wasn't wrong.

It was so fucking good, the way her muscles gripped my dick, tightening around me, pulling me into her body.

"Fuck," I rasped, rocking against her, chasing the high I knew would inevitably come.

It was sensation overload. The alcohol in my veins, Celeste's perfume, her tight little body beneath me. There wasn't room to think about anything else. There was only her. Us.

This.

I went harder, thrusting into her over and over, grabbing at her hips, sucking the skin under her jaw, biting and licking. Celeste made me unhinged in a way I never had been before. But thinking about her at some fancy dinner party with guys like her ex Miles drove me insane. I didn't want anyone else to experience this—to know how prettily she came apart.

I wanted that privilege to belong to me and me alone. But this wasn't some fairy tale where guys like me got the girl, and even if I did, I wouldn't know what the fuck to do with her. She was used to a life I couldn't ever give her. And this—here, now—was as good as it was ever going to get between us.

"Zane." It was a breathless moan. A whispered prayer. And my name on her lips made me feel like a motherfucking king.

"Yeah, I know, babe. I know."

A bolt of panic went through me, the buzz wearing off a little.

I dropped my face to the crook of her neck, pushing out the cold harsh bite of disappointment.

As if Celeste felt the change in me, she wrapped her arms around me, erasing every last sliver of space between us.

Something slithered through my gut, but I shut it down. She felt too good and there was no undoing what I'd done now.

There was no going back.

Even if I knew things would never be the same.

24

CELESTE

ZANE WAS STILL AND SILENT ABOVE ME, ONLY THE SOUND of his exerted breaths filling the space.

We'd done it.

We'd had sex.

I'd had sex with Zane Washington.

A warm rush of emotion flowed through me as I snuggled into his arm bracketed at the side of my head.

"Fuck," he hissed, pulling off me and slipping out of the car. He disposed of the condom and yanked up his jeans.

"It's okay," I said, unable to stop smiling. Because I'd had sex… with Zane. "Come back. I want to—"

"We need to go."

"Where?"

"Home. I need to go home."

"Okay," I sat up, pulling my dress down. I was sore between my legs but that was to be expected. "I can give you a ride. Maybe we can hang out with your grandma. It's not that late. I'm sure—"

"Stop. Just… stop." Zane cut me an icy look that made a shiver run through me.

Not in a good way.

"What's the matter?" My brows pinched, my heart crashing against my ribcage.

"I'm drunk and you're—"

"Drunk? You're… oh." Bile churned in my stomach. He was drunk. And I was basking in the afterglow of my first time with a guy who looked like he regretted every second.

"You should go. Get home before Mommy or Daddy realize you're missing."

"Zane, don't do that." I shuffled to the end of the seat, wincing a little, and reached for him. "Don't downplay what just happened. It was…" *Everything.*

"You don't get it, do you?" He snarled, snatching his hand away. "This, us, it's a game. You're a game to me, Einstein. A way to pass the time. That's all this is."

"I don't believe you." I shook my head, shoving off the sting of his words. "I felt it just now and I know you did too."

There had been a moment of clarity, when we'd both realized this was more than a game. I hadn't imagined it. He was just doing that thing guys did whenever they started to panic.

"Jesus, you're so fucking deluded, Celeste. This isn't a fairy tale. I'm not going to get down on one knee and profess my undying love for you." He ran a hand down his face, blowing out an exasperated breath. "It was sex. Unforgettable sex at that."

Pain lanced through my chest. He was lashing out, trying to protect himself by pushing me away. I knew enough about Zane by now to know that was his standard MO. He thought letting people in, trusting them, made him vulnerable. But he didn't need to worry with me. I wasn't out to hurt him.

I cared.

Couldn't he see that?

"Well, it was special to me," I whispered.

Because I'd chosen it. For once in my life, I'd made a decision based on what *I* wanted.

And yeah, maybe a small part of me wanted to rebel after the disastrous dinner party at the Sinclairs. But either way, I still wanted Zane.

His strangled laugh rumbled through me like a storm. "Go home, Celeste. And if you know what's good for you, you'll stay away next time."

He stalked off toward the trees that flanked the perimeter of the reservoir.

"Zane, wait." I hopped out of the back of the car and went after him. "We should talk about this. We should—"

He whirled on me so quickly that I lost my footing and tripped, landing on my hands and knees on the cold, dirty ground.

"Damn," I hissed, the skin on my knee smarting.

Zane glared down at me, his eyes hazy but hard. Was he really that drunk? He hadn't seemed that drunk when I'd first arrived, but he didn't exactly give me a chance to ask.

"Zane, please…"

He shook his head a little, disgust curling at his lips and then took off into the shadows.

Taking another piece of my heart with him.

I didn't go home.

I couldn't.

After Zane left me there in the dirt, blood trickling from the scrape on my knee, I'd forced myself back in the car and driven to Nix's place.

Harleigh took one look at me and breathed, "What the hell did he do?"

"I…" I glanced at Nix, and he held up his hands.

"I'll leave you two to talk. If you need me, holler." He disappeared down the hall, the door slamming was a sign that we were alone.

"You're hurt." Harleigh motioned to my knee, and I nodded, swallowing down the tears threatening to fall.

"Sit. I'll get something to clean you up." She went into the small kitchen and retrieved a first aid kit.

Part of me still couldn't believe my father had bought this place for Nix and Jessa. Especially knowing that Harleigh would end up living here. But maybe it was his only way of showing her that he trusted her to make her own decisions and path in life.

He had never afforded me the same freedom.

It was different, I knew that. I'd grown up in his world, under his roof. He hadn't had to earn my trust and adoration because it had been given freely—he was my father, after all. He had raised me and provided for me. It wasn't until the truth about Harleigh came out and I discovered I had a sister that things really started to change.

That I started to realize that maybe it was okay to want more from life. To chase the hopes and dreams that would make *me* happy instead of making the people around me happy.

"Here, let me have a look at it." Harleigh grabbed a cushion off the couch and shoved it under her knees. "Want to tell me what happened?"

"Will you scold me like a naughty child and send me back across the res?"

She let out a heavy sigh, lifting her eyes to mine. "I know things have been weird between us—"

"Understatement of the century," I murmured.

"But you have to understand that our lives are different, Celeste. Surely, you know that."

"Really, after everything we've been through, you're going to throw that in my face? I never once judged you or where you came from, Harleigh, not once."

"I know." She wrung out the towel and started dabbing my knee. I winced. "Sorry, I'll try and be careful."

"It's fine."

"Look, Celeste, I'm not judging you. You're a good person. One of the best people I know. But we both know that your mom doesn't want you hanging around with me, Chloe, and the guys. I don't want to cause you any more trouble than I already have."

"And what? I get no say in it? Do you have any idea what it's been like since you left? I have no one, Harleigh. I don't even have Miles anymore. I spend my days alone. Do you know how horrible that feels? To know you don't have anyone."

"I'm sorry."

"Yeah, me too."

Silence filled the space between us. Thick, heavy silence. In her own weird way, I knew Harleigh was only trying to protect me. Maybe even protect herself. But I was so fed up with everyone around me thinking they knew what was best for me.

"I had sex with Zane," I blurted.

"What?" Disbelief rippled over her expression, and I nodded.

"In the back of my car. And do you know what? I don't regret it. I don't regret it at all because I like him. And I think he likes me, even though he's too damn stubborn to admit it."

"Oh, Celeste." Harleigh gave me a sad smile, and I frowned.

"Why are you looking at me like that?"

"Because I warned you not to get tangled up with him."

"But we had sex, Harleigh." My stomach clenched just thinking about it, my cheeks burning. "That has to mean something."

He kept trying to push me away, but it was what boys did when they got spooked. And he wouldn't get spooked unless there was something there.

"Maybe you could talk to him or get Nix to talk to him. I bet his grandma is in my corner. She seems to—"

"His grandma? Zane's grandma?"

"Yeah, I went over there yesterday and took her some flowers and dinner. I wanted to make sure she was okay."

"Okay? Celeste, slow down. I don't understand what you're saying. You've been hanging out with Zane and his grandma?"

"Well, I wouldn't exactly say hanging out... So, will you do it? Will you or Nix talk to him? Because I think if—"

"No."

"No?" I stared at her with disbelief. "But I just told you—"

"Celeste." She took my hands in hers. "Listen to me. Whatever is going on between you and Zane, it isn't healthy. He's using you, babe. And I think in your own way, you're using him too."

"What? That's not true. I'm not using him. I like him, Harleigh. I really like him."

"Just think about it for a second. How does being around Zane make you feel?"

I snatched my hand away, a sinking feeling going through me. "You think I'm acting out."

"That's not what I said. I just think you're not thinking rationally about this. It's completely normal to want to experiment and be a little reckless. We've all been there."

"Experiment? You think this is an experiment? That I got up this morning and thought, 'I know, I'll give my virginity to Zane and see what happens.'"

"Tell me you didn't," Nix groaned from the hall.

"You… you weren't supposed to hear that."

He murmured something under his breath before stepping into the room. "Does he know?"

"I-I'm not sure."

"Did he hurt you?"

"What? No! Nothing like that. I wanted it. I just… I think he was drunk."

"You think?"

Embarrassment curled inside me.

"I didn't stop to ask. He seemed okay when I first got there, but then we… and he got all weird."

I didn't tell them what he'd said. That he'd left me on the cold, hard ground and walked away.

"And he definitely didn't catch on that you were, you know…"

"I don't think so. I tried to tell him, but things got out of hand. It's not a big deal." I shrugged.

Nix studied me, searching my eyes for the truth no doubt. But the truth was, I didn't know what to feel.

Everything was a mess.

I thought I'd been in control of the situation. I'd wanted to meet Zane, and deep down, I went knowing what he wanted. Because I wanted it too. But now everything felt wrong. Harleigh was acting like everyone else in my life, with her preconceived ideas about what was or wasn't good for me.

"Celeste," she said, softer this time. "This doesn't have a happy ending; you have to know that."

"But—"

"She's right." Nix came and stood behind Harleigh, sliding his hand under her hair and curling his hand around her neck. They were so in sync, like magnets. "Zane isn't the serious type. He doesn't trust anyone. Least of all a girl from Old Darling Hill."

"You're wrong," I said, defiance coating my words. "There's something there, I know there is."

"Even if there is, it won't matter." Nix gave me a sad smile, and for some reason his hurt a whole lot more than the one Harleigh had given me. "The only woman Zane has room in his life for is his grams. He'll never choose you, Celeste."

"But…" The words died, withering inside me like my heart.

My brain couldn't accept it. It was like every logical argument I had evaporated the second Zane kissed me.

If it had been any other girl acting like this, I would

have reeled off a ton of stats about failed relationships, rates of infidelity, and the rise of people entering non-monogamous relationships.

All the signs pointed toward the fact that what Harleigh and Nix shared was rare.

One of a kind.

It wasn't the norm.

I could kiss ten, twenty… thirty frogs and never meet my prince. Instead, I'd be stuck with someone like Cooper Sinclair, a rich, pretentious playboy looking for a trophy wife.

"Come on," Harleigh said, applying a dressing to my knee. "I'll drive you home and Nix can follow in his car."

"You don't have to do that." I sniffled, aware that she was already trying to get rid of me.

I glanced at Nix, wondering if he'd offer to let me stay here. He had before. But this time, he said nothing. Clearly drawing a line between us.

Him and Harleigh on one side.

And me on the other.

"Okay then." I got up, steeling myself.

He went and got his keys, leaving me with Harleigh once more.

"Will you be okay?" she asked.

"I'll be fine." I gave her a weak smile. She gave me a small nod but didn't offer any words of encouragement. I guess we'd surpassed that point in our relationship.

"Ready?" Nix asked, cutting the tension in half.

"Yeah." I glanced around the place before heading for the door.

Wondering if they knew how lucky they were. They had both had such a hard life, surviving things no teenagers should ever have to. But they had each other. Always and forever.

And that was a rare thing indeed.

A thing most of us would never get to experience.

Especially me.

25

ZANE

The vibration of my cell phone pulled me from the restless sleep I'd fallen into. Fumbling over to the side, I managed to grab it off the nightstand and bring it to my ear.

"Yeah?"

"We need to talk."

"Nix? The fuck?" A brass band was playing in my head, my mouth like cotton balls.

After stopping by the store to grab a bottle of the cheapest liquor I could, I'd stumbled back to the trailer, checked in on Grams, and drank it down until I was numb.

Until everything—including Celeste, *especially* Celeste —disappeared.

I'd fucked up.

Story of my life, making one bad decision after another. But I'd needed her so fucking badly. Because I knew she would make it all go away, and she had.

The second I'd pushed inside her, the world had gone quiet.

And then after, she'd looked up at me with stars in her bewitching blue eyes and it had hit me all at once.

It was real.

Whatever she thought she felt for me, whatever was developing between us, it was fucking real.

"I'm outside."

Something in his voice had me sitting up and pulling a t-shirt off the floor. "Yeah, give me five."

The second I stepped out of the trailer and saw his grim expression, I knew.

"Is she okay?" I asked, a strange unfamiliar sensation tugging in my chest.

He flicked his head to the old porch swing, and I followed him.

"You fucked her."

"I… yeah."

"You're an asshole, Z."

"It wasn't like she didn't want it. She was practically—"

"It was her first time."

"What?"

His words reverberated inside me because I couldn't possibly have heard him right.

"You heard me. She was a virgin."

"Nah, no way. Her and the Mulligan kid—"

"She came over covered in dirt and blood and told Harleigh what happened."

"She was a virgin?" The words tasted like acid on my tongue.

Nix nodded gravely.

"Fuck," I breathed. "I didn't know. I didn't…"

"She said you were drunk too."

"I'd had a few beers. It'd been a shitty day."

"So you thought you'd take it out on Celeste? Jesus, Z, what the fuck were you thinking?"

"I wasn't okay. I needed something to take the edge off and we—" I stopped myself. He didn't know, and I wasn't sure I wanted to tell him.

"Finish the sentence," he said coolly.

"We've been fooling around."

"You've been… Fucking hell, Zane. If her parents find out, do you have any idea what they'll do?"

"She's seventeen. The age of consent—"

"I'm not talking about the age of consent, asshole. I'm talking about her. Her mom and dad are already freaking out that she's throwing away her future because of Harleigh. Do you really think they're going to be happy she gave herself to…"

"Go on, say it. A guy like me?" My jaw clenched.

"That's not what I meant. Don't twist my words. You're a good guy, Z. One of my best friends in the world. But this thing between you and Celeste, it only ends in heartache."

"Because she can't possibly want me? Because it's just a game, right? A chance for her to live a little before Mommy and Daddy dearest marry her off to Vincent Moneybags the third."

"You say it like she'd be the one breaking your heart."

"What the fuck is that supposed to mean?"

"It means, asshole, something tells me Celeste is more like her sister than either of them realizes. And maybe, just maybe, she's prepared to give it all up for a broken boy from The Row."

"Speak for yourself," I spat. "I'm not broken."

Nix's brow arched and I let out a heavy sigh, dragging a hand over my jaw.

"Do you like her? Really like her? Because there's no middle ground here. Either you let her go, or you let her risk everything by choosing you. But this isn't Harleigh we're talking about, Z. Celeste didn't grow up in The Row. She's used to a certain life."

"Don't be fucking ridiculous. I would never expect her to pick me. We're just fooling around." But as I said the words, my chest tightened, my lungs straining for oxygen.

Choose me.

She would never choose me.

"So you'll have no problem telling her you made a mistake and that it won't happen again."

Something he'd said earlier snagged my attention. "When you said they think Harleigh is to blame for some of Celeste's recent behavior... is that why things are so weird between them?"

"I think so. Harleigh doesn't want Celeste to end up resenting her if things go to shit."

"I really fucked up, didn't I?"

"Yeah, you did." He slung his arm over my shoulder. "But I get it. There's just something about those Rowe girls."

"Harleigh will never be a Rowe," I said.

"No, but she's still a part of them. No matter how much she hates it."

"Harleigh needs to patch things up with Celeste. If I... end things"—not that there was really anything to end —"it's going to hurt her. She doesn't have anyone else."

"Shit, you care about her."

I shrugged but didn't commit to an answer. What was there to say? Even if I did care about her, it didn't change anything.

Celeste had her whole future ahead of her.

One that didn't include me.

WHEN I WOKE up the next morning, school was the last thing on my mind. After Nix had given me some hard truths, I'd crawled back into bed and tried to sleep my worries away.

Didn't fucking work though, and I felt like shit when I finally dragged myself out of bed.

I opened my bedroom and stuck my head out. "Grams, you good?"

"Just making breakfast."

I smiled. Of course she was. She was one of the most determined, strong-willed people I'd ever met. It was hardly a surprise that her and Celeste got on like a house on fire. They had a lot in common.

I shut those thoughts down. I had practice and school to navigate before I dealt with the shitshow with Celeste.

"Morning," I said, taking a seat at the table.

"How did you sleep?" Grams came over and grabbed my face, her crinkled eyes looking me up and down. "You seem a little p-pale. Were you drinking last night?"

"I had a couple of beers."

"Zane Thackeray. What have… I told you?" She tsked, but I didn't miss the way she grasped the counter, inhaling a weary breath. "Drinking on a school night."

"Relax." I stood up, dropping a kiss on her head. "You sit, I'll finish breakfast."

"I'm fine."

"Grams, please."

"Oh, okay."

I helped her get situated, making her a fresh pot of coffee while I tended the bacon and eggs. "How are you feeling?" I asked her over my shoulder.

"I'd feel better if I knew how Celeste is?"

"What?"

"Well, did you talk to her yesterday or not?" A knowing smile tugged at her mouth.

"She was fine, Grams. You don't need to worry about Celeste."

"I suppose I'll see her at the center in a day or two. I can ask her myself." She huffed, only ramping up the guilt I already felt.

I'd taken her virginity in the back of her Range Rover and now I had to tell her we were done. If she didn't hate me already, she would after that. Maybe Nix was right though—maybe it was for the best.

I'd let things go too far. Taken advantage of her strange infatuation with me. And although I couldn't undo things, I could end it before either of us got too deep.

Who the fuck was I kidding? I'd already gotten deep when I'd fucked her into the leather seat.

It was something I wouldn't forget in a hurry though. How good she'd felt, how eagerly she'd moaned my name.

I didn't know it could be like that. But I should have known that sex with Celeste would be intense. She was so different to the girls I was used to.

"Zane, dear?" Grams said, pulling me from my thoughts. "Are you okay?"

"Yeah, I might have some good news actually."

"I will always appreciate some of that."

"The shift manager down at the mill said I might be able to get some more hours. And it's the twilight shift so I'll get a better hourly rate."

"I thought we talked about this? I don't want you—"

"Grams. You need that treatment and I want to help. I'm *going* to help." She didn't need to know my story wasn't quite the truth. In fact, the less she knew, the better.

"Zane, dear, it isn't your job—"

"Stop with that shit, Grams. You looked after me for years when Mom left. It's my turn. I have to do this, okay? I need you to let me do this."

"O-okay." Tears clung to her lashes. "So long as it doesn't interfere with school or the team."

"It won't, I promise. I've already worked out a schedule, and he's willing to give me a month's advance." The half-lies rolled off my tongue but left a sour taste in my mouth. "Isn't that great?"

"You're a good boy, Zane Thackeray. You deserve so much happiness, my sweet boy."

"Okay, Grams. Don't go getting all teary on me. You know I don't like it when you cry."

"One day we're going to need to talk about it," she said, a sad, tired look in her eyes.

"One day, Grams."

But today was not that day.

"You look like shit," Kye said as we hauled ass into the locker room.

"I didn't sleep."

"Let me guess you got a hold of some strong liquor.

Don't think I don't know a hangover when I see one. Question is, why were you getting drunk home alone? Unless you weren't alone?" His brows waggled.

"Fuck off, Carter."

"Hey, Nix, do you know why lover boy is hungover?"

I glanced over at Nix, and he kept a neutral expression. "Nope."

"Hmm." Kye studied the two of us. "Why do I feel like you're not telling me everything?"

Coach chose that moment to enter the room. "Look alive, ladies. I want asses on the field in five minutes." He tapped his clipboard against the wall and headed out the door leading to the football field.

"This conversation isn't over," Kye said.

I chose silence. I didn't want to talk about it. Not with Nix, not with Kye, and definitely not in front of the rest of the team.

I pulled on my shoulder pads and jersey before shoving my feet into my cleats and bending to tie them.

"Better haul ass, Washington, or Coach will have us all running suicides again," Hench called, and I flipped him off over my shoulder.

My teammates began to file out of the locker room, but my cell bleeped, so I grabbed it out of my bag and read the message.

Unknown: I have it. Meet me at the same place. Midday. Don't be late.

Shit.

Me: Midday is a little difficult for me. Can we make it after three thirty?

Unknown: Midday. Be there or I'll assume you no longer need it.

Fuck.

I quickly texted back.

Me: I'll be there.

I just had to figure out how I was going to get out of school without raising the alarm.

26

CELESTE

I HADN'T HEARD FROM ZANE SINCE HE'D WALKED AWAY from me. But I hadn't texted him either.

I was trying to figure out what to say to him. How to put into words what last night meant to me.

Harleigh and Nix might have believed that we were doomed but I was choosing not to believe that.

We'd had *sex*.

Out of all the girls he could have called up, he'd called me. That had to mean something.

Didn't it?

"Mom?" I balked as I entered the kitchen.

"Don't sound so surprised, Celeste. I do live here too, you know."

"I just wasn't expecting to see you is all."

It was Monday morning, she was usually long gone when Max and I finally surfaced.

"Yesterday could have gone a lot better," she murmured, running her thumbs around her mug of coffee.

"You ambushed me, Mom." I let out a weary sigh. It was too early for this. "What did you expect?"

"I expected you to be the polite, acquiescing girl you've always been. You know, you could do a lot worse than Cooper Sinclair."

"We literally have nothing in common except Columbia."

"Because you didn't even give him a chance, Celeste. Not all relationships have that instant spark you know. It can take time to build."

I stared at her with utter disbelief. She was right. Cooper had tried to talk to me yesterday. By reeling off a list of his accomplishments. Class valedictorian. His impressive GPA. The time he spent shadowing a consultant at Albany Med over the summer. But not once at any part in our conversation did he think to ask me about myself. The whole thing had been super uncomfortable, not to mention awkward. It was at that point, I'd made my excuses and had gone to play with Pippa, Mrs. Sinclair's chocolate Labrador.

"What is it you want from me, Mom?"

"Excuse me?" She had the audacity to look offended by my question.

"It's not a difficult question."

"Don't take that tone with me, young lady," she scoffed. "Really, Celeste, it's like I don't even know who you are anymore."

"Because I'm finally thinking for myself? Because I've finally realized that maybe there's more to life than dinner parties, country clubs, and impressing the Vaughns and the Sinclairs and all your other friends?

"I'm seventeen, Mom. I want more. I want to try new things and make mistakes and get into trouble. I have my whole life to—"

"Stop." Her voice shook with barely restrained anger. "Just. Stop."

She took a big deep breath, flattening her palm against the counter. I hadn't witnessed Sabrina Delacorte's perfectly poised façade slip much. But lately —well, ever since Harleigh had come into our lives—it was happening more and more often. And part of me got it. It had rocked Mom's carefully constructed world when Dad had brought Harleigh here. But I couldn't understand her disdain for a girl who wasn't responsible for the actions of her parents.

If Mom's ire needed a target, it was my father. He was the one at fault here. Not Harleigh.

And certainly not me.

But love was a funny thing—made you do funny things. And maybe Mom was having some kind of existential crisis. Maybe watching her husband try to repair his relationship with his estranged daughter—a daughter who hadn't grown up in our world—brought to light some insecurities she'd long buried.

"It isn't fair, you know. To punish me because your own life is spinning out of control. Things change, Mom. People change, and that's okay. Harleigh is a good person, not the poisonous creature you think she is. I'm not acting out because of anything she has done or said. I'm acting out because I'm seventeen and I want to make my own choices. I want—"

"Enough," she snapped. "I have heard enough, Celeste. Mrs. Sinclair was kind enough to give you the volunteering spot at the center, and she has arranged a press release for Saturday afternoon. I told her you'd be there."

"Mom, I'm not—"

"This is non-negotiable, Celeste. You will be there, and you will be the amiable girl I know you can be."

Her words set my teeth on edge, but I didn't argue. There was no point when she got like this. So single-minded that she couldn't see past her own misguided expectations of how things should be.

"Fine," I said, heading for the door. I couldn't be around her for another second. My skin was too tight, the weight of expectation a crushing pressure on my chest.

I loved being at the center, helping out. Making a difference to the people I met and talked with. But I didn't want to be a pawn. A poster child for potential donors. It wasn't about that for me. It was about doing the work, actually making a difference. I didn't want to pose with my mother, Mrs. Sinclair, and Cooper just so she could parade me around, preening about all the good work I was doing.

Max appeared at the bottom of the stairs and smiled. "Hey, what's—"

"Leave me alone," I said, moving around him toward the door.

I grabbed my keys and shoved my feet into my sneakers.

"Celeste, wait up," he called after me, but I was already gone.

I'd rather be at school than spend another minute in a house with the woman I was slowly beginning to hate.

"HEY, SIS, WAIT UP."

"What, Max?" I whirled around, pinning him with an exasperated look.

"What's going on? You seem... pissy? I asked Mom what was wrong, but she wouldn't tell me."

"I'm just tired of it all."

"Being their golden child finally wearing thin?"

"Max..."

"What? I'm just saying it's taken you long enough to realize she's nothing more than a cold-hearted bitch."

"*Max!*" I gasped.

He shrugged. "It's the truth. She doesn't really care

about us. Well, she definitely doesn't care about me. All she cares about is her image and reputation."

"I… yeah, I'm starting to think you're right."

"Don't let her get to you." He nudged my shoulder with his. "Hey, listen, do you want to hang out with me, Toby, and the guys at lunch?" I gawked at him, and he frowned. "Why are you looking at me like that?"

"You know you just invited me to hang out with you and your friends at lunch, right? Like those exact words came out of your mouth."

"Okay, you don't need to get all hysteretic about it."

"Hysteric."

"Yeah, that's what I said."

"No, you said hysteretic which means something entirely diff—"

"You know this is why you have no friends, right? Nobody wants to hang out with a walking talking thesaurus."

"Bite me."

"Seriously? You are so fucking weird." He shook his head. "Do you want to hang out at lunch or not?"

"You don't have to do that, Max."

"Do what?"

"Pretend to care."

A strange expression flickered across his face. "It's not that I don't care. I'm just… I'm not good at this kind of stuff. I've spent years living in your shadow. It hasn't exactly been easy to like you."

"Max, that's not true."

"Yeah." He gave me a sad smile. "It is. But I'm over it now."

"If you say so." I smiled, and he grinned back.

"So lunch…"

"Thanks for the offer, but I'll be okay."

"If you're sure."

"I am."

"Well, okay then. I'll see you later, Sis."

"Bye." I lifted my hand in a small wave and watched him take off down the hall.

Maybe I wasn't as alone here as I thought.

I ATE lunch on my own in my car. I wasn't hiding, that wasn't it at all. I just didn't feel much like being around people.

I'd spotted Miles and Marcy making out on my way to the parking lot and while it didn't bother me, it did make my heart ache.

I didn't like Miles that way—maybe I never had. But I liked the idea of having someone. That one person who was yours. Who liked you—maybe even loved you—for you. Not because they wanted to change or fix you, but because your soul called to them.

Last night, there had been a moment when I'd thought Zane was that person. But his continued radio silence was making any hope I still had rapidly fade away.

Surely by now, he had *something* to say to me. Even if it wasn't what I wanted to hear.

We could figure this out. I knew we could. If he would only talk to me.

I grabbed my cell phone, silently willing him to text me. I was so focused on Zane, on the memories of last night that when it started to vibrate, it startled me.

"Crap," I breathed, taking a steadying breath.

Disappointment clanged through me when I realized it wasn't Zane.

Chloe: I don't suppose Zane is with you?

My brows furrowed as I texted her back.

Me: Why would he be with me? I'm at school.

Chloe: No shit, Sherlock. Kye and Nix are worried. He left school earlier, gave them some stupid excuse about feeling unwell. But now he isn't responding to their calls.

Me: Do you think something happened with Miriam?

Dread tossed in my stomach.

Chloe: I don't know. He'd tell them if it was about her though, wouldn't he?

Me: Maybe I should go over there. Check in on them?

Chloe: No, I don't think that's a good idea. I'll call Mom and ask her to check in. Just… if you hear anything, text me.

Me: I will.

I gnawed the end of my thumb. There were a hundred reasons Zane could have cut out of school. But none that would make him lie to Nix and Kye.

Chloe was right, I shouldn't go over there. It wasn't my place. Besides, I'd promised Dad I wouldn't cut class again.

But what if something was wrong?

What if they needed help?

I glanced at the clock on the dash. Lunch was over in twenty minutes, but I had study hall for the hour after that. I could be there and back before fifth period.

Decision made, I quickly texted Max and asked him to cover for me while I was gone.

Max: Where are you really going?

Me: I told you, I got my period and need supplies. I'll be back for my next class.

Max: Don't pursue a professional career in subterfuge. You're a terrible liar.

I smiled at that.

Me: I'm surprised you know what that means.

Max: I googled it. I'll cover for you.

Me: Thanks. I owe you.

Turning on the ignition, I backed out of the parking spot and thumbed Zane's address into my GPS.

Twenty minutes.

If I drove fast, I could make it in fifteen.

I HADN'T EVEN TURNED into Darling Row trailer park when I spotted Zane up ahead.

Relief slammed into me. He didn't seem to be in any hurry which meant Miriam was okay. But it didn't explain why he'd left school.

Slowing down, I pulled alongside him. He glanced over, scowling when he noticed me.

I cranked the window down and smiled. "Need a ride?"

"What the fuck are you doing here?"

"It's a funny story actually. If you let me give you a ride home, I'll tell you all about it."

Zane dragged a hand through his hair, glancing left and right before settling his tormented gaze back on my face. He blew out an irritated breath and yanked open the door.

"Hi," I said, tingles of anticipation vibrating inside me. "Are you okay? Chloe said the guys were worried and I thought—"

"What are you doing, Celeste?" His cold tone turned my blood to ice.

Not Einstein.

Not babe.

Celeste.

I didn't like it. It didn't sound… right.

"I came to make sure you and your grandma were okay."

"I didn't ask you to do that."

"I know, but Chloe seemed worried, and I thought… you're mad at me."

"You've got to stop with this shit, Celeste. We're not together. You're not my girlfriend. I thought I made that clear last night."

"I know… I just thought—"

"For fuck's sake, you're acting like a stage five clinger. We fooled around a couple of times and it's like you've gone and convinced yourself we're together or something."

His words landed like blows to my stomach, but I steeled myself. He was hurting, that much was obvious. His eyes lacked their usual menacing glint.

"I know what it's like to feel lost and alone, Zane. I

can help. Even if you don't want to be with me, we can be friends."

What was I saying? I didn't want to be friends. I wanted to be more than that to him. But maybe he needed time to get there. To see that none of the other stuff mattered.

All that mattered was how we felt about each other. And he cared. I knew he did. I'd felt it in the way he'd kissed me. The way he'd needed me.

I waited, giving him time to digest my words. Slowly, he lifted his eyes to mine and my heart catapulted into my throat at the pain there.

"Zane, what is it? Tell me what's wrong?"

"You," he breathed. "It's you, Celeste. This. Us. I never should have let it get this far. If I'd have known you were a virgin… fuck, I never would have touched you."

"Y-you know? But ho— Harleigh."

"Nix, actually. But it doesn't matter because you should have told me."

"I tried." Tears clogged my throat.

"Yeah, but not hard enough. Now I'm the bad guy for taking your fucking cherry and making you think it meant something—"

"It did mean something," I cried. "You keep talking about it like it was a mistake, but it wasn't. I was there, remember. I wanted you just as much as you wanted me. You're just too scared to admit it. You're a coward, Zane Washington. Whatever way you—"

"Are you done?" His eyes darkened as he cut with me another withering look.

"I… Zane, please. We can talk about this. I drove all the way—"

"I didn't ask you to be here. No one asked you to be here. This ends now." His expression turned hostile. "I don't want you here, Celeste. You need to stop turning up like some crazed stalker. It's pathetic. You're pathetic, and you need to stay away from me and my grandma."

I sucked in a sharp breath at his parting words. He didn't mean them. He couldn't.

But Zane shouldered the door and climbed out, giving me one final scathing look.

And this time when he walked away, he didn't take another piece of my heart with him, he left it broken into smithereens all over the ground.

27

ZANE

I KICKED THE DIRT AS I WALKED AWAY FROM HER. FROM the look of utter devastation on her face. But it was for the best.

Celeste Rowe was too good for me. Too good for a guy who had just sold his soul to the devil in order to make ends meet.

Leo D'Angelo owned me now. And in four weeks' time, if I didn't have his money with interest, he would demand blood. But it didn't matter. All that mattered was the wad of cash in my pocket. The money Grams needed to pay for her treatment.

I'd figure out the rest. Bust my ass at the mill or ask Bryson to be added to his roster. I could make it work.

I had to.

So although I felt like the world's biggest asshole at the things I'd said to Celeste, I needed her to hate me.

I needed her to stay the fuck out of my business.

Out of my life.

I couldn't have her anywhere near this arrangement with D'Angelo.

Nix had been right all along.

But as I climbed the ramp to the trailer, I couldn't stop thinking about the fact that she'd come for us again. That she was willing to risk the wrath and judgment of her parents if they ever found out, for me.

It didn't make any sense. I'd only ever been cruel to her. Even in the few times we'd fooled around, I'd spewed horrible, hateful words at her because I couldn't let myself believe any of it was real. That she could ever want a boy like me.

Broken down by life and circumstance, I had nothing to offer her. No money, no prospects … no future. And she had everything.

Why the fuck would she ever choose me over that?

"Grams?" I called, entering the trailer. Only to find my best friends sitting there with her.

"I knew it," Kye hissed under his breath.

"What's going on?" I looked between them.

"They were worried," Grams said, giving me a concerned look. "Something about you feeling sick and coming home to rest?"

"Actually, I was at work. Morris managed to get me an extra shift, so I said yes. It's not a big deal." The lie came easily as I headed for the kitchenette to grab a glass of water.

Nix followed me. "Where have you really been?"

"Like I said, I did an extra shift—"

"Zane..."

I shook my head, glancing at Grams. "Not here, okay."

"Fine, but we are talking about this."

"Not here, not yet. You need anything, Grams?"

"A cup of tea wouldn't hurt. You boys are going to send me to an early grave."

My fingers tightened around the glass in my hand.

"Grams, that's not funny," Kye said.

"Oh, hush now. It is the only one inevitability of life. We are born and we die. Everything else is just part of the adventure."

"Still, none of us are ready to lose you just yet, we have too many adventures in our future." He winked at her, their laughter lightening the tense mood.

"Coach will kick your ass when he finds out you cut class," Nix said.

"No one cares I wasn't there, Nix. I'm not his star player."

"He cares. We all do. You're just too damn stubborn to see it."

"Can we not do this right now? I don't want her to worry any more than she already is thanks to you two assholes."

I made Grams a tea and went and joined her and Kye.

"Here you go," I said, placing it on the little table beside her favorite armchair.

"You're a good boy, Zane Thackeray." She smiled at me like I was her world.

Her everything.

I only wondered if she knew she was mine too.

"So… SPILL IT," Nix said as we sat in Kye's yard.

After we'd sat with Grams for a while, she'd wanted a nap. So I'd made sure she was comfortable and headed over to Kye's house with the two of them.

"I went to Leo D'Angelo."

"D'Angelo … Leo D'Angelo. Why does that name sound famil—D'Angelo, as in the loan shark?" Kye balked. "You went to a fucking loan—"

"Shh." I glanced back at the house. "I don't need that shit advertised. You know Leo likes to work under the radar."

He was a whispered myth around The Row. The man people went to for a quick injection of cash when they were all out of other options.

"Bryson got you the introduction," Nix said as if it was the only thing that made sense. I nodded, and he cussed under his breath. "What the fuck were you thinking?"

"I was thinking that Grams needs the treatment. She's getting worse and it kills me. It fucking kills me that I can't fix it for her. So yeah," I blew out a frustrated breath. "That's what I was thinking."

"Shit, Z, man." Kye gave me a weak smile. "I'm sorry."

"Yeah, me too."

"You should have talked to me first. I could have talked to Bryson, Jessa, and Colt. Between us we could have figured something out. You didn't have to go to Leo."

"Look, I appreciate it. I do. But this isn't your burden, Nix. It's mine. One I'll gladly pay if it means Grams gets the care she needs."

"But what about paying him back? It's not an interest-free loan, Z. It comes with some serious consequences if you can't repay him."

"I'll find the money."

"We'll find the money," Nix said. "If you think we're leaving you to shoulder this alone you clearly don't know us at all."

"Nix is right. We're behind you, Z. Every step of the way."

"No."

"No?" Nix glowered. "It wasn't a question. You made a deal with the devil, and you expect me to just let that fly without doing something to help?"

"Yeah, I do." I kicked the ground with my boot. He glared at me, and I glared right back.

"Okay, guys, while under normal circumstances I'd enjoy this little pissing contest, we need to stick together over this. Not let it tear us apart," Kye huffed.

"He started it," Nix murmured.

"Can we please change the subject? It's been yet another shitty day."

"Fine. Have you talked to Celeste?"

I dropped my head back, running a hand over my face. "She turned up here, like you two assholes."

"She did?" Nix frowned.

"Yeah, although she didn't make it to the door. I sent her away."

"Wait a second," Kye said, looking between us. "What am I missing? Are you and Celeste… Shit, you are. You dirty dog. You've been—"

"Kye." Nix shook his head, and Kye's expression dropped.

"There's more to this story, isn't there?"

"I ended it. Told her not to come around here again."

"You think she'll listen?" Nix asked.

"Oh, I'm pretty sure she'll never want to see me again after some of the things I said."

Kye let out a low whistle. "That bad?"

"It wasn't pretty." My chest constricted remembering the hurt in her expression, the look of absolute betrayal.

"It's for the best." Nix nodded, his eyes full of understanding and regret.

"I can't believe she came for you," Kye said in half-disbelief, half-awe. "That's pretty epic. She's so… and you're so…"

"Fuck off, asshole. And I'm done talking about this, so drop it."

It had been one of the shittiest days of my life. All I wanted was to drown my sorrows in beer and weed and pray to a God I didn't believe in that tomorrow would be a better fucking day.

Nix's phone started ringing and he dug it out of his pocket, checking the screen. "I gotta take this." He got up and walked off.

"Pussy-whipped," Kye coughed, chuckling, and Nix flipped him off over his shoulder.

Silence enveloped us and Kye reclined his chair, tucking his hands under his head. "Can I ask you something?"

"Depends. Is it going to make me want to punch you?"

"Probably, but I'm going to ask anyway. If Celeste wasn't Harleigh's sister, do you think you would have ended things?"

"Bro, come on. I said I didn't want—"

"Yeah, yeah, I know. But I've known you my whole life, Z, and you've never, not once been like this about a girl. Surely, that's gotta mean something."

"Yeah, means I picked the wrong fucking girl."

He craned his neck, glancing over at me. "But that's just it, what if she's the right girl?"

"She's not."

She couldn't be. We were from two different worlds. We might as well have been water and oil.

Kye pulled out a blunt and leaned over. "You look like you need this more than I do."

"Thanks." I took the lighter out of my pocket and lit

the end, taking a long hit, letting the smoke roll through me.

"You know if you want to talk to me about her, you can."

"I don't."

"Yeah, but if you did—"

"Carter?"

"Yeah, Z?"

"Shut the fuck up."

THE REST of the week dragged. Between school, practice, and picking up extra shifts at the mill, I kept myself busy enough not to think about Celeste.

At least, that was the lie I told myself.

The truth was, she infested my thoughts. Grams asked about her constantly. Especially, since she hadn't been at the group Wednesday night. But I kept it vague.

I didn't know.

I didn't plan on texting her.

No, I didn't care.

By Thursday, Grams was hardly talking to me. But she had finally gotten her appointment through for her first infusion, so I could suffer her old lady tantrum so long as she didn't have to suffer unnecessarily.

We had a game tomorrow night; our final game before the playoffs started in two weeks' time.

"Good practice," Coach Farringdon boomed across

the locker room. "Get showered and changed and get out of here. I'll see you all bright and early tomorrow. Washington, a word in my office please."

Shit.

What did he want?

Kye flashed me a curious look, but I mouthed, "It's all good."

Coach didn't know anything, and if he did, it was none of his business.

I followed him to his office and went inside.

"Take a seat, son."

"What's up, Coach?"

"Sit," he said, and I did. "Miss Kyrie informs me you still haven't submitted any college applications."

"That's right, sir."

"Want to clue me in as to why?"

"College isn't in the cards for me, you know that," I said.

"What I know, Zane, son, is that college is in the cards for each and every one of my boys. But you have to want it. You have to make the effort and fill out the application."

"Look, Coach, I appreciate your concern, I do, but I have more important things to think about right now." I stood up, done with this conversation.

"More important than your future? I checked your transcripts, Zane. With your GPA you could get into a good school. Just think about it, okay? You still have a few weeks, and a bunch of colleges have late submission."

"Can I ask you something, Coach?"

"Sure, son."

"Why do you even care?"

He whipped off his ball cap and dragged his fingers through his hair. "Because you're my boys, the whole damn bunch of you. And someone's got to want more for you. You change your mind and need some help with things, you come to me, okay?"

I gave him a non-committal nod. "You're a good man, Coach. I wish I had a different answer for you."

"Me too, son." His expression sobered. "Me too."

28

CELESTE

"CELESTE," MAX CALLED. "THERE'S SOMEONE HERE TO SEE you."

My brows pinched as I peeled the cushion from my chest, my heart pitter-pattering beneath my rib cage.

The stupid fickle thing wanted it to be Zane. But my head knew better.

I knew better.

He'd made it perfectly clear on Monday that he wasn't interested in giving us a chance. I'd given him my first time and he'd thrown it back in my face.

I never would have touched you.

A shudder went through me, one I felt all the way down to my soul.

"Celeste!"

"Coming. I'm coming." I hurried downstairs, surprised to find Chloe standing on my doorstep.

"Hey." She lifted her hand in a small wave. "Can we talk?"

"Uh, sure, come in."

"I'm going out so you two have the house to yourselves." Max grabbed his jacket off the rack. "Text me if you need me."

"Okay."

"Bye, Maxy." Chloe called after him with a smirk and he flipped her off over his shoulder. "So friendly," she murmured.

"What are you doing here, Clo?" I asked.

"You've been ignoring me, so I thought I'd come and make sure you were okay."

"I told you, I'm fine."

"I know, but you see where I come from, 'I'm fine' is just another way of saying everything is not fine." She gave me a knowing smile. "So why don't you make us both a cup of hot chocolate and you can tell me all about it."

"There's really nothing to tell."

"Okay then, I'll tell you what I think I know, and you can tell me how I've done."

"Fine. Come on, the kitchen is this way."

Chloe followed me, 'oohing' and 'aahing' at Mom's expensive wall art. "Your house is like something out of a magazine," she said. "I mean, I knew this place was big, but I didn't know."

"It's just a house, Clo."

"You would say that. But I look at this and I see a different world to the one I live in."

"A perfect house doesn't mean a perfect family."

"No, I guess you're right." Her expression sobered. "I'm sorry if I'm being weird."

"It's fine. I get it. I just don't like it." Because this house, this life, my family, was the reason I was so lonely.

It was part of the reason Zane had ended things.

Money didn't buy happiness; it didn't buy friends or a happily ever after. It made things easier, sure. But it also tarnished things. It made it difficult to know who to trust. It made it difficult to make friends… and keep them.

I set about making Chloe and I a mug of hot chocolate each with marshmallows. She chatted about her day. Told me all about Warner, the guy she'd chatted to at the diner after the football game, and their first big date.

"You know, Greg told Warner that Zane basically told him to stay away from you."

"Clo…"

"What? I'm just saying, he's mightily protective of you for someone who doesn't care."

"He isn't protective of me." If he was, he wouldn't have broken my heart without a second thought.

"Are you going to tell me what happened between the two of you? Because I've heard bits and pieces but—"

"What bits and pieces?" I gawked at her.

"I know you had sex, and I know you drove to The Row Monday to check in on him and Grams. But Kye won't give me any details."

"This is so embarrassing."

"What, why?"

"Because! I was a virgin, Clo. I was a virgin and I let him…"

"Was it good?"

"*What?*"

"The sex." She rolled her eyes.

"I'm not sure that's the thing we should be focusing on right now." Because the second I thought about it my body grew hot all over.

"Did he at least make it good for you?"

"I feel very uncomfortable having this conversation with you. He's practically your brother."

"Okay, let's talk about the fact you've been ignoring me all week then. Which is strange since Zane has been MIA a lot too."

"If you're hoping to learn all Zane's secrets, you're asking the wrong girl," I said. "He isn't talking to me at all."

Chloe rolled her lips together, drumming her fingers on the counter.

"What?" I asked, noticing her obvious torment.

"If I tell you something, do you promise not to a) freak out and b) tell anyone else?"

"Okay," I replied, feeling a sense of unease at her tone.

"You know how Zane's grams needed that new treatment?"

"New treatment?"

"Yeah, she needs some infusion therapy, but I overheard my brother talking to Nix and I think Zaneborrowedmoneyfromaloansharkandnowtheyrereallyworriedabouthim."

Chloe inhaled a ragged breath, rubbing her chest.

"He did what?" I asked, hardly able to believe what she'd said.

"If I'm right, and I'm pretty sure I am, then there's only one person he could have gone to, and Leo D'Angelo is not a good person, Celeste."

A loan shark. It didn't make any—

"Miriam. He borrowed the money for Miriam."

Chloe nodded slowly, sadness glittering in her eyes. "Apparently the insurance wouldn't cover it, so he went and found an alternative way."

"Oh my God." My heart ached for them. Zane and his grandma. The boy who would do whatever it took to make sure the woman who raised him didn't suffer.

"How much did he borrow?"

"I don't know. I'm not sure anybody does. But I'm worried about him, Celeste. We all are." She toyed with the hem of her sweater. When her eyes finally lifted to mine, I saw a flicker of regret there.

"Chloe?"

"There's something else," she said. "But I'm not supposed to tell you."

"Okay." I braced myself for it.

"Your mom told Harleigh to stay away from you."

My eyes grew to saucers "She did what?"

Chloe nodded, reaching for my hand. "I don't know the specifics, but she told Harleigh to back off and leave you be."

"I… she really did that?"

Another nod. "Harleigh told Nix that it was your dad. But she confessed to me that it was your mom. She's trying to keep the peace."

I don't know why I was surprised. Mom had taken an instant dislike to Harleigh the moment she had moved in with us. But it cut deep knowing that my own mother would rather see me sad and lonely than let me have a relationship with my sister.

"Mom has never been an easy woman to navigate." I sighed. "But this is… I can't believe she did that."

"Harleigh loves you, Celeste. She just doesn't want to get in the way of your life, your future."

"I don't care about any of that."

Chloe's brow crinkled. "You really mean that, don't you?"

"I want to go to college and get a degree and a good job, but not at the expense of who I am and the people I care about."

"You're a good person, babe. And I'm so fucking angry at Zane for pulling that shit with you."

"We're too different." Pain coiled around my heart. I'd tried more than once to show him that I cared—that the fact we were from different worlds didn't matter to me. But it wasn't enough.

I wasn't enough.

"Do you really believe that?" Chloe smiled but didn't reach her eyes.

"It doesn't matter what I believe because he does. He believes it, Clo." And there wasn't anything I could do about it.

"So that's it? You're just going to give up?"

"I don't know what else to do." I threw my hands up in defeat. "I kept telling myself that he lashed out because he was scared, but you didn't hear the things he said to me, Clo."

Shame washed over me. He'd said some truly heinous things to me. Things that deserved my anger. But I couldn't just switch off my feelings so easily.

"Boys are fucking clueless at times. The fact that he didn't tell Kye and Nix about what he was going to do speaks volumes. Zane really thinks he had to deal with this alone and that's bullshit. We all love Grams. She's family. God, I hate this."

"What will happen… with the loan shark?"

"I don't know." She sucked her bottom lip between her teeth, letting it pop. "But it's never a good idea getting tangled up with somebody like Leo D'Angelo."

"I don't know what I'm supposed to do here."

"Nothing. I didn't come because I thought you could fix it, Celeste. I just thought you would want to know."

"Thank you. I'm guessing no one knows you're here?"

"What do you think?" She gave me a small knowing smile. "But the way I see it, you're one of us too, Celeste. Screw what anyone else says."

"Thank you." I squeezed her hand. "That means a lot."

"You know, you could always go out with Greg. Something tells me that would push Zane toward admitting how he feels about you."

"I'm done playing games, Clo."

Because for once I wanted somebody to fight for me. To choose me. Not because I was Celeste Rowe-Delacorte, but in spite of it.

"Yeah, I think I'm over the whole dating thing too."

"But I thought you liked Warner?"

"Warner is nice enough. But he isn't…"

"A certain mysterious guy that just happens to attend DA?"

"Am I that transparent?" She gave me a shy smile.

"You know, you could just try asking him out?"

"I've made it more than obvious I like Nate. He's clearly not into me."

"Impossible. You're beautiful and smart and sassy. Guys dig that."

"Guys, right. Except the only guy I want."

"He's a complicated guy. Maybe you need a less obvious approach," I said, as if I was any kind of expert.

"Why is this stuff so hard?" Chloe let out a heavy sigh.

"Because love isn't supposed to be easy, Clo."

"Yeah, I know," she said around a sad smile, "but does it have to be this hard?"

BY THE TIME Friday rolled around, I needed to talk to somebody.

Max was already gone when I got up, and the last person I wanted to talk to was Mom or Dad. So I headed into school and hunted down Nate.

"Rowe, this is a surprise," he said, slamming his locker closed. "I thought after our Teller Valley adventure you'd iced me out."

"Can we talk?" I rushed out.

"Uh, sure. You want to go somewhere a little more private?" He glanced up and down the hall.

"Yeah, that would be great."

"Come on."

I followed Nate out of the building and around to the athletic field. "Up you go." He motioned for me to climb the bleachers, and I slipped past him, opting for a row near the back.

It was cold out, the wind picking up, so I burrowed into my coat, waiting for him to join me.

"What can I do for you?"

"Can I trust you?"

"I don't know, can you?"

"Nate," I sighed.

"Relax. I'm not looking to spill all your deepest, darkest secrets to anyone. Even if I wanted to, it's not like I have anyone to tell." He shrugged.

"Sorry, that was rude. I'm just a little on edge."

"Things with Washington not going well?"

"I… what?"

"Come on, it wasn't hard to figure out. The two of you are—"

"He decided I wasn't worth it."

"Ouch. For what it's worth, I'm sorry."

"Thanks. But I didn't bring you out here to talk about my relationship with Zane. I need some advice."

His brows furrowed. "You have met me, right? I'm not sure any advice I can give you is—"

"Zane's in trouble. At least, I think he is. And I'm trying really hard not to get involved because he made it clear that he wants nothing to do with me. But it's not in my nature to do nothing. Not when my friends are in trouble."

And Zane was more than a friend. Even if I would never be more to him. Even if he didn't want it, he owned a piece of my heart now.

"I'll remember that in the future." Nate winked, and I rolled my eyes.

"Can you be serious for just a second?"

"Shit, sorry." His expression sobered. "Go on, I'm listening."

"Chloe said—"

"Of course little Carter is involved somehow. I swear to fucking God, she's trouble wrapped up in a—"

"NATE!" His eyes widened at the sheer frustration in my voice. "This is serious. Zane borrowed money off a loan shark and Chloe is worried about what might happen. They all are."

"Fuck, that's…" He dragged a hand down his face. "Fuck. It sounds all kind of messed up, yeah. But I'm not sure what you want me to do about it."

I wasn't until this moment. But then it hit me, like the sunrise burning off the lingering morning haze.

"I'd offer to help him out," he went on. "But my parents don't exactly give me free reign of my trust fund. I'm not deemed 'trustworthy' enough." He air quoted the word.

"I'm not asking you to give him money," I clarified as the plan unfolded in my mind. "But I do need your help."

29

ZANE

"Tell me I'm seeing things." Kye said, wiping his forehead with the back of his hand.

It was the end of the third quarter, and the Hawks were leading by two touchdowns.

But my head wasn't in it. So much so, Coach had benched my sorry ass after the first quarter when I got into a scuffle with one of the visiting team's players.

"Chloe invited Miller?" Nix asked, accepting a bottle of water off another player. He popped the cap and chugged half the thing down.

"Thirsty?" I asked, quirking a brow.

"Unlike some of us, I actually work my ass off on the field."

"That pussy had it coming." I shrugged with indifference. He shouldn't have gotten all up in my face and then maybe he wouldn't have found my fist cracking against his nose.

Asshole.

"It's news to me if she did." Kye went back to our original conversation.

"Maybe Harleigh invited him," I said, earning me a death stare from Nix. "What? I thought you were good with Miller hanging around since you and B are so secure in your relationship."

"You're a real asshole sometimes, Z. You know that, right?"

I'd avoided looking at the crowd at my back as much as possible. Because I didn't want to look for *her*, especially when I knew she wouldn't be there.

It was weird—I'd never had anyone in the crowd cheering for me. Grams had done all that when I was little, but once I'd reached junior high, it got harder for her to be in crowds. I was just happy knowing she was at home, safe and comfortable. And the few times Celeste had been there with Harleigh and Chloe, I'd told myself she was an unwelcome distraction. But now she was never going to be there again, and it fucking sucked.

The fourth quarter got under way, and I watched my team kick ass. Nix was on fire, throwing the perfect ball pass after pass. The crowd was amped, aware that this was the last game until the playoffs. The win wasn't important—we were already guaranteed a place—but to everyone supporting us, it was hopefully a sign of things to come.

I should have been celebrating with my team, excited about a shot at the championship. The chance to go end my high school football career on a high.

But I felt nothing.

Just the bitter sting of regret and the lingering sense that I'd made a huge fucking mistake.

"Didn't expect to see you here," I said to Nate as we joined everyone outside the building.

"What can I say? I'm a stage five clinger."

It was a joke.

He was joking, and yet, I couldn't help thinking back to what I'd said to Celeste on Monday.

"How is she?" The words slipped out, and Nate frowned.

"She's been better. Listen, can we talk?"

"If this is about Celeste, I'm not—"

"It isn't."

"Sure, I think everyone's heading to the res, but I need to check in on my grams first."

"How about I give you a ride?"

"Fine."

I didn't have the energy to argue, and I wasn't sure I wanted to party tonight, not when every time my friends looked at me, I felt their concern. Their disappointment.

They were worried about Leo. But they didn't need to

be. I had it under control. I was working every extra hour I could.

"We're going to take off," I said to no one in particular. "Miller is going to give me a ride."

"Oh, I thought..." Chloe started, but quickly stopped herself. "It doesn't matter."

"Maybe we'll stop by the res later."

"Z, man, come on," Kye said. "We can't party without you."

"I'll be there."

I wouldn't. But I didn't want to make a big deal out of it. They would go to the res, the drinks would flow, and they would forget all about my sorry ass.

Harleigh shrugged out of Nix's arms and came over to me. "You made the right choice, you know. I'm not talking about Leo... that's... I get it. Why you did it." Her eyes softened with understanding. "But you should have talked to us first. I'm talking about Celeste. I know the two of you—"

"B?"

"Yeah, Zane."

"It's all good. I'm fine. I'll be fine."

She gave me a small, apologetic nod. As if she was somehow responsible for the shitshow that had become my life.

This was exactly why I didn't get involved with anyone, because it only led to one giant fucking headache.

"Come on, I have some really great weed in the car," Nate said.

"Lead the way." I motioned for him to go on ahead.

When we reached his car, he paused, turning to me. "I want to say Harleigh is right, but you look as miserable as fuck, and I know Celeste is—"

"Don't, okay. I made my choice."

"And it wasn't her?"

"No, it wasn't."

The words sliced through me.

Inside his car, the tension was almost unbearable.

"You wanted to talk?" I said.

"Yeah, listen. I got wind of your little problem."

"I don't know what you're talking about."

"The loan shark."

"Did Harleigh tell you?" I bristled.

"Uh, not exactly. It was… Chloe."

"Chloe? Fuck, she knows?" I knew Nix would confide in Harleigh. I'd given him my blessing on that front. But we'd decided to try to keep Chloe out of it.

"She overheard Kye and Nix talking and she's worried."

"So she called you?" I stared at him in disbelief.

"I… we talk sometimes."

"Does Kye know about this?"

"It's not like that."

My brow lifted. "It's *always* like that."

"It's not important. She's worried and needed to talk

to someone. But it got me thinking. I think I can help you out."

"Let me get this straight, you came tonight because you want to offer to be my fairy godmother or something?"

"Look, I'll level with you. My family is about as dysfunctional as they come. I'm pretty sure they all hate me. But they're kind of stuck with me, you know?" He shrugged. "Anyway, I'm not allowed to access my trust fund until I'm twenty-one, but I do get a monthly allowance that just sits there. I want to give it to you."

"I'm sorry, what? Because it sounds like you just offered to give me your allowance every month."

"Pretty much." A faint grin traced his lips.

"Why the fuck would you offer to do that?"

"Because I don't need it. Because they think they can buy my silence. Because I couldn't help my sister, but I can help you and your grams."

"Your sister?" I asked.

"Yeah, Penny. She overdosed when I was a kid."

"Shit, man, I'm sorry."

I'd heard rumors but I didn't know the specifics. It made a lot of sense now—why he and Harleigh had developed a friendship.

"Look, if it makes you feel better, you can consider it a loan without interest and you can pay me back as and when you can."

"Shit, Miller, I appreciate it, I do. But I can't accept it. It's too much."

"Bullshit. You can accept it and you will. What do you think will happen if you can't make the repayments to this guy? What will happen to your grams then if you're hurt, or worse, dead."

A shuddering breath rolled through me, making my stomach turn over. He was right—of course he was. But I'd been desperate. And asking Nix and Harleigh, or Jessa, or Kye and his mom hadn't felt right, not when they all had so much of their own shit to contend with. But Miller was different. He could afford it. And it wasn't charity because I'd pay him back every cent and then some.

"You really want to be my loan shark, Miller?"

"I've been called worse things in my time." He smirked. "Let's just call it a friend helping another friend out."

"I'll figure out a way to pay you back every month, I swear. And once I graduate and get a job, things will be easier."

"It's all good, man. I'm just glad I can help."

"You're sure—"

"Wouldn't have asked if I wasn't."

"Thanks, man. I owe you."

A weight lifted off my shoulders. I didn't relish the idea of taking handouts off someone like Nate, but maybe it was hearing him say his sister had OD'd that gave things a little perspective.

I'd grown up hating Old Darling Hill and everyone in it. They had it easy, I'd thought. They had money and security and big, posh houses. But maybe I'd underestimated that the illusion didn't always show what was going on inside, behind closed doors.

Guilt churned deep inside me, but I ignored it.

It didn't change anything where Celeste was concerned.

Sometimes when you cared about someone—and maybe I did care about her in my own twisted way—the only way to show them was to set them free.

One day, when she was living the dream at college, dating some wealthy med student or lawyer-in-training, Celeste would realize that.

THE SECOND we pulled up outside my trailer, I knew something wasn't right.

"Expecting a visitor?" Nate asked me, eyeing the car parked out front.

"Not that I know of."

Dread slicked down my spine as I climbed out of Nate's car and headed up the ramp. "Grams?" I called out, my senses on high alert as I slipped around the door.

"Oh, Zane, you're home. Your friend was just about to leave, but I told him you were coming home to—"

The ground went from under me as Leo D'Angelo stood, a wicked glint in his eyes. "Zane, just thought I'd stop by and see how you're doing."

"We're fine." I moved closer to Grams right as Nate came through the door.

"Hey, what's up? I'm Nate. Nate Miller."

"I'm… a friend." Leo smirked.

A crackle went through the air and Grams glanced up at me. "Zane, dear, what is going on?"

"Nothing, Grams. Leo was just leaving. Isn't that right?"

"Sure am. It was good to meet you, Miriam. Maybe I'll see you around again sometime soon."

An icy chill went through me. Nate caught my eye, a silent understanding passing between us. But I didn't suspect Leo was here to cause any trouble. He was just asserting his authority, reminding me of what I stood to lose if I didn't pay up on time.

Fuck.

I was in way over my head, but the severity of the situation didn't hit me until I saw him sitting opposite Grams like he was an old friend of the family.

"We'll walk you out," Nate said, surprising the shit out of me.

Leo nodded, shoving his hands deep into his pockets. "Miriam."

"Goodbye." She cast me a weary glance and I gave her shoulder a reassuring squeeze.

"I'll be right back."

I followed Leo and Nate outside, trying to keep my cool. Closing the door behind me, I made sure to move away from the trailer before I said, "What the fuck do you think you're doing coming around here?"

Leo smirked. "I like to scope out my investments. Take an inventory as such."

"You stay away from here. I swear to God, if you—"

"Relax." Nate shoved a hand into my chest and pushed me back a little. "How much?" he asked Leo.

"Excuse me?"

"How much to settle his debt, right here, right now."

"You don't have that kind of money, kid."

"Try me." Nate stepped forward, pulling his wallet out of his pocket.

"Miller," I hissed but he ignored me, pulling out a stack of one-hundred-dollar bills.

Leo's eyes shone with alarming interest. "Well, well, isn't this a surprise."

"How. Much?"

"That's not how our arrangement works."

"It is now." Nate didn't back down even an inch. It was impressive from the guy who always seemed so indifferent about everything. And although it didn't sit well with me that he was bailing me out, I was fucking relieved he was here to stop me from doing something stupid.

"Name your price to get the fuck out of here and never come back."

"Two large."

"Bullshit," I spat. "That's not what we agreed."

"The terms just changed. Call it an early repayment fee."

Nate tsked but started counting out twenty one-hundred-dollar bills. "There." He shoved it at Leo. "Consider your arrangement with Zane over."

He studied Nate for a second before checking the cash. "You should give me a call sometime, kid. I could make good use of your deep pockets."

Nate tensed. "Nah, I'm good, thanks. But you should probably forget this ever happened. My money's good with other people too," he said coolly. Calmly. Like he walked in this world all the time. "People who probably don't like people like you."

Leo narrowed his gaze for a moment and my heart jumped into my fucking throat. But then he said, "It was a pleasure doing business with you." He saluted us with the wad of cash and climbed in his car.

"Fuck, that was intense," Nate loosened a breath, his shoulders sagging with relief.

I waited for the car to disappear down the dirt road before I replied, "I can't believe you just did that." Disbelief coated my words.

"You owe me, Washington." He winked, heading back into the trailer like he hadn't just saved my ass ten times over.

30

CELESTE

"Celeste, Sabrina, so glad you could make it," Mrs. Sinclair greeted us with air kisses and shoulder squeezes.

I played the part of the dutiful daughter, smiling in all the right places and giving polite answers when spoken to. But inside, I was a simmering volcano on the verge of exploding.

It was all Mom's fault.

She'd poisoned Harleigh against me. And in turn, my friends—Harleigh's friends—had started to keep me at arm's length.

I'd always known I was different to the woman who had raised me. I had a kind soul. Gentle and open. I didn't look at someone and judge them on their station in life or how I could use them to my own ends. But I had never spent too much time worrying about it because I'd been raised to play a role. To fit my parents' expectations for me. And I'd played it well. I'd been complicit in it.

Well, screw that.

I wasn't a puppet. I was a young girl with feelings and dreams and aspirations of her own. Harleigh had taught me it was okay to stand up for what you believed in, to go after what you wanted. She'd been offered a place in our world, and she'd given it all up for the boy she loved. But it was more than that. She'd given it up because accepting her place in our family meant giving up a piece of her soul—of who she was. And she hadn't been prepared to compromise on that.

Harleigh had given me a glimpse of what life could be outside the confines of rules and expectations. A world where I could be anything. Love anyone. Mom would never accept Zane. Just as she would never truly accept Harleigh and Nix. But I'd been prepared to choose him anyway. And even though he didn't want me—even though he didn't think I was worth it—I didn't regret a single moment of it.

So standing here, with Mrs. Sinclair and my mother and Cooper, smiling and playing the role I'd played so many times before, killed a little part of me. But I'd do it because this was different.

This was a means to an end.

I just needed to buy some time to figure out a few things before I confronted her.

"Cooper, you look positively dashing." Mom grabbed his shoulders and kissed both of his cheeks. He shot me a cocky grin; one I didn't return. Because I had a line I would not cross and letting Cooper Sinclair believe he stood a chance with me, was on the other side.

"Thanks, Mrs. Delacorte."

"Oh sweetie, please, call me Sabrina."

"So, I've got us set up in one of our smaller meeting rooms. The reporter wants to go over a few things and then he'll have us join Claudia's group for some candid shots. We want to keep things as natural as possible."

All while name dropping my mom no doubt. I resisted the urge to roll my eyes.

It was good publicity, I knew that. But I couldn't help but think they were going about it all the wrong way. A fundraiser would have been more inclusive and less tacky. A silent auction with some big donors or a charity ball to raise the profile of the various projects the center delivered. Real stories and real people. Not some stuffy press release with me, Mom, and Cooper smiling stiffly at the camera.

"You might want to try smiling," Cooper whispered to me as Mrs. Sinclair led my mom down the hall.

"Don't you think it would be more beneficial to do something real and meaningful," I said. "This feels so… staged and fake."

"Come on, Celeste. Don't tell me you're one of those social justice warrior types."

I gawked at him. "Excuse me?"

"It's cute you think you can make a difference." He bopped my nose like I was his plaything, and I swatted his hand away. He'd been an ass at his grandmother's house last weekend, but he hadn't been this obnoxious.

"Look, a word of advice, smile at the camera, bat your eyelashes, look pretty, and watch the donors roll in."

A shudder went through me. "That is so gross."

"It is what it is." He shrugged. "We should go out soon. Give the oldies what they want."

"No, thank you." Irritation rippled down my spine. He really was a piece of work I had no interest in spending time with.

"If they"—he cocked his head toward my mom and his grandmother—"get their way, this thing between the two of us is going to happen. We might as well try to enjoy it."

Cooper reached for me, brushing a strand of hair out of my face, then letting his thumb linger on my jaw. I was so stunned at his brazen act, that I was rooted to the spot.

Until a door slammed down the hall, jolting me from my surprise.

"Excuse me." I brushed past him, needing to get the hell out of there before I screamed. Or worse, kneed him in the balls.

Hurrying down the hall, I didn't see the person come out of the men's bathroom.

"Shit," Zane grunted, grabbing my shoulders. "Celeste?"

"Oh… hi." Awkward tension filled the space between us, crushing my lungs.

"What's wrong?"

"Nothing, I'm fine." I stepped away from him, needing to put a safe distance between us. "You're here with Miriam?"

"Yeah, she's in with the others." He tipped his head to the double doors leading to the main hall. "I noticed you weren't here Wednesday…"

"I wasn't feeling so good."

"Oh." Zane ran a hand through his hair and down the back of his neck, his eyes fixated on my face.

It was too much. His proximity. The intensity with which he looked at me. He opened his mouth to say something but panic saturated my veins.

"I should go," I blurted out, moving around him.

"Wait, can we—"

"Goodbye, Zane," I said, hurrying away from him and ducking into the women's bathroom.

Diving into a stall, I closed the door and leaned against it. Of course, I should have known Zane might be here. But I'd been so incensed after finding out the truth about Mom that I hadn't stopped to consider it.

And now he was here, on the other side of the door.

Ugh.

I waited for a few minutes, giving him time to move on. Or to at least let me escape without the embarrassment of running into him again.

Sure enough, when I finally left the safety of the bathroom, the hall was empty.

And Zane was gone.

"CELESTE, THANK GOD," Miriam said as I approached her table. She was busy playing four in a row with Martha again. "I've been worried about you."

"About me?" I frowned.

"Well, yes, d-dear." She gave herself a second. "You did such a sweet thing, coming to visit, but then you disappeared without a trace."

"I'm sorry, things have been kind of busy."

"Too busy to see my grandson?" Her brow lifted.

"Why would you think—"

"I may struggle to get my words out occasionally, young lady, but I can assure you my brain is... is still functioning. You think I don't know when a young lady is trying hard to impress a boy?"

"I..."

"Four in a row," Martha blurted, and Miriam muttered something under her breath.

"You should call him, dear. He isn't doing so good." She gave me a knowing wink.

Mrs. Sinclair and Mom chose that second to enter the room with Cooper and the photographer in tow.

When I'd suggested coming to talk and meet with the group, Cooper and Mom had been very vocal about waiting until the photographer was ready.

"Okay everyone, if we could have your attention, please." Mrs. Sinclair stood front and center. "We have a very exciting opportunity today. The local newspaper is going to run a feature on the center and our newest board member Mrs. Delacorte, and my grandson Cooper have kindly agreed to be in some photos to highlight all the fantastic work we do here.

"Claudia has some release forms for you all to sign and will answer any questions you have."

"Sounds like a bunch of horse crap if you ask me," Miriam scoffed.

"I quite like having my photo taken," Martha fluffed her hair.

"Ladies," Claudia greeted us as she came over. "Celeste." Her disdain was palpable, but so was her displeasure at the press release. I'd seen the slight curl to her lip when Mom stepped into the room.

Maybe we had more in common than I first thought.

"Do either of you have any questions about the photoshoot?"

Miriam waved her off, taking the release form and scanning it briefly.

"Well, if you're happy to participate, I just need you to fill out the form and sign it. Celeste will help if you need her to."

Well, okay then.

I glanced over to where Mom was deep in conversation with the photographer, completely in her element offering direction and ideas.

Mrs. Sinclair welcomed another group of people into the room and my heart sank at the sight of Zane. His expression said it all, he didn't want to be here. But before he could voice his protests, Claudia hurried over to them with more release forms.

Surely, he wasn't going to be a part of this?

Zane Washington. The boy least likely to ever participate in organized activities.

I didn't get a chance to ask him, or even try and eavesdrop on his conversation with a couple of other regulars I noticed from helping out Lewis the other day. Because Cooper appeared behind me.

"And what are you lovely ladies up to?" he asked, laying his hand on my shoulder. I flinched at his possessive touch and Miriam caught my eye, frowning. Cooper was oblivious though, squeezing gently, awkwardly massaging my shoulder in some gross display of ownership.

"You know, y-young man... it's rude to touch a woman without her permission."

"Oh, Celeste doesn't mind, do you, babe?"

My eyes grew to saucers, hardly able to believe my ears. "Actually." I shook him off and moved my chair forward a little. "I would prefer it if you didn't do that."

"Don't be such a spoilsport." He chuckled. "Oh, I think that's our cue."

"Excuse me," I said to Miriam and Martha. Miriam was still looking at me with a strange expression and I tried to silently reassure her I was fine. Cooper didn't intimidate me, even if his touch was unwelcome.

"Ah, Celeste, you're here, good," Mom said as if she

hadn't seen me right over there, talking to Miriam and Martha.

Because it occurred to me, she didn't care. All she cared about was getting the perfect photo for the press release that would hail her as some kind of philanthropist. A woman of the people.

Please.

Cooper stepped up beside me as the photographer directed us into his desired pose. We were too close, too familiar.

"Okay, Sabrina and Jeanine, if you can get in behind Celeste and Cooper." Mom stepped up beside me and Mrs. Sinclair joined Cooper on his left side. "Good, that's great. Big smiles."

My brows knitted. It all felt very unnecessary. I searched the room and saw the same disapproval on Claudia's face. But it was Zane's expression that made my heart stutter in my chest. His eyes zeroed in on where Cooper's hand brushed mine, flaring with jealousy.

"And maybe slip an arm around her," the photographer said, but I barely heard the words over the roar of blood in my ears as Zane watched us.

Watched me.

Cooper banded his arm around my waist, startling me.

"What the hell are you doing?" I said.

"It's just for the photo. Smile." He smirked down at

me, the *click click click* of the camera going off in front of us.

"Perfect. Now look directly at me—"

A door slammed loudly, and the room seemed to pause, glancing over to see what was happening.

But I already knew.

Because Zane was gone.

___

31

ZANE

I BLEW OUT OF THE CENTER IN A CLOUD OF ANGER.

He'd touched her. That pretentious asshole with the smirk had put his hands on my girl.

Except she isn't your girl.

Fuck.

I'd clocked the way he watched her, like a predator stalking his prey. I wasn't the only one. Grams had pinned that fucker with one of her 'I've got your card marked' looks too.

I paced back and forth, trying to temper the storm raging inside me.

Seeing her was like a blow to the stomach, but seeing him touch her like that, like he had ownership over her, made my fucking blood boil.

He was exactly the type of guy her parents would want her to be with. Entitled, smug, a rich boy who walked into the place like he owned it and everything in it.

Jesus. It was fucking with my head.

She was fucking with my head.

The door opened and Claudia's voice filled the air. "I swear to God, Tina, if I have to watch Sabrina flaunt her daughter around the place like she's the second coming for a minute longer, I will scream."

Shit, that was Celeste's mom? I mean, now that I knew, I kind of saw the resemblance. But they were so different.

Quietly, I slipped around the corner, pressing my back to the wall.

"She's not interested in the work we do here," Claudia said to whoever was on the other end of her cell phone. "All that woman cares about is making herself look good. She's practically got Celeste married off to Cooper. Makes you wonder if she planted her here in hopes of setting them up."

I went rigid.

"Apparently, he's taking her to Winter Formal, but anyone would think it's their engagement party. The whole thing is just gross."

My fist clenched against my thigh but it wasn't enough. She was going to date that asshole because he was parent-approved. Something I would never be.

A sticky trail of shame snaked through me. I would

never be good enough. It was staring me right in the face, it always had been.

Pain ricocheted through my knuckles as my fist connected with the wall, but I didn't balk, I relished it. Welcomed it into my body, my soul, letting it feed the darkness inside me.

I was an idiot for ever letting myself get tangled up with Celeste. Because she would move on.

Already had by the sounds of it.

And I'd be left to watch from the shadows as some asshole like Cooper gave her everything she deserved and more.

***

"You're quiet," Grams said as we drove home in Nix's car.

"Just thinking."

"About all the stupid decisions you've made lately?"

"Grams, come on. I said I was sorry about Leo—"

"Do not say that name in my presence. He is a criminal, Zane Thackeray. A low-life criminal who preys on people like you. And if that good boy Nate Milton hadn't—"

"Miller," I corrected her. "It's Miller."

"Milton. Miller. It doesn't matter." She inhaled a thin shaky breath. "I know… I know your heart is in the right place, dear. But you can't put yourself at risk like that. Not for me. Never for me."

"I didn't know what else to do." I gripped the wheel, frustration bleeding from my words.

"You could have talked to me. We could have figured it out together. You carry the weight of the world on your shoulders, dear, when a problem shared is always—"

"A problem halved," I muttered.

She reached for my arm, laying her frail bony hand on me. "Oh, Zane Thackeray, what am I going to do with you? When your mom left... I was in a dark place for a long time. I was so unwilling to let anyone help us. To risk your heart again. I couldn't stand the thought of someone coming into our life and hurting you. But I didn't think..." Tears rolled down her cheeks, hitting me right in the stomach.

"It's okay to let people in, Zane. Not everyone is out to get you."

"I don't need anyone, Grams. I have all I need right here." I squeezed her hand gently.

"And Celeste? What about her? Because I know heartbreak when I see it, and that girl is hurting."

"You saw that circus today. That's her life, Grams. Her world. I don't belong there."

"I wish you could see yourself the way I see you. My selfless, sweet boy."

She didn't say any more about it, so we rode the rest of the way in silence. Her words weighing heavily on my mind.

Once we got home, I got her inside and made sure she was comfortable.

"I'm going out," I said, grabbing my keys. "Will you be okay for a bit?"

"I'll be fine. It's you I'm worried about."

"I'm fine. I'll ask Chloe or Mrs. Carter if they can check in on you later."

"Oh, hush now." She waved me off. "Go. Just promise me you'll make it home in one piece."

"Always." I dropped a kiss on her head and got the hell out of there.

"Maybe you've had enough," Kye said, eyeing the bottle of vodka in my hands.

"Nah. I can still see that asshole touching her."

"Why don't you just call her. I'm sure—"

"Not going to happen. She made her bed, she can fucking lie in it."

"I don't want to be the one to point this out, but weren't you the one who broke things off?"

"We didn't have a thing," I spat, taking another long pull of vodka, letting the bitter taste dull all the other emotions coursing through me. "We had... nothing. We had nothing."

Because I was nothing.

"Jesus, you're a mess." Footsteps crunched somewhere in the distance and Kye sat up. "Hello?"

"I come in peace." Nate stepped into the sliver of moonlight.

"Miller, get your ass over here."

"You invited him?" I asked Kye.

"Figured he deserved it after saving your ass."

"Yeah, I guess you have a point. Take a seat, Miller. We're drinking away our shitty existences."

"That's something I can always get on board with. But I thought since D'Angelo is off your back, things would—"

"Celeste has a new guy."

"She does?" His brows went up. "That doesn't sound like Celeste."

"What do you know of it?" I growled.

"Easy. I'm just saying, I think you've got your wires crossed."

"I saw it with my own eyes. The fucker was all over her."

Anger welled inside me again, but it was chased by something else. Something I still didn't want to acknowledge, even now.

"Apparently he's taking her to Winter Formal," Kye added.

"You're sure?"

"Doesn't matter," I murmured, sinking further into my chair. The vodka had taken the edge off, but it wasn't enough.

Only one thing could quiet the roaring in my head, and I'd lost her.

I'd ruined her, pushing her straight into the arms of some rich, pretentious douchebag.

"Fuck," I hissed, kicking the ground. Dust sprayed up around me and the guys choked.

"Watch it, asshole," Kye muttered. "I need to take a leak." He got up and stumbled toward the tree line.

"You two are really partying hard tonight, huh?"

"It's been a shitty day, Miller."

"Listen, there's something you need to know." He sat forward, running a hand over his jaw. "The money—"

"Shit, you need it back?" I sobered suddenly. "I can work something out. I'll pull extra shifts at the mill, see if I can get on the roster at—"

"No, no. It's not about the money... shit, okay." He blew out a steady breath and a strange sensation curled through me. "It's about where the money came from."

"What do you mean where it came from? You said—"

"I know what I said, but she made me promise..."

No.

No fucking way.

"Tell me she didn't," I growled, anger swelling inside me like a tidal wave. "Tell me you didn't fucking let her—"

"Whoa, I didn't *let* her do anything. She wanted to help but she knew you wouldn't let her. So I agreed to be her cover story. I promised I wouldn't tell you, but I think you need to know the truth."

"The truth about what?" Kye stumbled back to his chair.

Nate glanced at me, and I nodded. Maybe Kye could make better sense of what he was saying than I could. Because it didn't make any sense.

It didn't.

"I didn't bail Zane out."

"You didn't? I don't understand. I thought—"

"It was Celeste." Her name echoed through me like thunder. "She withdrew the money and gave it to me to give to him."

"Shiiit." Kye flopped back into the chair. "That's—"

"I need to see her," I said, shooting up from my seat. But the world spun, the vodka and fresh air choosing that moment to hit me. I tripped back into the chair and tried to get my bearings. "Maybe tomorrow, I'll go see her."

"Yeah, tomorrow. Tomorrow it's ooon," Kye whooped. "Tomorrow, Z-man goes to get his girl. In the meantime, Miller, you got any of the good stuff on you?"

Nate slipped his hand into his pocket and smirked. "I never go anywhere unprepared."

But I was too caught up on Kye's words to hear him.

Because he'd called Celeste my girl too.

But she wasn't.

And she wouldn't ever be.

"Fucking move," I grunted, shoving the hairy leg off me.

"W-what?" Nate murmured, his head poking up

between the floor and Kye's bed. "Holy shit, I feel like something crawled inside me and died."

"Stop talking, it hurts," Kye groaned. "Everything hurts."

"That's what you get for drinking your body weight in vodka and smoking your lung capacity in weed." Chloe stood in the doorway of Kye's room. "What the hell happened to you three last night anyway?"

"Ask Z. It's all his fault."

"Fuck you, asshole," I breathed, hauling myself off the floor. "I need water and Tylenol."

"Grams is fine by the way," Chloe added. "I checked in on her last night and again this morning."

"Shit, what time is it?"

"A little after nine thirty. I'm making pancakes if anyone wants any."

"I'll take some of those and a coffee," Nate said. "Strong black coffee."

Chloe chuckled. "Let's go, Miller. You can fill me in on what the hell happened last night."

"Z realized he made a huge fucking mistake letting Celeste go and we spent the night trying to come up with a way for him to win her back. At least, I think we did. It all gets a little hazy after the second bottle of vodka."

"Took you long enough." Chloe flashed me a sly grin. "So what epic grovel did the three of you manage to come up with? Because I have got to hear this."

"Actually, we didn't." Nate finally sat up, revealing his

bare chest. Chloe's cheeks flushed and she looked everywhere but at him.

"So I'll uh… I'll be in the kitchen." She hurried off. "But I want to hear all about your plans to win her back."

"Why does she assume I even have a shot?"

If I was Celeste, I would never want to talk to me again.

"I love you, man," Kye said. "But sometimes, you really are a clueless fucking idiot."

32

CELESTE

"THE PRESS RELEASE WAS A HUGE HIT," MOM SAID OVER breakfast Wednesday morning.

It had been three days since the photoshoot, and two days since the paper had printed the story.

I refused to read it.

"Jeanine has already had two calls from potential donors."

"That's great, darling." Dad dropped a kiss on her head.

This was new. Them both sticking around for breakfast. A lame attempt at getting me back on side, no doubt. But it wasn't going to work. I was done being their golden child, their trophy, their pawn.

Unbeknown to them, I'd spent the last two days making some choices about my future.

"Isn't that great, Celeste?" Dad attempted to draw me into the conversation.

Things had been strained to breaking point between me and Mom. But I still couldn't get over the fact that she'd sabotaged my relationship with Harleigh.

"Celeste," Dad repeated, and I blinked over at him.

"I have some news," I blurted out. I'd been waiting for the right time to tell them, but there would never be a right time.

Better to rip the Band-Aid off and face the consequences.

"I've decided on my major."

"Whatever do you mean?" Dad frowned.

"I don't want to study medicine. I want to study psychology."

"Psychology?" Mom balked. "But that isn't the plan."

"Plans change, Mom," I snapped.

I'd been thinking about the future a lot since my first session at the center when I'd watched Claudia lead the talking circle. Being a doctor was only one way to care for people. Counseling and therapy was another.

"Michael, talk some sense into your daughter. She's being ridiculous."

"Why? Because I'm making a decision for myself? Is that not okay, Mom? Do you want to choose my career, my boyfriend, and my friends? Speaking of the fact I have no friends, does Dad know what you did?" I looked her right in the eye so she could see exactly what I thought of her schemes. "One of the reasons why my sister won't hang around with me anymore?"

The words—the *accusation*—pierced the air. Mom's perfect mask slipped just a fraction. But I saw it. I saw the cracks.

And I reveled in them.

"Sabrina?" Dad said, casting a suspicious eye on her. "What on earth is she talking about?"

"I did what needed to be done to protect our daughter," Mom sneered. "Harleigh and her friends are bad influences, Michael. Your daughter is not good for Celeste, so I took matters into my own hands."

Thunder flickered across Dad's expression. "You talked to her. You talked to my daughter behind my back. After everything we've been through, you—"

"WHAT ABOUT ME?" Her voice was shrill, making my blood curdle. "What about *our* children and their futures? Harleigh came into this family and turned everything on its head. She stole you. She stole you away from me and I won't just stand by and let her destroy us. So hate me all you like but I only did what you're too weak to do." Mom's defiant gaze slid to mine. "Your big heart has always been your weakness, Celeste. This world is ruthless. You have to think with your head, not your heart. You have to—"

"Stop, Mom. Just stop." Sadness coated my words. "Are you really that cruel that you would rather see me unhappy and lonely than accept Harleigh into your life?

She is not a bad person. This isn't her fault, and you can't keep punishing her for Dad's mistakes."

Mom silently fumed, a tumultuous storm swirling in her eyes.

"Unbelievable." Dad let out a weary sigh. "I thought we were finally making progress, that you understood that it isn't a choice between you and Harleigh, Sabrina. You're my wife. My *wife*. I made vows to you. Ones I intend to honor. But Harleigh is my daughter and I have already made so many mistakes with her. She is a part of this family whether—"

"She will never be a part of *my* family." Mom snarled the words, her perfect mask slipping, revealing the ugly woman beneath. "And if you can't see that, Michael, if you can't see the damage you've done by ever bringing her here, then you are not the man I married." She stormed out of the kitchen, taking the air with her.

Dad watched her go, rubbing a hand over his stubbled jaw. When his gaze finally found mine, his expression broke. "Oh, sweetheart. I am sorry. I'm so, so sorry." He came to me, pulling me into his arms and I fell against him. Because although he wasn't innocent in all of this either, right now, I really needed someone to hold me and tell me everything was going to be okay.

I needed my dad.

MOM LEFT and didn't come back. By Thursday night, the atmosphere in the house was oddly calm. Dad asked me and Max to have dinner with him. Mrs. Beaker prepared all of our favorite things, the spread far too excessive for three people.

Until the doorbell rang and Dad gave me a conspiratorial smile. "I'll just get that," he said.

"What's going on?" Max asked, snagging a smoked salmon canapé off one of the plates.

"I don't—"

"I thought it might be nice if Harleigh joined us," Dad said from the doorway.

I turned a little to find my sister standing there, apology glittering in her eyes.

"Hi," she said.

"Hi."

"I hope you're hungry," Dad ushered her toward the table, "Mrs. Beaker made all of our favorites."

"That's… she didn't need to do that."

"No, she didn't. But I asked her to. I wanted to enjoy a meal with my kids."

It was awkward at first, the three of us sitting there with Dad. But then he cleared his throat and said, "Me and your mother have decided to separate for the time being."

"Well, shit," Max breathed.

"Max, language, please."

"What does that mean, Dad?" I asked. "What's going to happen?"

"Honestly, sweetheart, I don't know. Your mother and I have a lot to work through. But for now, I think it's best that we do that separately."

"I'm sorry, Dad." I gave him a weak smile. Part of me was relieved that I wouldn't have to deal with Mom every day, but she was still my mom, and he was still my dad.

"I'm sorry if I caused trouble," Harleigh said quietly, looking at her plate. "That was never my—"

"Harleigh Wren, look at me," Dad said. "You are my daughter and I have already made so many mistakes where you are concerned. But I'm done making excuses. If Sabrina can't accept you as part of this family, then that's her choice. But you are my daughter, my flesh and blood." He looked at me and then Max. "I know I haven't been perfect or present nearly enough but that all changes today."

"Sounds good to me, Dad." Max shrugged. "Can we eat now?"

"Yes, let's eat."

Dad and Max chatted and joked like he hadn't just announced he and Mom were separating. But Max seemed lighter somehow. It was weird.

"Hi," Harleigh slid into the seat beside me.

"Hi."

"Celeste, listen, I am so sorry. I've been such a bitch to you over the last few weeks, but Sabrina said—"

"Don't. Don't do that. I know she's to blame, I do. But you could have talked to me, Harleigh."

Devastation flickered across her expression. "I know. I'm so sorry. Honestly, I think a part of me believed her. Believed that you were better off without me."

"Harleigh, I have never thought that, not once. You're my sister, I love you."

"I know and I'm so lucky to have you." She hugged me. "And Zane would be lucky to have you too."

I pulled back, frowning at her. "But you said—"

"I know what I said but I was scared, Celeste. I've never had to worry about someone else's feelings before. I didn't want you to get hurt and Zane is a complicated guy."

"You're telling me." I smiled but it quickly dropped when I remembered that he hadn't gotten in touch this last week.

When I'd seen the flash of jealousy in his eyes at the center, I'd thought he might try to see me. Or in the very least, text me. But he hadn't.

"You know he—"

"Harleigh, it's okay. I'm okay. Do I wish he'd have given me a chance, yeah." My heart squeezed. "But it's okay. I just hope he and his grams are okay."

I knew they would be. Nate had helped me to make sure they were. I still needed to explain that little fact to my father, but I figured today was probably not the right time for it.

Besides, it was my money. If I wanted to help a friend out, that was my prerogative.

"Miriam is doing okay. She's pissed that Zane 'chased you off' though."

Laughter pealed out of me, and Dad and Max glanced to our end of the table.

"What are you two whispering about?" Max smirked.

"Oh, nothing," I said with a smile of my own. "Nothing at all."

Harleigh grabbed my hand under the table and squeezed gently.

She was here.

And for the first time in weeks, I felt like things were finally going to be okay.

"Celeste, you have visitors," Max bellowed from downstairs.

It was Friday night. Winter Formal.

Nate had offered to go as my date, but I'd politely declined. I didn't want to go and watch from the sidelines while everyone else had the time of their lives with their dates and friends. Besides, I felt better about things after our impromptu dinner with Dad and Harleigh last night. It was nice—we'd never done that before. The four of us together, a family. There was still a lot to sort through with Mom, but we'd all decided to shelve that for another day.

She'd hurt me, really hurt me, and I wouldn't be ready to forgive her anytime soon.

Before I could get to my bedroom door, footsteps sounded out in the hall accompanied by laughter. Lots and lots of laughter.

"Max, what is— Harleigh? Clo?" My brows furrowed. "What are you guys doing here?"

"Surprise!" Chloe grinned. "We're taking you to Winter Formal."

"You are, but why?"

"Because, Cinderella"—she breezed past me and threw her bag down on my bed—"it's junior year and you shall go to the ball."

"Clo." Harleigh chuckled. "Maybe tone it down a little bit."

"What? Can't a girl be excited? I've never been to a rich people dance before. I bet it's a damn sight better than our poor excuse for a school dance."

"You don't have to do this," I said to Harleigh. "You hated it at DA."

"But I love you." She smiled, "And Clo's right, you deserve this. So let's get dressed up and do this."

Harleigh and Chloe steered me toward my closet, rifling through the few dresses I had. "Hmm, I don't know. The green or the black?"

"Black," Harleigh said, a mischievous glint in her eye. "Definitely black."

"I think you're right. Hair up with a sexy choker and some red lipstick." Chloe grinned with excitement. "You'll look killer."

"We don't have to go over the top. It's not like I'm out to impress anyone."

"Babe, you never know when you might meet your prince. A girl can never be too prepared." Chloe winked at me, and I rolled my eyes at her ridiculousness.

"Thank you," I said, wrapping my arms around them both. "Thank you for doing this."

"Of course. But if we don't hurry, we're going to be late. And we don't want you turning into a pumpkin on your big night."

THE DARLING ACADEMY gymnasium had been transformed into a winter wonderland complete with dry ice sculptures, fake snow, and metallic blue and silver streamers.

"Wow, now this is what I'm talking about." Chloe let out a low whistle, taking it all in.

"Everyone's staring," I whispered, noticing the way everyone seemed to stop to watch me and Harleigh enter the room together.

"Let them stare," she said with a dismissive shrug. "Drinks or dancing?"

"Maybe a drink."

We weaved our way through the crowd, the music pulsing through my body. Miles spotted me, his arm wrapped around Marcy's waist. He gave me a warm smile and I smiled back. There was no denying they looked good together.

"I'll be right back," I said to the girls and made my way over to them.

"Hi."

"Hi," he said.

"Hey." Marcy looked me up and down. "Did you want something?"

"Can I talk to Miles for a second? I promise it's nothing to worry about. I'm really happy for you guys, and I love your dress, it really brings out the color of your eyes."

"Uh, sure. Okay." She gave me an uncertain smile. "I'll be over there with the girls." Marcy went up on her tiptoes and made a show of kissing him.

I fought a smile at her attempt at marking her territory. "Someone is a little possessive," I said as she walked away.

"She knows our history."

"Yeah. Listen, Miles, I owe you an apology."

"No, Celeste, you don't," he said. "You gave me a chance and it didn't work out. I get that now. We're friends. Best friends. I miss you."

"I miss you too. But I don't want to tread on anyone's toes." My gaze flicked to Marcy.

"I don't think that will be a problem when she realizes you're already spoken for."

"What do you mean?"

Miles pointed over my shoulder, and I turned slowly,

the air whooshing from my lungs when I spotted Zane standing awkwardly underneath the balloon arch. But despite his obvious discomfort, he looked so good. The black dress shirt hugged his chest and shoulders and he'd rolled up his sleeves, revealing the intricate ink swirling up his forearm. His hair was styled out of his face, his expression hard and uneasy. Until he found me across the room and some of the ice in his gaze thawed.

"Miles, I…"

"It's okay, Celeste," he said, giving me a little nudge. "Go get your guy. He looks like a fish out of water standing over there all alone."

"You're a good guy, Miles Mulligan."

"And you're one of the best people I know. Now go. Before he makes a run for it." His mouth quirked up at the corner.

Everything slowed down as I walked toward him, the sounds and laughter all melting away until there was nothing but the sound of my heart beating wildly in my chest.

"Zane," I breathed, stopping right in front of him.

God, he looked so good.

"A little birdie told me I might find you here." He gave me a crooked smile.

Zane smiled and it was like everything turned right with the world.

"What are you… I don't understand."

"Fuck, Einstein." He reached for me, plucking a loose curl between his fingers. "You look incredible."

"You look nice too."

He barked out a laugh, his hand slipping to the side of my neck, his thumb brushing my skin. My eyelids fluttered as I sucked in a sharp breath. "Zane…"

"I was wrong." He stepped closer, erasing the sliver of space between us. "I don't hate you, Celeste. I couldn't hate you if I tried. But I fucking hate that I lost you."

"Everyone's staring," I blurted, too overwhelmed to make any sense of what was happening.

Zane leaned closer, dipping his face to mine. "Let them stare. I don't give a shit about anyone but you. You're mine, Celeste." He touched his head to mine, breathing me in. "And I don't give a fuck what anyone else thinks about it."

33

ZANE

My heart thrummed in my chest, making it hard to think straight. But Celeste looked… fuck, she looked like every guy's fantasy come true.

The black satin dress hugged her waist, flaring over her hips and finishing just above her knee. Her hair was gathered in a high ponytail with the ends curled, drawing attention to the thick black choker sitting at the base of her neck.

Fuck. That was hot.

I could imagine tugging on that while I—

"Zane."

My name on her lips yanked me from the less than innocent thoughts running through my mind.

Celeste's lashes fluttered as her cheeks flushed, an

adorable red blush that matched her lips, as if she knew exactly what I was thinking about.

Jesus, I was in trouble.

So much fucking trouble.

The entire room watched us, but I only had eyes for her. Even if I was aware of the DA football team all glaring in my direction. But none of them dared to approach or say anything. Because while Celeste might not have been popular at DA, she was still Michael Rowe's daughter and that gave her some level of protection. I wasn't sure it would ever stretch to my presence on DA territory, but I didn't care.

I was here for her.

Only ever her.

This kind, strong, tenacious girl who wasn't scared to go after what she wanted and put her neck on the line for the people she cared about.

I still couldn't believe she had given Nate the money to give to me. To Grams.

"You take my breath away," I said, brushing my lips over her cheek, my heart crashing in my goddamn chest.

A soft sigh escaped Celeste as she turned toward me, our mouths aligning, sliding together. She laced her hands behind my neck, choosing me in front of her classmates, her teachers, maybe even the odd parent chaperone.

I'd grown up believing I didn't need anyone except Grams, Nix, and Kye. But this—feeling her soft lips on mine, her curves beneath my hands—was more than I could have ever imagined.

She didn't care that I was the broken boy from The Row, barely keeping my head above the surface. Celeste didn't care. She never had. I just hadn't wanted to believe it.

Hadn't thought I deserved it.

"Zane," she breathed, kissing me softly before pulling back to look at me. "What are you doing here?"

"You are so fucking beautiful. Dance with me."

"D-dance… you want to *dance*?" She glanced over at the half-empty dance floor. Most people were still gawking at us, but still, I couldn't take my eyes off her.

"You keep stealing my firsts, Einstein, you might as well have another."

"You know, you can't really call me Einstein anymore."

"What's wrong with Einstein?" I grinned, and she gave me a pointed look. "Fine, how about I call you mine instead?"

She ran her hands up my chest. "I really like the sound of that."

"Good because I like the sound of it too." My hands dropped to her ass, pulling her closer.

"Zane, we can't—"

"Okay, lovebirds, let's not get thrown out of the dance because Z can't keep his hands off his girl."

"Kye," Celeste gasped. "What are you doing here?"

"Looking good, Celery." He winked.

"Celery?" She gawked at him before swinging her eyes to me. "What does that—"

"Don't ask." I chuckled, drawing her closer, breathing her in. "We all came." Turning her a little, I pointed over to where Nix and Nate stood with Harleigh and Chloe.

"I can't believe you did all this."

"A wise old woman told me I needed to make a grand gesture. So here I am, at a fucking DA school dance, for you, babe. Only ever for you."

"I don't know what to say, Zane. I'm speechless."

"I don't need you to say anything right now." I moved my mouth to her ear and whispered, "But later, I'll need to hear you scream my name."

Her breath caught as she pressed into me. "You said something about our first dance?"

Celeste gazed up at me with nothing but lust and longing in her eyes. It hit me then, that this is what it felt like to find your person. The one person who saw past all the armor and bullshit. The one person who wanted you regardless of your flaws.

"I did." I tugged her onto the dance floor, wrapping my arms around her and swaying us to the sultry beat. Other couples and groups of people danced around us, finally bored at my surprise appearance.

After a little while, our friends joined us. Nix danced with Harleigh, while Chloe danced with Nate and Kye, the three of them laughing and joking. We were proof it didn't matter if you were from The Row or Old Darling Hill, we were all teenagers with our own baggage, dealing with our own shit. Sure, we might have been different, we might have had different experiences of the world, but cut us open and we all bled the same.

"I'll warn you now," Celeste said, grinning up at me like a fool. "I'll probably fall in love with you, Zane Thackeray Washington."

Her words fisted my heart, squeezing the air right out of my lungs. "You think you might fall in love with me one day, Einstein?" I barely got the words out over the giant fucking lump in my throat.

She rolled her eyes, fighting a smile. "I think it's a real possibility, unless you keep calling me that. Then all bets are off."

"Is that so?"

"Don't test me, Zane. Or I might run."

"It doesn't matter. Even if you run, I'll come after you. Always. You're mine now."

Celeste Rowe was mine.

And I didn't plan on ever letting her go.

"I GOTTA SAY IT, Z, I never thought I'd see the day." Kye slung his arm over my shoulder as we stood over by the buffet table, watching the girls dance.

"You're telling me," I grumbled, tugging at the collar on my shirt. The thing was so fucking tight I could hardly breath. "How much longer until we can leave?"

He barked out a laugh. "Aww poor baby, feeling a little out of your depth?"

"Fuck you, asshole."

"She's worth it though, right?"

I watched Celeste, arms thrown in the air, a smile painted on her goddamn beautiful face. "Yeah," I said, swallowing hard, trying to tamp down the urge of possessiveness I felt over her. "She's worth it."

"What are we looking at?" Nate and Nix joined us.

"Just watching Z's girl do her thing on the dance floor." I elbowed Kye in the ribs and he bent over, grunting in pain. "What the fuck was that for?"

"Keep your eyes to yourself, asshole."

"I wasn't… Fuck you, Z. Is this how it's going to be now?"

"You asked for that," Nate added with a smirk.

"Says the guy who hasn't stopped looking at Clo since we arrived," I pointed out.

"What the fuck, Miller? You been checking out my sister?"

"What? No. I don't—"

The girls made a beeline for us. I reached for Celeste, pulling her into my side.

"Why are you all standing over here?" she asked.

"Just enjoying the view." I nuzzled her neck, nipping the soft skin there. "Are you having fun?"

"It's been… everything. But honestly, I'm ready to leave."

"Thank fuck," I said a little too enthusiastically and everyone laughed.

"Such a charmer." Celeste pressed her hand against my cheek and kissed me softly. "Take me home, Zane Thackeray," she whispered.

"Actually, we have plans."

"We do?" Her brows crinkled.

"Yeah, come on." I glanced at Nate and he gave me a small nod.

The guy was an enigma, but he'd proved himself more than once now, and I was so fucking grateful to have him in our corner.

A few people watched us leave, but I didn't give two fucks about them. The only people who mattered were the ones by my side and the girl in my arms.

"Oh my God," the girls all shrieked with excitement as we exited the building and headed toward the stretch limo waiting for us.

"I think I just died and went to heaven," Chloe said, bouncing precariously on her skyscraper heels. How the fuck she walked in those things, I would never know. But she grabbed Harleigh's and Celeste's hands, yanking them toward the door.

"Mr. Miller," the driver said. "Everything is inside, just as you requested."

"Thanks, Cliff." The two of them shook hands before Nate helped usher the girls inside.

"Fuck me," Kye let out a low whistle. "He wasn't kidding when he said he could pull this off."

"I owe him big time," I murmured.

I didn't like being beholden to anyone. Especially not the likes of Nate Miller. But I'd wanted to give Celeste one perfect night—the kind of night she deserved—and he'd been more than willing to help. In fact, he'd insisted.

"I hate to admit it, but Miller is a good guy," Nix said.

"Good enough for Clo?" My brow arched playfully, but Kye didn't look impressed.

"No one will ever be good enough for my baby sister."

"Try telling her that." I flicked my gaze to the limo door where we could just make out Chloe and Nate chatting inside.

"Come on, assholes," Nix said, motioning for us to get in. "I need some one-on-one time with my girl."

"You have one-on-one time with your girl every night. It's me you need to feel sorry for." Kye pouted. "You both have regular pussy now and what do I have? Nothing. I have nothing."

"Maybe stop sleeping your way through the girls at school and one of them might actually give you a chance."

"Nah, I'm good." He grinned. "I need to get in some more practice before I meet my forever girl." Kye slapped me on the back before following Nix into the sleek black car.

I glanced up at the sky, breathing in deeply, letting the frigid air fill my lungs. Growing up, I'd never let myself believe in happy endings because I'd been convinced my story wouldn't have one. But maybe it was time to rewrite the narrative? Maybe with Celeste by my side, I could finally believe what Grams had been trying to tell me.

That I deserved something good in life.

I flopped into the leather bench seat beside Celeste and slipped my arm around her shoulder. "What do you think?"

"It's… I don't know what to say."

"I wanted to give you one perfect night."

"And it is." She gazed up at me.

"What you did for me Celeste, no one has ever…" I couldn't find the words to explain to her what it meant to me and Grams that she'd wanted to help.

That she'd chosen us.

"It's okay." She smiled, the emotion glittering in her eyes punching me dead in the chest. "I want to help, in anyway I can. I care about you. Both of you, Zane."

"You are incredible." And I still couldn't fucking believe that I got to call her mine.

Music poured out of a hidden speaker, giving us enough privacy to talk freely. Kye shoved a beer into my hand and a glass of champagne into Celeste's. "Enjoy." He winked before moving back to the other bench.

"What are you thinking?" I asked her as she took a small sip of her drink, uncertainty shining in her eyes.

"I need you to know that I don't need all of this, Zane. I only need you."

"I know that." Cupping her face, I brushed my thumb

along her jaw. "But maybe I want to be able to walk in your world sometimes."

"There isn't any 'my world' and 'your world' here. You know, I realized something lately, we get to make our own rules. Our own world." She grinned at me.

"What about your old man?" I touched my head to hers. "He won't approve—"

Her mother definitely wouldn't. But I'd heard that Sabrina had moved out, so maybe I wouldn't have to deal with her scrutiny yet.

"Let me worry about my father," she said, full of blistering conviction. "I choose you, Zane Washington." She scraped her fingers against my jaw, kissing me. "I. Choose. You."

34

CELESTE

I WAS FLOATING ON CLOUD NINE. OUR FRIENDS' LAUGHTER rose above the music as the limo drove us to a surprise location. Surprise, because no matter how many kisses I pressed against his lips, Zane refused to tell me where we were going.

"You're not playing fair." I flashed him puppy dog eyes.

"Me?" His brow went up. "I think you decided to play unfair the second you put this dress on." His fingers trailed up the inside of my knee, sending shivers skittering through me.

"Maybe I wanted you to suffer. Just a little bit." A smirk tugged at my mouth. He leaned in to kiss me, but I stayed out of reach, chuckling at his adorable frown. "Will you tell me where we're going?"

"It's a surprise."

"I don't like surprises."

"Everyone likes surprises."

God, I liked this version of Zane. Playful and flirty. He hadn't taken his eyes off me all night. Not when I'd danced with Harleigh and Chloe, and especially not when I'd danced with him.

Zane dancing. Now there was something I didn't think I'd ever get to see. But he did it.

He did it for me.

To give me one perfect night.

The look on my classmates' faces had been priceless as the seven of us had danced, soaking up everything Winter Formal at DA had to offer. I'd seen a few of them on their phones, snapping photos and texting their friends and families no doubt. I half-expected Mom to start blowing up my phone any minute because hot gossip traveled that freaking fast in Old Darling Hill.

But I didn't care if she found out. Just like I didn't care what my dad had to say about it. Who I dated—who I gave my heart to—was my decision, and mine alone.

I pressed my face against the glass window again, trying to figure out our destination.

"It won't matter," Zane whispered against my ear, his hand still resting on my thigh. "You'll never figure it out."

"We've been in the car for about eleven minutes, traveling on average twenty-five to thirty miles an hour. That means we've probably traveled around five miles. A five-mile radius with the school at the epicenter would put—"

"Who are you right now?" Zane gawked at me.

Heat crept into my cheeks. "What?"

"Better brush up your skills, Z, if you're going to keep up with Little Miss Genius over there." Kye snorted, and Zane flipped him off.

"I like numbers." I shrugged. "And words. And problem solving."

"I think it's cute," Chloe said.

"Hey, at least she can help you with your homework," Kye added.

Zane grumbled something under his breath, a scowl painted on his face as he sank back against the bench seat.

I leaned over him, hovering my mouth over his. "Ignore them."

"Easier said than done, Einstein." His mouth twitched, his eyes darkening with lust. "Fuck, I want you."

"I'm yours."

"You mean that?"

I nodded, my mouth dry, my heart crashing wildly in my chest.

"Hey, lovebirds," someone called, breaking the spell we were under. "We're here."

"Thank fuck," he breathed. "Come on, I need to get you alone."

I'D BEEN to Nate Miller's house a couple of times before with Harleigh. But I never expected to be standing here after Winter Formal with Zane beside me.

"This wasn't quite what I was expecting," I murmured as Zane took my hand and tugged me toward the door.

"His family are away for the weekend, so we have the place to ourselves."

Except, we weren't alone, because Harleigh, Chloe, and the guys were all here.

Noticing my expression, Zane squeezed my hand. "Trust me, okay?"

I nodded, because what else could I do? Despite wanting to be alone with him—and I *really* wanted to be alone with him—I was still excited to be here together with our friends. It didn't feel weird or awkward. In fact, being with Zane was as easy as breathing.

Nate jumped in front of us all, producing a key from his wallet and a baggie of weed. "Welcome to the after-party." He opened the door and we all filed in, Zane's hand on the small of my back as we walked down the hall.

"Everyone, if you want to head into the kitchen where I have prepared some snacks and a smorgasbord of drinks."

"Smorgasbord. What the fuck does that mean?" Kye snorted.

"It can mean either a range of open sandwich type canapés... and nobody cares." I flushed bright red. "I blame the champagne. I ramble when I've had a drink."

And maybe, just maybe, it was the nervous energy coursing through me.

Zane banded his arm around my waist and dipped his face to the crook of my neck. "You are so fucking cute right now."

Everyone headed into the kitchen, but Nate hung back. "And for the special couple." He dangled a key in front of us.

Zane snatched it off him and said, "Thanks, man. I owe you."

"Have fun." Nate winked, before he disappeared into the kitchen.

"What was all that about?"

"You'll see, come on." Zane took my hand and moved down the hall until we were at the back of the house.

We entered a utility room and slipped out of a door leading to the yard. The Millers' pool shimmered under the moonlight as we crossed the yard to the beautifully lit pool house.

"It's so pretty," I said, a trickle of anticipation going through me. Because we were alone at last.

Zane unlocked the door and turned to me, his eyes simmering with hunger. "I know it's not a fancy hotel room," he hesitated, "but I thought…"

"It's perfect. Take me inside, Zane."

No more words were spoken between us as we entered the pool house. Zane closed the door and slipped his arms around my waist again, dropping his chin to my shoulder. "I wanted us to have a do-over."

"A do-over?" I craned my neck to look at him.

"Your first time… you deserved more."

Turning in his arms, I rested my palms against his chest. "I don't regret it, Zane. Not for a second."

"Still, I want to make it up to you."

A shy smile formed on my lips. "I wouldn't say no to that."

"We have the place to ourselves for the night. If you want to—"

"I do. I really, really do."

"Thank fuck. Come here." His hand curved around the nape of my neck so he could draw me closer. Our breaths mingled, our eyes saying everything we wouldn't yet.

"I want you, Zane Thackeray Washington. I want you so much."

"You're mine." He kissed me hard, licking his tongue deep into my mouth, making my stomach clench with need.

Zane's hand dropped to the backs of my thighs, and he lifted me up, carrying me further into the pool house and down the hall. He nudged a door open and lowered me to the floor.

I glanced at the queen size bed and inhaled a shaky breath, desire swirling through me.

"Hey, we go at your pace, okay?" Zane stroked a finger along the curve of my jaw and along my collarbone.

"I don't want to take it slow," I whispered, my fingers

going to the buttons on his shirt, popping them open until my palms found his smooth, warm skin. My dress was next, his hands making light work of the zipper in the back.

When we were both naked, Zane picked me up and carried me over to the bed, lying me down and falling on top of me. "Hi." He nudged my nose, stealing a kiss.

"Hi."

"Tell me what you want, Celeste."

I threaded our fingers together and trailed our hands down my stomach to the apex of my thighs. He took control, sliding his fingers through my wetness and dipping two inside me.

"God, Zane," I whispered, arching into his touch. Running my hands up his arms and over his shoulders, I reveled in his lean, defined body.

He didn't take his eyes off me as he worked me with his fingers, curling them deep and slow.

"I want you," I whimpered, leaning up to nip the underside of his jaw.

"Come for me first."

"Zane… ah," I cried as his thumb joined the party, rolling circles over my clit.

"You look so beautiful like this. I want to watch you fall apart, Celeste. Come all over my fingers, babe."

"Yes," I panted, fisting the sheets. "God, yes."

A wave built inside me, hurtling toward shore until it crashed over me, unrelenting and powerful. My entire body shuddered as I quietly moaned his name.

Zane… Zane… Zane.

He pushed my thighs open, falling against me, his hard length brushing my stomach. I reached between us, grasping him.

"Wait, shit, we need a condom."

"I want to feel you. All of you."

"I'm clean," he said gruffly.

"I'm on birth control."

"Thank fuck." His body trembled as he lifted my leg around his waist and pressed into me. Inch by glorious inch. "You feel incredible." His eyes pinned me in place, their intensity taking my breath away. Zane looked at me like he couldn't believe I was his.

But I was.

Every single piece of me.

"Move, Zane," I choked out. "I need you to… move."

He pulled out and waited a second before sliding back in, deeper this time, making us both moan. "This—this should have been our first time," he said.

"Don't you know, I'll take you anyway I can get you." I grinned.

He gazed down at me, thrusting into me with slow, shallow strokes. "I'm so fucking gone for you."

"Show me." I hooked my arm round the back of his neck and kissed him.

And for the rest of the night, Zane showed me exactly what I meant to him.

My eyes fluttered open, a lazy smile tugging at my lips as my gaze found Zane.

"Morning," he said, his hair all mussed up and sexy. "How did you sleep?"

"Like the dead. Somebody wore me out."

A playful smirk tugged at his mouth as he leaned in and kissed me. "It's not my fault I can't keep my hands off you."

"It was amazing." I stretched out beside him, feeling a delicious ache between my thighs. "We really owe Nate, huh?"

"We?" Zane leaned over me, arching his brow.

"Well, yeah." I frowned. "We are a we now, are we not?"

"If that's your really obvious way of asking if you're my girl, then that would be a hell fucking yes." Zane rolled me underneath him, caging me in with his arms. "If we're quick we probably have time to—"

"Okay, lovebirds, time's up," a voice boomed. "We're heading to Crêpe-a-licious for breakfast. You have fifteen minutes to move your asses."

"Fucking Carter, cockblock."

"We need to find him a girlfriend," I said. "Then we can all group date."

"Have you met Kye? He goes through girls quicker than Miller goes through weed."

"You make a good point." Whoever set out to tame Kye had their work cut out for them. But he was a good guy, his heart was in the right place. "I tamed you, didn't I?"

"More like cast a spell on me," Zane said. "Feel free to break it at any— ouch, what the fuck, Einstein?"

I released his nipple and smirked. "That'll serve you right."

"Jesus, you crazy woman."

"Correction, I'm *your* crazy woman."

"Hey, assholes, let's go!" Kye banged on the door again.

"He isn't going to stop until we show our faces," I sighed.

"Fine," Zane huffed. "But after breakfast I want you all to myself again."

"Or... we could go hangout with Grams. I've missed her."

Zane froze, staring at me with a strange expression.

"What's wrong? Did I—"

He crashed his lips down on mine, kissing me so hard I felt a little dizzy.

"Wow, what was that for?" I asked a little breathless.

"Want to know a secret?" he whispered. "I think one day I could fall in love with you too."

CELESTE

After breakfast with Zane and our friends, Nate gave me a ride home. I felt nauseous at the thought of telling Dad about Zane, but I refused to hide our relationship. Who I dated was my choice. And while I didn't need his permission, part of me—the part raised to be the perfect congenial daughter—did want his blessing.

"You okay over there, Rowe?" Nate asked as we pulled up outside my house.

"Yeah, I'm fine."

"Are you sure? Because you look like your blueberry pancakes are about to make a reappearance all over my leather."

"I'm *fine*."

"You know, Celeste, even if he's pissed, what's the

worst that could happen? He disowns you for a while. Cuts off your allowance. You'll figure it out."

"Are we talking about my life here or yours, Nate?"

"Ouch, you wound me, Rowe. Wound. Me." His eyes twinkled with humor, but I saw the lingering shadows there.

"I'm joking," I said. "Besides, you have a point. We have each other. And Harleigh and Nix and the guys… even Chloe." My brow lifted.

"*Don't* go there."

"I should go there. But thanks, Nate. For everything."

"Yeah, yeah. You know I should start charging for all my worldly advice. That's Harleigh and Nix, and now you and Zane."

"Maybe it'll be your turn next."

"Un-fucking-likely."

With a chuckle, I shouldered the door and climbed out, heading inside the house.

"Dad, I'm home," I called.

"In here, sweetheart." I found him in the kitchen. "How was the dance?"

"It was fun, thanks."

"Good, I'm glad. You deserved it."

"Dad, can I talk to you about something?"

"Sure." He laid down his papers and looked at me. "What's up?"

"I need to tell you something, but I'm worried about what you'll say."

"Does this something have to do with a boy by any chance?"

I nodded. "I'm… involved with someone."

"From the way you're dancing on the spot, I can assume it's not Miles."

"Definitely not Miles."

"Okay, someone else from school then?"

"Not exactly. You remember Nix's friend Zane—"

"Celeste, I'm not sure I like where this is headed…" His brows bunched with concern.

"Just hear me out, please. I know you and Mom had this idea that I would end up with someone like Cooper Sinclair, but honestly, I'd rather stick pins in my eyes. But Zane… he makes me feel alive, Dad."

"And how long has this been going on?"

"A few weeks, but it only got serious recently."

"Serious… I see. Your mother will have something to say about this, Celeste."

"I know." My stomach sank. She would never accept Zane.

"But your mother isn't here anymore." His expression softened. "That said, if you're going to be dating Zane, I have a few ground rules."

"Okay." I nodded.

"I want to meet him. Bring him over for dinner and I'll have Mrs. Beaker make something for us. That point is non-negotiable. If I'm going to hand responsibility of my daughter to someone, I want to look him in the eye and see his intentions."

"Fine." I rolled my eyes. "But I have rules too."

His brow arched.

"If you embarrass me, yourself, or try to intimidate Zane, I will never forgive you. Ever, Dad. I mean it. Zane might come from The Row, but he's a good person with a lot on his plate. The last thing he needs is you judging him when you know nothing about his life or what he's been through."

"Fine."

"Fine." Tension crackled between us.

"You know, sweetheart." He let out a defeated sigh. "I have only ever wanted what is best for you and your siblings."

"And I get that, I do. But sometimes, you have to trust that we know what that is, Dad."

He gave me a small nod. "I'm glad you told me."

"I didn't want to lie or keep this a secret. But there is one more thing…"

"Yes…"

I inhaled a deep breath, fidgeting with the zipper on Zane's hoodie. "So, uh… Zane's Grams needed a new treatment for her MS, treatment her medical insurance wouldn't cover it. So I gave it to them, Dad. I—"

"You gave them money?" His frown grew. "Celeste, I don't know if that's appropriate. Is this why he's dating you, to get to your—"

"No. He didn't even know. I just wanted to help. I met his grams at the center, and I'm going to keep helping so long as she needs it, Dad. I'm also going to continue volunteering at the center." Because I liked being there, spending time with people like Miriam and Martha. I wanted to make a difference.

"We need to talk about this, sweetheart. You can't just give—"

"You did it for Harleigh. For Nix and Jessa. I don't see how it's any different. I care about Zane and his grams a lot. We have the money, they don't. You keep talking about wanting to change, to do better by us. Then prove it, Dad.

"Zane is my boyfriend. He's part of my family now too. This isn't some schoolgirl crush. I care about him, Dad." *I think I might be falling in love with him.*

My father stared at me, and I'm sure I detected a hint of pride there. "As an adult you think you know everything, but you and your sister are constantly opening my eyes and teaching me new things."

"Is that… a good thing?"

"Yes, sweetheart." He smiled. "I think it is."

I SHIFTED NERVOUSLY on my feet, the flowers and bag of takeout heavy in my arms. The door swung open, and Zane appeared. Just the sight of him made my heart ratchet.

"I brought dinner and flowers." I thrust the bouquet at him.

"Flowers, again? If you're not careful, Einstein, I'll start thinking you're into me."

"Zane Thackeray, who's out there?"

"You didn't tell her?" I whispered.

"No." He grinned. "I wanted it to be a surprise. Come on."

Zane took my hand, and I went to enter the trailer, but he stopped me at the last second, ducking his head to kiss me softly. "Hi."

"Hi." Warmth spread through me.

"Did you bring dessert?" he asked, and I shook my head. "Too bad. Guess I'll just have to eat you then."

"Zane!"

His laughter wrapped around me as we moved inside.

"Grams, there's someone here to see you." He gave me a little nudge, and I went over to her.

"Hi, Miriam."

"Oh, Celeste, thank God, dear. I've been worried."

"I'm okay." I gave her a warm smile. "I brought something for dinner, and I got you a fresh bouquet of flowers."

"You didn't need to do that, dear. I'm just happy to see you."

"I'm happy to see you too, Miriam." My gaze lifted to Zane, something passing between us.

"What is going on here?" Miriam glanced between us.

Zane came over and pulled me into his arms, standing behind me. "Celeste agreed to be my girl, Grams."

"Well, about damn time." Her whole face lit up. "I

knew there was something going on between the two of you that first day we saw her at the center. Never seen my boy look at a girl the way he looked at you, dear."

"Grams," Zane groaned, dropping his chin to my shoulder. "You don't need to tell her all my secrets."

Miriam huffed. "Maybe you'll be able to talk some sense into him, Celeste. Maybe you'll be able to make him believe he's good enough for something better than working at the mill his whole life."

I glanced up at him, smiling. "I'm sure I can work on it."

We hadn't talked about the future yet. This thing between us was too new, too fragile. But there was one thing I was certain about.

Nothing in my life had ever felt more right than standing wrapped in Zane Washington's arms with his grams beaming up at us.

EPILOGUE

CELESTE

"Come back here," Zane hooked his arm around my waist and pulled me onto the bed.

"Zane! We're going to be late."

"We have time." He trailed hot wet kisses up the side of my neck, grazing my earlobe with his teeth. "Happy Thanksgiving, babe," he murmured, his hands skating down my stomach to the hem of the Hawks jersey covering my body.

"Zane Thackeray, don't make me shout for Grams."

"You wouldn't dare." His eyes narrowed.

"Try me, mister." Untangling myself from his arms, I pressed a soft, lingering kiss on his mouth and climbed off the bed.

"Damn, you look good wearing my number."

I flashed him a demure smile over my shoulder. "You

know, if you consider applying to college, maybe I'll get to wear your number next year too."

"Einstein," he warned, his expression hardening.

I was pushing it, I knew that.

It had barely been a week since he walked into Winter Formal and claimed me in front of the entire junior and senior classes. But I was already thinking about the future. *Our* future. Columbia wasn't hours away, but I couldn't imagine being apart from Zane. At least, we had next year together before we needed to make any big decisions.

I pressed my lips together and pretended to lock them and throw away the key.

"If you don't want me to come over there and get you naked, I suggest you run." His words sent a thrill through me, and I smirked. "I'm not kidding, babe."

"Relax, I'm going." I blew him a kiss and slipped out of his bedroom and into the bathroom across the hall.

Dad hadn't been too happy when I'd asked to stay here last night, but he'd finally agreed after grilling Zane for the most awkward thirty minutes of my life. He could hardly refuse my request when Harleigh literally lived with her boyfriend.

After quickly doing my business and washing up, I slipped out of the bathroom only to find Zane's bedroom door open.

"You know, Zane Thackeray," I heard Miriam say. "I'm so proud of the young man you're becoming. Celeste is a beautiful soul, and you'll do well to remember that."

I smiled, creeping down the hall to watch them, my heart almost bursting at the sight of Zane helping his grams add creamer to her coffee.

"Good morning," I said, not wanting to eavesdrop any longer than necessary.

"Good morning, dear. Did you sleep well?"

"I did, thank you."

Zane caught my eye, his lips twitching.

"*Behave*," I mouthed, hoping to God Miriam didn't notice our heated exchange.

"What time are we going over to Nix's? I want to help Jessa with the pie," Miriam asked.

"We can leave whenever you're ready," I said.

"Perfect. I need to curl my hair first. Zane usually helps me with the stubborn ones, but I… I was thinking maybe you could help me, dear."

"I would love that," I said over the ball of emotion in my throat.

Zane kissed her cheek and then came over to me. "You help Grams and I'll grab a shower. And thank you," he whispered.

"Whatever for?"

He stared at me intently. "For choosing us."

ZANE

"So how was your first sleepover?" Kye asked as we hung out in Nix's living room while the girls and Grams helped Jessa with the food.

"The best kind of torture."

"That good, huh?" He smirked, and I bit down on my lip, shaking my head.

Having Celeste in my bed had been perfect. I'd loved feeling her pressed up against me as she slept. But trying to fuck her with Grams down the hall was a bit of a mood killer.

"I'm happy for you, Z. You deserve a little bit of good in your life. And look at the two of them, as thick as thieves already." He glanced over to Grams and Celeste.

My heart swelled as I watched the two of them laughing while Celeste helped Grams roll out a sheet of pie crust. "I don't deserve her," I murmured. "But I'm sure as fuck going to find a way to keep her."

Kye gripped my shoulder. "Something tells me you won't have to try very hard."

"What are you two assholes talking about?" Nix dropped down on the couch, Max and Nate joining us. Nate had blown off his family to spend the day with us, and Max had nowhere else to go since Michael was going to see Sabrina.

"Z's girl."

"Seriously? That's my sister, Carter." Max glowered at me.

"Name a time and place, kid." I smirked.

"Asshole," he muttered.

"Colt seems like a decent guy," I said. We'd met Jessa's boyfriend a couple of times, but it was the first time we were spending any length of time with him.

"He is," Nix said. "He treats her right and makes her happy. That's all I want for her. Do you think your mom will make it?" he asked Kye.

"Your guess is as good as mine." He shrugged but I saw the pain in his eyes. "Miller brought plenty of the good stuff for later."

"Keep your voice down," Nate said.

"Relax, it's all good."

"What's all good?" Chloe perched on the end of the couch next to Nate.

"Nothing for you to worry about, Clo."

"Any word from Mom?" she asked Kye.

"Not yet."

"Her loss."

"Hi, boyfriend." Familiar hands slid over my shoulders and Celeste pressed a kiss to my cheek.

"Hey." I brought one of her hands to my mouth and kissed her knuckles. "How's Grams doing over there?"

"She's doing good. Don't worry, I'm keeping an eye on her."

"I know."

Celeste knew we came as a package deal; it was one of the things I loved most about her.

Shit, had I really just thought that?

"Zane, what is it?"

"Nothing," I choked out.

Kye caught my eye and mouthed, "*You are so fucking screwed,*" amusement dancing in his eyes.

But I didn't bother to argue.

Because he was right.

I was screwed.

Celeste had somehow managed to burrow under my skin and thaw the layers of ice around my heart.

And now that she was there, I never wanted her to leave.

CELESTE

"Can somebody get that?" Jessa called.

"I'll get it." I hurried over to the front door and opened it. "Dad, what are you doing here? Sorry, I mean—"

"It's okay, sweetheart." He smiled. "I know I'm turning up unannounced, but I wondered if perhaps there was room for one more?"

"I thought you were meeting with Mom today?"

His expression turned crestfallen. "I didn't want to do this here. Now. But I want to be honest with you, sweetheart. Me and your mother will be separating, officially."

"Oh." I didn't know how to feel about that. "Come in. I'm sure we have room for another one."

"Mr. Rowe." Zane came over to us and held out his hand. "Happy Thanksgiving, sir."

"You too, son. This looks like quite the gathering." He ran his eyes over the two tables pushed together, mismatched chairs crammed around it. It was a tight squeeze, but it didn't matter. This was family. The kind you chose. The kind that you loved unconditionally. The kind of family everyone deserved to have.

"Dad?" Harleigh said.

"Harleigh Wren, I wondered if perhaps I could join you all?"

Nix wrapped his arm around Harleigh. "I'm sure we can make room."

"Thank you."

"Come on," Harleigh said. "I'll introduce you to everyone."

He gave me and Zane a gentle nod and followed Harleigh and Nix.

"You good?" Zane asked me.

"They're separating, officially."

"How do you feel about that?" He pulled me into his arms.

"Okay, I guess. Things haven't been right for a while. But she's still my mom, you know?"

"I never got the chance to make things right with my mom, but you still have that chance. If and when you're ready." He brushed the stray hair from my face.

"When did you get so smart?" I asked him.

"Oh, it's from hanging around with this girl I know. She's kind of a genius."

"She is, huh?"

"Yeah." He leaned in, brushing his mouth over mine, not caring one bit that the house was full of our friends and family. "She's beautiful." *Kiss.* "So smart." *Kiss.* "Compassionate." *Kiss.* "Stubborn as a mule." *Kiss.* "And I told her that one day I was pretty sure I could fall in love with her."

"You did, huh?" Zane's teasing words sent my heart into overdrive, and I couldn't stop smiling.

He nodded. "But I've got a confession to make. I lied. Because I'm pretty sure I'm already falling."

"Want to know a secret?" I whispered.

"Always."

"I'm pretty sure I'm falling too."

PLAYLIST

Wrong – Zayn, Kehlani
Break My Heart – Hey Violet
Power Over Me – Dermot Kennedy
Find What You're Looking For – Olivia O'Brien
Eyes Closed – Halsey
I Still Wait For You – XYLO
Romantics – Tove Lo, Daye Jack
Bad Life – Sigrid, Bring Me the Horizon
I Want You So Bad – Glades
Bad Habit – Royc3
Six Feet Under – Billie Ellish
Take My Heart – Birdy
Lonely Together – Sofia Karlsberg
Pray For Me – The Weeknd, Kendrick Lamar
Favorite Crime, Olivia Roderigo

ABOUT THE AUTHOR

Angsty. Edgy. Addictive Romance

USA Today and *Wall Street Journal* bestselling author of over forty mature young adult and new adult novels, L. A. is happiest writing the kind of books she loves to read: addictive stories full of teenage angst, tension, twists and turns.

Home is a small town in the middle of England where she currently juggles being a full-time writer with being a mother/referee to two little people. In her spare time (and when she's not camped out in front of the laptop) you'll most likely find L. A. immersed in a book, escaping the chaos that is life.

L. A. loves connecting with readers.

The best places to find her are:
www.lacotton.com